THE GIFT: BOOKS 1, 2 & 3

THE GIFT: BOOKS 1, 2 & 3

THE BILLIONAIRE'S LOVE STORY

LILY ZANTE

PUBLISHED BY:

Paperback Edition

Lily Zante

The Gift, Books 1-3 (The Billionaire's Love Story)

ISBN: 978-1-914467-52-3

AUTHOR'S NOTE

'The Billionaire's Love Story', is a contemporary billionaire romance serial set in New York and consisting of nine 25K-45K installments. This boxed set consists of Books 1, 2 & 3 of The Gift, the first of part of the story. The other books in the series are:

The Promise (FREE)
The Gift, Book 1
The Gift, Book 2
The Gift, Book 3
The Gift, Boxed Set (Books 1, 2 & 3)
The Offer, Book 1
The Offer, Book 2
The Offer, Book 3
The Offer, Boxed Set (Books 1, 2 & 3)
The Vow, Book 1
The Vow, Book 2
The Vow, Book 3
The Vow, Boxed Set (Books 1, 2 & 3)

Reading Order

The Gift, Book 1
The Gift, Book 2
The Gift, Book 3

THE GIFT, BOOK 1

The Billionaire's Love Story (#1)

CHAPTER ONE

Screaming children wreaked havoc in the toy store, and their cries of laughter rang straight through Tobias Stone's ears.

Not much excited him these days but it was hard not to get caught up in their excitement, hard not to feel their joy, hard not to hear their high-pitched shrieks. Hard to dismiss the wonder on their faces as they played with the display toys and stared wide-eyed at the shiny new boxes that were displayed so enticingly on the shelves.

It made him feel better about himself and made Christmas more bearable to know that he was spreading a little happiness. Or rather, his foundation was. The huge toy store had been closed to the public for the evening while the Tobias Stone Foundation invited children from the city's adoption centers to visit the department store and select a toy of their choice.

But he was also aware that he'd had to miss an important meeting that had suddenly come up. Luckily, Matthias was standing in for him but he would need to return to the office soon. His multi-million dollar hedge fund didn't stop running just because Christmas was coming.

His eyes darted around the place, and he glanced at his watch again, getting anxious and needing to leave. Contemplating his escape, he looked towards the exit and saw a child peering through the glass doors.

"I'm going," he told Candace, his hard-as-nails assistant.

"Not yet, Tobias. It's barely been an hour. Smile." She flashed him her false one. "At least make it look as if you're having a good time."

"I *am* having a good time but I'm in the middle of important negotiations, in case you'd forgotten."

It was all very well hosting an evening for these children—and it made him feel good about himself for a change— but he still had a business to run.

"People need to see your face, Tobias. It's good publicity for you to be seen mixing with all sorts of people—especially these poor kids at a time like Christmas. It adds credibility to your philanthropy."

He didn't mind giving his wealth away. If anything, he thrived on it and there was no way that he was going to get through his millions in his lifetime. He liked to think that he didn't spend too extravagantly, but he had the usual billionaire playthings—luxurious properties around the world, a private jet and a private island, to mention a few.

Even though he enjoyed the finer things in life, he worked damn hard and preferred to remain low-key, as much as was possible for a man with his wealth and history.

While giving away his wealth made him happy, making money did too.

"If we could just have a few shots of you with the children, sir," said the photographer herding a group of children together and leading them towards him.

"What a brilliant idea," agreed Candace and took his arm. "How about near the tree?" She led him over to a beautifully decorated Christmas tree lit up with warm, golden-colored lights.

"Smile, everyone," the photographer ordered.

"Is this necessary?" Tobias asked, giving the man a tight-lipped smile.

"Smile," said Candace, through her gritted teeth. Tobias obliged as a group of young children, barely reaching his waist, gathered around him as though he was Santa Claus.

"You are so kind, Mr. Stone," gushed one of the women from the adoption centers. "It is so very generous of you, taking the time to give these children a Christmas present."

He nodded at her, barely hiding his look of unease. Being thanked for doing something like this made him uncomfortable.

"Would you mind if we had a photograph taken together? People will be so much more interested to read it if they see your picture." She smiled at him sweetly. "Vanessa? Hurry up!" She called out to her colleague, another matronly woman who looked as though she'd be more at home baking pies.

Tobias returned a fast smile, conscious of time slipping away. It would be the morning of the next day in Hong Kong and he was anxious to sit in on the negotiations.

"Thank you, ladies, but I really must leave." He broke away from the group, determined to disappear before Candace asked him to do something else. She was like a fiery Doberman, silky, fast, super alert and she made sure he was seen in the right places with the right people at the right time.

"You're still making the most eligible bachelor lists," she told him. But he had no interest in these things. He preferred to pay for sex, seeing it as nothing more than a transaction which required payment. There was no emotional attachment that way.

"I'm leaving," he growled; he'd been here an hour already but as he turned around and headed towards the exit, he saw the same child still peering in. "Has nobody let him in?" he muttered, striding towards the large glass doors of the store.

"It's a win-win deal, Tobias," Candace had told him. "You buy those poor kids a toy and come out looking like a saint." Tobias grimaced at the thought. He wasn't a saint. Not by a long shot.

But that wasn't the reason he'd gone along with her idea of giving Christmas gifts to children less fortunate. He'd done it because for the longest time he'd hated Christmas and had avoided the festivities. Christmas was about being with loved ones and Tobias was alone.

It could have all been so different.

This had been the second year they had run this event, and this year he'd even looked forward to it. But he was now anxious to return to the office because he didn't have much else to occupy him. His millions couldn't buy him peace, love or happiness, though whiskey and Naomi made the world tolerable.

He walked up to the door and the sight of the child looking through the glass, wide-eyed with wonder, reminded him of himself; of how he'd been at that age. He had been dirt poor once and remembered the time when he used to stare at other kids who had the things he never had.

"Where are you going?" Candace tottered up on her heels behind him.

"I'm letting him in."

"But we're closed to the public this—"

"Where the fuck is his mother?" Tobias snarled. The security guard nodded at him as Tobias flung the door wide open and peered at the child who stared back at him with fear in his eyes.

Immediately, his hardness melted. "Do you want to come inside?"

The child's body language perfectly illustrated his dilemma. One foot was poised as if he was ready to enter but his solemn face indicated no immediate desire to make a move.

"Don't just stand there," Tobias said. "If you want to come in, then come in." He looked around for signs of the boy's parents and saw a woman with her back to the child, talking on her cellphone. She turned around just at that moment, her gaze landing on the child, before moving to him. She rushed towards them and stopped at the door, just behind the boy. The child stared at his mother but said nothing.

"Jacob, we can't go inside," the woman said.

"Can I have just one look? Please, Mommy?"

Tobias watched the exchange; the woman appeared to waver and then stared at Tobias.

"Are you open?" she asked him.

"Yes." He pulled the door wide open and moved away.

"Pleeeease, Mommy? Just a look?"

The woman appeared to consider it. And the longer she took, the more the child's anticipation grew. It annoyed the heck out of Tobias.

"Why don't you let him in and put the kid out of his misery?" He gave her the once-over, taking in her scuffed shoes and the huge tear in her stockings.

"He's not miserable," she retorted, fast as lightning.

"He doesn't look too happy to me."

She narrowed her eyes at him. "Ten minutes, Jacob. No more." The boy smiled so brightly that it brought a smile to Tobias's tight expression.

He remembered that look and wished he still could feel that level of excitement about anything. Even winning new deals and reaching the next milestone in his business had lost its sparkle.

Nothing mattered much, anymore.

Christmas, with its gaudy commercialism, packaged and dressed up in dazzling bright baubles and sparkling lights, had lost its allure for him years ago because now it reminded him of the life he could have had. He would still have been insanely successful, disgustingly rich, but he'd have had someone to share his wealth with.

Now he carried too many memories of the wrong kind.

He watched as the woman—the boy's mother, he presumed —stepped aside warily and looked around the store. Candace sidled up to him. "We're *not* open to the public, Tobias," she seethed. "You can't just let any strays in. This is specifically for kids from the adoption centers."

"It doesn't matter," he replied, noting that the boy wore a coat that was obviously one size too small for him.

The boy's mother walked up to them. "Is something going on in the store?"

"We're not open to the public," Candace replied.

"You're not? I'm sorry, we'll leave."

Tobias walked over to the boy who was happily sitting on the floor playing with an Iron Man figure and a fighter jet.

"So you like Iron Man, huh?" Tobias asked, crouching down.

The boy nodded. He held the fighter jet in one hand and the figurine in the other.

"Did you write your letter to Santa?"

"Yes."

"What did you ask for?"

"Coloring books."

"Coloring books?" asked Tobias in surprise. "So you must already have an Iron Man?"

The boy shook his head.

"Would you like to have Iron Man?"

The boy stared down silently and shrugged.

"Did you know that tonight is a very special night?" Tobias asked, eager to get the boy talking. "You can pick anything you want from here and it will appear under your tree on Christmas Day."

The boy frowned as he stared back at Tobias. "You're not Santa."

"No. I'm not, and I'm sure you'll get your coloring books from him. But, see all of these children here?" Tobias waved his hand around. "They're all going to pick a toy and they get to open it on Christmas Day. You can, too."

The boy looked at the floor again, as if he didn't trust Tobias. Just then Tobias's cell phone rang and he answered it, standing up slowly.

It was Matthias. "It's not going too well. You should get back to the office. There are a few things we need to discuss."

"I'm coming," replied Tobias and watched as the woman rushed over to her son and told him they had to go. He hung up and walked back to Candace. "Why did you do that?" he growled at her. "How much trouble is one extra child going to be?"

"If you let one in, you won't be able to stop the rest."

Tobias didn't care too much for Candace's opinion. He was too busy staring at the child. He saw the boy's face drop, saw him leave the toys he'd been playing with and get up slowly.

"Fucking ridiculous," he hissed under his breath, then walked over to the mother and son. "You should let the poor kid stay," he told the boy's mother.

"He's not a *poor* kid," the woman threw back.

"Well, it certainly looks to me as if he doesn't want to leave just yet."

"That other woman told us we had to—"

Fucking Candace. "I don't care what she said," Tobias snapped, a little too angrily.

"Tobias, let me handle this." He felt a tightness in his chest as Candace suddenly appeared by his side again.

She put on what he now knew to be her best and most false, over-the-top persona and explained, "Tonight is a charity event hosted by the Tobias Stone Foundation for a few of the city's adoption centers. This store is closed to the public for a few hours. Why don't you come back tomorrow? You can shop all you want then."

Tobias ground down on his teeth. If he lost his temper now, it would give the wrong type of publicity for the Stone Empire. Before he had a chance to say anything to his PA, the boy suddenly spoke up. "I saw you on TV," he said shyly.

"I don't think you did, honey." The boy's mother gave Tobias an apologetic look.

"I did, Mom. He *was* on TV." For the first time Tobias tried to hold back a smile. The woman slipped her hand through the boy's. "Come on," she said, obviously not believing a word. "Let's go."

"I did, Mom." The boy turned to him. "You were on TV, weren't you?"

But the woman appeared to be in a hurry. "I'm sure you saw him, honey. Come on. We need to get back."

Tobias watched as they walked out of the store. Just outside the door, the woman bent down and pulled something out of her bag then handed it to the boy. When the boy put it to his mouth, Tobias realized it was an inhaler.

He glared at his assistant. "Was that really necessary?"

CHAPTER TWO

She walked past the glistening shop windows of the blue-canopied Tiffany store, her annoyance spreading, almost as fast as the hole in her stockings.

The day, which had started off badly, had become progressively worse. Savannah stared down at the huge tear which had now spread out to her knee. It had been small and inconspicuous when she'd left home this afternoon to pick Jacob up from school. She'd been hoping it would have held but the more she tried not to think about it, the more she kept touching it, to make sure it wasn't getting bigger by the millisecond. In doing so she'd turned the tiny hole into a crater the size of her thighs.

"I didn't get it?" She wailed in frustration at the news that another job interview hadn't worked out. She stared despondently at the rush of traffic before her. New York, three weeks before Christmas, was both a shopper's heaven and hell.

Money was tight and she couldn't afford to buy a lot, yet she was determined to make this a special Christmas for her boy. But she was still looking for a decent job; a mission she'd been on since mid-November. She had traipsed around different agencies handing out her resumes and talking to the professionally dressed, tight-lipped women, trying to convince them that she had good office skills, and that she'd been an office manager back in North Carolina and was competent with most of the PC software.

She could do better than stocking shelves at the supermarket which had been her job until recently, when looking for a decent job had become a full-time job in itself.

The traffic snaked angrily across the road as she grabbed Jacob's hand and waited for the traffic lights to change. She'd been hopeful of getting some holiday work but it was proving to be difficult. An office job in the city would be better than working in the supermarket near where she lived. While it was ideal for its location and proximity to her cousin Kay's apartment and Jacob's new school, working in the supermarket didn't pay enough.

She needed a decent job that paid decent money. Kay still paid the rent on her apartment because she still needed a place to come back to, and her company was providing accommodation for her in Hong Kong. But Savannah still had to buy food and pay the bills. And she hadn't considered just how much more expensive things in the city would be compared to what she was used to.

It had seemed like a brilliant idea at the time, when Kay offered her the use of her apartment in Sunnyside for one year while she worked abroad. Savannah had jumped at the chance, having spent last Christmas with her cousin here, and she and Jacob had moved in over the summer when Kay left.

New York was a world away from the small town where she grew up in North Carolina. She'd left that behind, her parents too, and ventured out here, via a short stint in Pennsylvania where she'd stayed for a few months with Kay's mom.

She'd come all the way here, not for the bright lights of New

York—that dream from her childhood was gone—but because she hoped to make a fresh start and her cousin thought the city would be good for her.

She had responsibility now; she had Jacob to take care of. The boy had seen enough pain during his short years and she wanted to put a big distance between her and her ex-husband. Now that the divorce was final, she wanted to forget the ugly past and make a fresh start.

"Jacob!" She turned around, horrified to see her son standing in the entrance to a fancy big toy store, lit up like a firework. With its shiny decorations and shimmering window displays it looked like a set from a Disney cartoon, leading children in like a Pied Piper.

She'd tried to steer Jacob away from these kinds of stores, knowing she couldn't afford anything inside them. They were a child's dream come true but a parent's worst nightmare.

That was why she'd taken him to the tree-lighting ceremony at Rockefeller Plaza, where they had waited with thousands of others. It was a free event, full of Christmas spirit. She couldn't afford to take him to the Winter Village at Bryant Park, no more than she could take him ice skating, even though she loved ice skating and Jacob had started to learn back when they were in North Carolina. She'd almost had a heart attack when she saw the prices to rent skates.

She had assumed that a visit to see the tree-lighting ceremony would have been enough, and buying him a thick and creamy hot chocolate from one of the stalls at the Christmas market along the way would seal the deal.

But she'd been won over by the magic and splendor of the streets and had made the mistake of turning onto Fifth Avenue. Glittering Christmas lights and sparkling snowflakes, purple, silver and blue danced along the storefronts. It was a magical, mystical, fantastical wonderland, and both she and Jacob were caught up in its shimmering spell.

She shuffled along, listening to the lady from one of the recruitment agencies she had visited earlier, regarding an interview she'd attended two days ago. She hadn't gotten that job either.

"Did you dress professionally?" the woman on the phone asked her.

"Of course I did."

"Then I don't understand it. You have the qualifications and you're only looking for temporary work. You just have to keep trying."

"I don't understand it myself." She stopped for a moment and panicked. *Where was Jacob?* He'd let go of her hand for a second and disappeared out of sight. She looked around frantically until she saw him standing at the door of a toy store. Complete relief swept over her. The shop looked big and glitzy and it broke her heart to see him standing there.

Who was that talking to him?

She marched up angrily, unsure whether she was angry with herself for not being able to afford anything, or angry with the man for trying to entice her son inside.

The salesclerk was tall and solemn-looking and he'd opened the door for Jacob but she knew her son well. She knew he wouldn't go inside because she'd taught him not to talk to strangers. But even so, she knew he would be standing there, almost salivating. She walked up to him and, just as she predicted, Jacob waited patiently, not going in yet desperately wanting to all the same. One look at his face confirmed exactly why she'd been deliberately avoiding these big stores.

They couldn't afford to go into stores like this, Jacob knew that. They could browse, but she was in a hurry to get him home and feed him. It had been a long day for him, coming to the city right after school. It took just under an hour but after a whole day at school, this trek into the city—where she'd tried to combine a visit to Rockefeller Center with a few visits to recruitment agencies—had tired him out completely, and this cold and chilly weather only exacerbated his asthma.

Jacob looked at her with his big excited eyes and she had to give in. The salesclerk eyed her coldly but the sheer look of delight on her boy's face warmed her heart on this chilly Friday evening. The more Jacob pleaded with her, the more she relented. But when the man told her to put the kid out of his misery, she felt the blood rush to her temples.

"He's not miserable," she replied defensively, her nostrils flaring as she stared into the man's cold, blue eyes.

"He doesn't look too happy to me," the man replied, looking at her coldly. She ignored him and told Jacob that he could have a look but no more than ten minutes. Her son's face instantly lit up as she stepped inside, feeling comforted as the rush of warm air heated her chilled hands and face.

She'd come here once, last Christmas, when Kay had told her to spend the holiday with her. Kay had bought Jacob a small remote control car which had given him hours of pleasure; something they had both needed on their first Christmas away from Colt.

Jacob sat on the floor and started to play with some toys and she looked around the store, noting that it was full of lots of children and that there was a man going around taking photographs.

There didn't appear to be many parents. She wondered if there was a special event going on; one that she and Jacob had unknowingly crashed. Savannah walked over to where the rude salesclerk was standing, and saw a woman talking to him.

"Is something going on in the store?" Savannah asked.

"We're not open to the public," the woman replied. She had

shiny dark hair and shiny shoes. Savannah felt instantly mortified. "You're not? I'm sorry," she apologized only to discover that the man was now talking to Jacob.

She rushed over just as the man got up to answer a phone call.

"I'm sorry, honey. We have to go," she said to her son, and saw his face drop. "I don't think we should be here. The salesclerks don't look too happy. I think they're having some sort of Christmas party for the children."

"Aaaaw, Mommy." His look of disappointment cut her heart into two. The idea of pulling him away just when he'd found something that made him so happy pricked her as sharply as a needle.

No wonder the man had looked at her with such contempt. He'd taken pity on Jacob and let him in because he felt sorry for them.

"You should let the poor kid stay," the man said, creeping up behind her. She didn't like the way he looked at her, at the way he was eyeing her clothes. Suddenly she felt more conscious than ever of her ripped stockings.

"He's not a poor kid," she replied, turning her back on him so that he couldn't see the ugly tear in her stockings.

Jacob stared at the floor quietly.

"Looks to me like he wants to stay."

"But the woman said—"

"I don't care what she said." The man's voice had a hard edge to it.

And I don't care what you say, she thought. The moment had been ruined and she didn't want to be here any longer. The two salesclerks were obviously having a disagreement among themselves. Then the woman approached her and told her about tonight being a charity event for children from adoption centers.

Savannah was now desperate to leave. Not only was she humiliated for having shown up at an event they weren't invited to, but she now also felt drab and dirty in front of this woman. With her matching red suit and shoes and handbag, and her perfect hair and her perfect makeup, she appeared to have the perfect life; a life so different than the one Savannah had.

Jacob said something about seeing the man on TV but Savannah wasn't paying attention. She felt the color rise to her cheeks.

"No, I don't think you did, honey," she said quickly, wishing they were outside. She didn't like the cold stare the man gave her. It made her feel unwelcome.

But Jacob was insistent. "I did, Mom. He was on TV."

Savannah raised an eyebrow. "Oh, really, honey? Come on. Let's go." She threw a contemptuous look at the man who smiled at Jacob as they swept past him.

Outside on the cold, frosty streets again, Savannah breathed easier. But she could see that the chill in the air wasn't so good for Jacob. "Here," she said, handing him the asthma inhaler. "Remember how to do it?"

"One puff," he told her, then put the piece into his mouth and pressed, breathing in long and slow.

"Better?"

He nodded.

"It won't always be like this," she told her boy, as they walked along in the cold, desperate to get home. One day she'd be able to walk into this store and buy him whatever he wanted.

"I know, Mommy. It's okay."

His words brought a lump to her throat. She was bringing him up properly, with values, manners and gratitude. Despite the dark memories from his childhood, she felt confident that he wouldn't be scarred for life. She was trying to build happier memories for both of them and had given herself one year to get her life back together.

She sensed Jacob had retreated into himself once more. "Honey," she said, trying to cheer him up. "You've gone quiet again. What are you thinking?"

"You didn't believe me."

"I didn't believe you about what?"

"About that man."

"What man?"

"The man in that store. I told you he was on TV."

"Okay, sure, I believe you." But her mind had already wandered and she was thinking of the things she needed to do tomorrow in order to find work.

"Can we go back there next week?"

"What, honey?" Her thoughts had drifted to more important matters. She didn't particularly relish the idea of wandering around the cold streets of New York visiting more recruitment agencies, yet sending her resumes out wasn't yielding much success either. If she didn't find something soon, she'd have to go back to waitressing in the evenings, something she didn't want to do because it meant leaving Jacob at Rosalee's until late evening.

As nice as Rosalee was, Savannah didn't want to burden Kay's former cleaning lady too much. Savannah now cleaned the apartment herself but used Rosalee every so often for childcare.

She could start waitressing again but it was an option she left as a last resort, when she could no longer put food on the table.

"To the toy store, Mommy. Can we go back?"

"I'm not sure. Let's see." She hated denying him things and tried to do her best. But the toys in that store were extortionate and putting food on the table mattered more.

CHAPTER THREE

The highlight of their weekend had been putting up the small two-foot-long Christmas tree that Savannah had bought from Wal-Mart. It was gaudy and fake, but she and Jacob had decorated it with excitement and joy, munching on Oreos and pretzels and dancing to songs on the radio.

Things turned even better on Monday when luck smiled down. One of the agencies called her first thing in the morning as she got ready for another day of wandering around New York.

Her self-esteem hovered somewhere between mildly hopeful and cautiously realistic. But the call from the agency telling her that an urgent last-minute job had come up was the best Christmas gift she could have hoped for.

Was she interested?

She most certainly was.

The work would be boring and tedious basic administrative tasks. Did she mind?

She didn't care as long as they paid her.

Could she take it?

Oh, god, yes!

Could she start today?

She was already there.

Savannah stared at the tall skyscraper and took a deep breath in. A few weeks of filing at this place? She'd clean the toilets here willingly if they asked her.

She stepped inside the cool metallic and marble interior of Stone Enterprises and stared at the pale gray walls and the leather and steel furnishings that surrounded her. White porcelain vases full of lilies adorned the place.

The recruitment agency had told her she'd need to look super sharp in a place like this even if she was only doing menial tasks.

Savannah gave her name and the name of the person she was supposed to work for to the cool blonde at reception. The woman looked so smart and stylish that Savannah stared at her own clothes in dismay. She'd worn her black suit. It had never been a suit, just separates, but the color seemed similar enough that her ensemble could pass as a suit, even though the material of her skirt was different than that of her jacket.

"Please take a seat," the blonde receptionist told her. "Someone will come down for you shortly." Noting the woman's blonde pony-tailed hair, Savannah fingered her own mousy brown hair gingerly, trying to smooth it. She looked around as people strode in purposefully. Not only was it the wrong color, it wasn't even within an inch of being as groomed and as shiny as the hair of the women who worked here.

She stared in further dismay at her shoes which she'd polished on the weekend but which now exhibited telltale splashes of Jacob's orange paint on one of them.

How come she hadn't noticed that earlier?

She considered going to the ladies room but decided to

postpone that until later, after her boss had shown her the tasks. She sat down on the soft padded leather sofa, waiting nervously and feeling out of place as time went by.

It's only filing, she reminded herself. *I can do this.*

The elevator doors in front of her opened and the noise of sharp, high-heeled footsteps followed.

"Ms. Page?" A redhead in a pristine black and white suit appeared before her. "Hello," she put out her hand for Savannah to shake. "I'm Briony Marsh."

"Nice to meet you," Savannah replied, getting up from her seat.

"I hope you're not afraid of heights," said the woman. "You'll be on the twenty-first floor."

Savannah shook her head and followed the woman into the elevator which was half full but it emptied by the time they reached the twenty-first floor.

"This way," said Briony and led Savannah through a long corridor that had identical doors leading off it.

The floor was carpeted in deep black and she could feel its thickness even through her shoes. The walls were papered silver and black and she wondered if all the floors were the same. The whole building and everything inside it, the people and the furnishings, screamed rich and extravagant.

With trepidation, she followed Briony to the end of the corridor, to a smaller room on the right. The office was small, but it had everything she needed; a computer with an attached scanner, a printer and a phone.

"You'll be working in here for the next three weeks."

Three weeks? Savannah's heart did a triple somersault. She'd been so excited to have a job that she hadn't even asked the agency about her hourly rate or how long the contract was for.

"Is that all right with you? It'll take you right up to Christmas Eve. Can you work Christmas Eve?"

Savannah knew she couldn't because Rosalee was going to her son's over Christmas and this left her without childcare, but she found herself nodding in response. "Yes," she replied, grateful for extra work.

"We usually close half day that day, but this project is important and it needs to be done quickly."

"It's fine," she replied. It was freaking amazing, or it would be, once she figured a way around her childcare problem.

Christmas Eve. Maybe she'd be able to buy Jacob a few decent Christmas presents this year.

"It's straightforward enough." Briony pointed to the big, bulky plastic boxes that were piled one on top of another and reached just above her head.

"You'll need to go through those boxes and take a few bundles of files and work through them in order. Let me show you. Take out a bundle. It's paperwork for one client. Some might have many bundles to their names. Scan each sheet like this," she slipped the sheet of paper into the scanner. "Then save it like this. When you've scanned one bundle, put everything back in order back into the boxes. I've got some empty ones in that corner for you to start with."

How long was this going to take? Savannah wondered. It looked simple enough.

"They're more or less in alphabetical order. Start with these, see, they're numbered at the sides. The scanning is what will take the longest time."

That's all she had to do?

"I'm sure you'll be fine, there's nothing much to it. Just work your own system. Go through these boxes first." Briony pointed to the three boxes that were spread out on the floor. "I had the maintenance men get them down for you. Do these first before you start on those." She pointed behind her and Savannah looked at the three piles of stacked boxes piled high and wondered how she was going to get them down.

"I think three weeks should be enough. See how you do."

"Thanks," said Savannah.

"I'm on extension 3279 if you need me. It's just a few doors down." She smiled and slipped out super-fast, before Savannah had even had time to ask her anything.

Savannah stared around her in a daze, knowing nothing about what department this was, who she was working for, how long she had for lunch or where the ladies room was. It was as if she'd been left to her own devices. Still, she could hardly complain.

She had an office job in Lower Manhattan, in the Financial District. She was here for three weeks which meant three weeks of income. The thought made her smile as if she'd just heard one of Jacob's jokes.

She took off her coat and scarf and smiled at the idea of having her own office with nobody else to worry about. She wasn't sure she'd fit in anyway; not if the rest of the people who worked here looked like the models from the Paris catwalks. She smoothed down her skirt; at least she had new stockings and they weren't torn. Yet.

She set to work quickly, knowing that the work was easy to do and that it beat working at the supermarket. She was grateful for the good things that had at last started to show up in her life: an apartment in New York, for which she had to pay no rent, a wonderful babysitter and now this.

The best thing of all? No Colt. Nobody to tell her she was a worthless piece of shit. No nasty scenes for Jacob to witness.

She and Jacob were safe and happy, and she felt lucky to be here.

Before long, she'd finished the first box. Staring out of the window to take a breath, Savannah observed the ant-like images of people crawling around on the sidewalks below. The Christmas decorations looked garish without the magic of the dark sky but it didn't matter. She was happy. Even graffiti would look good to her the way she was feeling.

This building was huge and she had no idea how many floors the company she worked for occupied but once this contract ended, she could ask Briony if any of the other departments might need a temp. It was an exciting possibility and for now, the money worries that usually plagued her at night and clung to her soul like mildew during the day were temporarily pushed away.

Reenergized, she set to work with gusto and by lunchtime was almost through the three single boxes which had been lying on the floor. If she didn't slow down, she would get through the rest of them far quicker than three weeks. If she wasn't careful, she'd do herself out of a job. She had to slow down.

It was time for lunch and her homemade sandwiches but she paid a visit to the ladies room first. As she made her way back to the office, she heard a voice behind her.

"Are you lost?"

She turned around to see a woman frowning at her.

"No," Savannah replied, and was about to go into her office.

"Do I know you?" the woman asked, leaning in and peering at her. "You look familiar."

Savannah recognized her instantly. Morticia Addams in a business suit. How could she ever forget? It was the woman from the toy store. All of a sudden, Savannah wasn't so sure that she was a salesclerk.

"I'm working here for a few weeks," explained Savannah, feeling the need to justify her presence since the woman looked at her as though she'd caught her stealing.

"Here?" The woman's eyes scanned her appearance from

top to bottom. Was that a look of pity that flashed behind her eyes? Savannah couldn't tell.

"I'm working for Briony Marsh." *Why don't you go ask her if you don't believe me?*

"You are?" The woman's steely blue eyes sparkled with amusement, heating Savannah's skin for the wrong reasons. "Welcome," she said, and headed back towards the elevator bank.

"Thanks," murmured Savannah under her breath, and hoped she wouldn't run into her again.

CHAPTER FOUR

Tobias noticed the smirk on her face as soon as Candace strutted into his office to hand him his lunch. "What's so funny?"

"It seems we take on just about anyone."

Puzzled, he lifted an eyebrow.

"That woman," Candace continued, "from the toy store last week; the one with the kid you took pity on."

Last week was a lifetime away in Tobias's life. "What woman?"

"At the charity event at the toy store ... for the adoption centers. The woman with that big hole in her stockings. She's in room 218."

Now he remembered. The woman whose son had wanted to stay. The one with the inhaler. "She's working here?"

Candace nodded. "That's exactly what I thought. She's working *here*. Can you believe it?"

He shrugged, not sure he understood what she was getting at. "What's so strange?"

Candace stifled a laugh and wrapped her shiny nails around

the fur collar of her coat, holding it snug against her neck. "She doesn't even look the type."

"I didn't know we had a *type,*" Tobias responded smoothly. He hadn't been a *type*—this local boy from Queens. But someone had believed in him, had mentored him and given him a chance. Someone had seen something in the young, dyslexic child whom teachers had given up on. He had a fast and clever brain and a killer instinct for making million-dollar deals.

For all her talk, the only thing Candace had going for her was that she was his PA, and that in itself gave her prestige.

"She's wearing a cheap ten-dollar suit. It doesn't look to me as if she's even run a brush through her hair. And you should see her shoes. Covered in orange paint!" She wrinkled her perfect nose.

"If she can do the job, I don't care."

"I don't understand why Briony couldn't get one of her regular people to do that job. It's those customer files you wanted scanned and digitized. It's something a three-year-old could do."

"I don't want a three-year-old or anyone who works for this company, for that matter, to go through my customer files. I want someone to come in and quickly finish the job." He unwrapped his corned beef sandwich and waited for her to leave.

Candace hoisted her slim and slender fingers on her hips. "I'd forgotten how paranoid you are, Tobias."

"I don't trust anyone."

"Don't worry," she turned to walk out of his office. "I doubt that woman can even read." She gave him a wicked smile, confirming her bitch status.

She did a good job for him though, and so he let her be. He tore into his sandwich and considered the idea of the woman who now worked on the same floor as him. For a moment, he wondered how her son was but just as quickly the thought was dismissed as his attention quickly drifted to his emails.

It was only later, when he got out of the elevator after meeting with one of his managers, that Tobias's curiosity got the better of him. Instead of returning to his office, he walked a few doors down to Room 218. The boy so reminded him of himself that Tobias's interest in him drove him to hover outside the door, wondering how to casually walk in and inquire about the child.

Not one to make conversation with people at the best of times, he decided against it. While he was interested to hear how the boy was doing, he had no desire to talk to the boy's mother. He started to walk away but the sound of something big and heavy falling, punctuated by a frightened shriek at the end, stopped him.

He rushed back and flung the door wide open.

"Oh...shit!" The woman lay sprawled on the floor with her legs akimbo and surrounded by a heap of plastic boxes that had fallen. Only one stack of boxes remained standing.

"Are you all right?" he asked, crouching by her side. She stared up at him, eyes wide, her hair falling around her shoulders.

She scrambled up to a sitting position. "I'm fine." She brushed her hand over her clothes, as if trying to smooth them down.

"Are you hurt?" He glanced over her, clearly noticing that her skirt had ridden up to her thighs and that the middle button of her shirt had come undone.

"I was trying to get one of those boxes down."

The boxes were heavy and she could have been hurt. "Are you insane?" he asked, not without a hint of irritation. He held out his hand and pulled her up.

Once standing, she let go of his hand as if it was on fire, then smoothed her skirt down again. "They were piled on top of one another and I'd finished the others—"

He wasn't interested in explanations. "You could have hurt yourself."

"I'm fine, really, I am."

"A lawsuit is the last thing I need."

She let out a cry of indignation. "I would never—"

"Your blouse," he said, his gaze falling to her chest and the button that had gaped open revealing an off-white bra. He turned away as she colored the shade of blood red. She turned her back to him as she did up her button. Now wouldn't be the time to tell her that the back of her stockings had a hole in them. Again. "How's your son?"

"My son?" She turned around, a look of surprise on her face as she smoothed down her skirt and her hair, and tried to put herself together again. "I thought..."

"You thought?"

"I thought you worked in that big toy store."

He raised an eyebrow.

"You're not a salesclerk?" she asked.

Briony walked in just then. "What happened in here?" she asked, looking around at the pile of boxes that had tumbled onto the floor. Papers from a few of them had fallen out, scattering all over.

"She was trying to get it down," Tobias explained.

"You finished the other boxes?" Briony looked surprised.

"They were half-full."

"Didn't you go through the safety rules with her?" Tobias asked Briony.

"I—" Briony's face flushed.

"It wasn't her fault." The woman jumped to Briony's defense quick as a flash. "I thought I could lift the lid off and get a few bundles out."

Briony shook her head. "Next time, call maintenance on 1111 and get someone to lift the boxes onto the floor for you. Or come and see me if you need anything. I'm in 222."

"I will. Sorry about the mess."

"Don't worry about the mess. Let me introduce you both," said Briony. "This is Tobias Stone, and this is Savannah Page. She's with us for three weeks."

They looked at one another and exchanged forced smiles.

"That will be all, Briony," Tobias said, turning to Briony, who nodded and left the room.

"It wasn't her fault. You shouldn't jump to the wrong conclusions so quickly."

"Jump to the wrong conclusion?" Tobias frowned. "That's rich, coming from someone who thought I worked at the toy store."

"It's even worse that you didn't work at the store and spoke to my son. I've taught him not to talk to strangers and you should have known better than to tell him to come inside."

"You were so busy on the phone, you weren't even paying attention to him. Anything could have happened." He could see that she didn't like the sound of that, the way she narrowed her eyes at him. He stepped towards the door and opened it, then turned around. "Jacob—how is he?" He still wanted to know.

"He's fine. Why?" She looked at him as if to ask what business it was of his. The way she stood with her hands on her hips, it was obvious that she couldn't wait for him to leave.

"I was just wondering, that's all. I saw he needed his inhaler." No matter how much she tried to smooth her hair down, there was a curl that always fell forward into her eyes. "It was too much unnecessary excitement over toys." She made it sound like an accusation. He hadn't known asthma to be brought on by excitement and chose not to reply to her comment.

"Candace tells me that you're working here for a few weeks."

"Until Christmas. What are you doing here?"

Amusement filled the smile he gave her and he watched her brush the dust off her sleeves.

"I work here, too."

Displeasure twisted her features and she looked away, as if considering what impact this might have on her. "It's a small world, isn't it? Nice to meet you, but I have work to do."

"As do I," he said, sliding his cell phone out of his back pants pocket. "If you'll excuse me." She bent down to pick up the papers that had fallen everywhere as he left the room.

Four hours of back-to-back meetings this morning had left him feeling tightly wound up and maybe he would slot Naomi in later this evening.

CHAPTER FIVE

"If you'll excuse me."

Savannah shrugged, relieved to see the back of the man she'd mistaken for a salesclerk. She bent down and collected all the papers together. When she had tidied everything up, she left her office and knocked on Briony's door.

"You don't have to knock," said Briony, when Savannah walked into the large one-room office where three other women sat with a desk in each corner, all of them facing the middle. Savannah braced herself, ready to make her apology.

"I'm sorry about what just happened." The last thing she wanted was to displease Briony and she couldn't afford to get off to a bad start. She needed this contract and hoped that many more offers of work would follow. "I didn't mean for you to get into trouble on my account."

Briony chuckled. "Don't worry about it. Tobias isn't the easiest of people to work for."

"He's your boss?"

"He's the main man," Briony replied. "He owns the company."

"Which company?" Savannah asked, thinking she had misheard.

"Stone Enterprises."

"*He* owns this *entire* building?"

"Didn't you know?"

Savannah shook her head. She had no idea that the hard-faced and cold man she'd met was even capable of making friends, let alone running a company as large as this.

"How long have you been in New York, Savannah?"

"Since summer."

"And you've never heard of Tobias Stone? Or the Stone building? Which is this one, by the way."

"My son said he'd seen him on TV."

"Your son is way more clued in." Briony laughed "On a more serious note, if you need help to get the rest of the boxes down, you must call maintenance. You can't risk hurting your back or incurring some other injury."

"I will. I'm sorry it happened."

Briony got up and put her coat on. "You're a fast worker. I like that." She nodded her head approvingly. "We need people like you, just don't injure yourself."

Her praise brought a smile to Savannah's face.

"Call maintenance when the others need shifting." Briony reminded her.

"I will. Thanks."

"Now that you're here, would you mind going to the tenth floor? I'm going to lunch but you could go ask for your security badge at reception there. That way you'll be able to walk right in tomorrow morning without me needing to come get you from ground floor reception."

"Sure." She left Briony's office feeling happier, and saw that the elevator doors had opened. She rushed to get in and it was only as the doors shut that she saw the elevator was going up.

Damn.

Seeing that the button to the thirtieth floor had already been pressed, she decided to wait until the elevator arrived at that floor before she pressed the button to descend again.

"Where are you going?" The moment she heard the voice, she instantly regretted getting in.

Trust her to get into the same elevator as Tobias Stone. She stared up and looked into his narrowed eyes which were now the color of slate.

"I—uh—I'm going up," she replied, trying to keep her voice level. Knowing who he was suddenly made her tread carefully and she didn't feel as well equipped to shoot off snarky comments.

"You're coming to my penthouse? With me?" His voice was laced with a mocking tone and yet his words sent electric shivers down her spine.

His *penthouse?*

On the thirtieth floor?

There was no way to get out of this except to come clean. "Seeing that I didn't know you had a penthouse on the thirtieth." *Seeing that I didn't even know who you were until a few moments ago.* "I think we both know that I need to go down."

"Go down?" His lips curled up, and it was the first hint of a smile, albeit a very naughty smile, that he gave her. She sensed that Tobias Stone was a man of hidden meaning and innuendo. But it didn't explain why it made her stomach dance as though the wings of a butterfly had brushed against it.

"I—I—" she cleared her throat. "I need to pick up my security tag from the tenth floor."

He said nothing, but even without looking at him, she felt him giving her the once-over. She suffered in silence the awkward and slow ride to the topmost floor and kept her attention on the elevator buttons, avoiding eye contact with Mr. Stone. Yet heat prickled slowly along her skin. Something about him, about being in a confined space *with* him, was causing her body to react in a strange way.

The door opened and he walked out, leaving her to slowly exhale and slump back in relief against the elevator wall.

If she was curious for a glimpse into his penthouse, she was disappointed. She saw only a hallway, carpeted this time in light gray, with black wallpaper. At the end of the hallway was a door. She continued to stare as Tobias Stone reached the door, her heart rate accelerating like wildfire. He paused before it and she wondered if he would turn around.

Her mouth fell open and crazy thoughts swirled around in her head. She knew that he knew she was watching him, and she quickly forced herself to press the button to close the doors. She hit the button to the tenth floor. Overcome with relief as the elevator slowly descended, Savannah felt her stomach do a crazy dance. What was it that had sent her heart rate rocketing? Was it the idea of what lay beyond the doors to his penthouse, or the smell of power that automatically came with so much wealth?

She didn't want to know.

When the elevator stopped at the tenth floor, she walked out, feeling slightly giddy. It reminded her of the early days when Colt had first kissed her, way before his fist had left blue marks all over her body.

CHAPTER SIX

Tobias walked into his penthouse and poured himself a shot of whiskey.

He didn't usually drink in the afternoon. But he'd just heard that this morning's negotiations had fallen through and it didn't look as if they were any closer to doing business with this company. It always pissed him off when a multi-million-dollar deal slipped through his hands.

He loosened his tie and threw off his jacket, letting the dark, grassy taste of whiskey slide down his throat as he stared out of his high-rise penthouse. He saw nothing but small specks of dirt down below; people scurrying around like busy ants. Instead of looking down, he much preferred to look out at the New York skyline, to see the city lying before him and to know that he was in the upper echelons of it; he who had been a poor dyslexic child whom most people had been convinced would amount to nothing.

And look at him now. He had everything.

Almost everything.

There had been a time years ago when he had believed he

had almost everything. But no more. He'd lost it in the blink of an eye. Had lost them.

He poured himself another shot of whiskey since he had no meetings or any other business lined up in the afternoon. Walking around the cool white marble floor, he stretched out his neck, trying to get the muscles to loosen up. It was peaceful here. The wide-open apartment gave him a sense of solitude when he craved peace. When he'd bought the building, one of the designers had laughingly suggested that he could have the topmost floor as a penthouse suite. It was an idea that had excited him and he'd decided to go for it, much to the surprise and delight of the designer.

Though he never slept here, it was a good, open space, *his* own space to escape to. Or when he liked to screw.

Excitement coursed through his body and he considered whether to call Naomi over tonight.

His was the type of tightness that she was good at releasing, and paying her by the hour meant he didn't have to go through the rest of that romancing crap. He didn't even have to talk to her. Staring at his watch, he tried to estimate whether to go home for the day. Losing the deal had ruined his mood, and he could do with Naomi setting the world to rights for a few hours. She didn't ask questions, she just serviced him, and that was the best thing about their arrangement.

She was the only other person who had the key to this floor—it was the only way to get here and since the employees only needed to go as far as the twenty-ninth floor, there was no chance any of them would ever go as far as the penthouse. He found it amusing that the new temp had managed to catch a glimpse of the floor that very few people had access to.

When his cell phone rang, and he saw Candace's name on it, he was tempted to ignore it. But he knew she only contacted him if it was an important matter. Reluctantly, he answered it.

"Yes?"

"Where are you?"

"In my penthouse."

"Tobias, you have a meeting in an hour's time with Oliver Rothschild."

Fuck. He'd forgotten. It had only been arranged this morning.

"The driver's coming for you in ten."

"I'll be down shortly."

Oliver's meetings often ended up in a strip joint once the business portion was over, and he had no desire to go there. He drained his glass and knew he needed mouthwash. After the heavy meeting with Oliver Rothschild, he knew he would need to call Naomi to his private residence later.

CHAPTER SEVEN

"Mommmeeeeee!"

Savannah ran out of the kitchen and almost tripped as she rushed to the living room. Jacob sat, excitedly pointing to the screen.

"What is it, Jacob?"

"Look, Mommmy. I told you." He smiled his widest, cheeriest smile.

"The billionaire hedge fund wonderkid, Tobias Stone, lost the..." She stared at the screen, still wearing her rubber cleaning gloves. There, in all his glory, was Tobias Stone. A journalist had intercepted him as he was walking towards a building. Watching him, she could see that he barely looked at the camera, choosing to look away, and his responses were concise, to the point. He barely smiled. The all too brief clip showed him then disappear through the revolving doors of the building. The subheading mentioned a multi-million-dollar deal falling through and then the next TV clip showed Tobias Stone with children around a Christmas tree. It looked as if they were in the toy store, the night she had met him.

She stared, speechless.

"See, Mommy. See, see. Told you, told you." Jacob started to sing.

Savannah walked over to him and sat by him, slowly taking off her wet gloves. "So you did, Jacob. I'm sorry I didn't believe you."

"I like him."

"You don't even know him."

"I know he's kind."

"How do you know that?"

"Because he let me come into the toy store. He said I could pick whatever I wanted."

"He did?"

Jacob nodded.

"That's not really a good reason to like someone, Jacob."

"Why not? He was being kind and nice, and you always said be nice to people. I was nice to him and he was nice back."

"But you don't know him."

"I do! He works in the toy store."

"That's just it, Jacob. He doesn't."

"So why did he tell me to pick what I wanted? Was he lying to me, Mommy?"

"Ah-no, sweetie, he was...uh...he was—"

"Was he lying to those other kids too? One of them told me that he was going to get a present from him, too."

Savannah's eyebrows pinched together. "He wasn't lying, honey. Mr. Stone was going to buy all those children a gift and I think he must have decided to buy you one as well."

"So he's really nice then, isn't he?"

She stared into space, wondering how to explain.

"Isn't he, Mommy? He's really nice." Jacob insisted.

"I guess he is. But you still don't know him. And you shouldn't be talking to strangers. You don't know what people are like. They act all nice to you and then you might find out they're not so nice after all."

"Like Daddy, you mean?"

Her heart thudded to a stop.

"Daddy used to be nice, until he turned horrible. I bet Mr. Stone isn't as nasty as Daddy."

She nodded her head. "No, I don't think he is."

"I don't ever want to see Daddy again."

"I know. That's why we're here. We're happy here, aren't we?"

"I like it here."

She didn't want to leave her son with bad memories, the very things she had tried hard to get rid of. "Did you know that I work for Mr. Stone's company now?"

Her son's eyes grew large, like green-colored flying saucers. "You work with him?"

"I don't actually work *with* him, Jacob. I'm just one of many people there."

"And one day you'll marry him and then we'll be happy. Isn't that right, Mommy?"

"We're happy now, aren't we?"

He nodded.

She got up. "Mommy just works there, honey, and she has no plans to ever get married again. Besides, Mr. Stone is probably already married."

Even if he wasn't, the idea was still ludicrous.

CHAPTER EIGHT

Towards the end of the second week, Savannah had worked her way through most of the boxes. Her work was nearly done and even though she'd tried to work at a snail's pace and drag out the time on the last few boxes, the day came when she had nothing to do.

Luckily, Briony seemed to have recognized her willingness to work and had lined up a few more tasks for her to complete, but this meant moving into the office where Briony worked. She didn't mind, though she much preferred having a room to herself. Instead she now sat at a small spare desk adjacent to Briony's. She was inputting data onto the system; it was yet another tedious job but it was a change from filing and scanning.

"Ease up," Briony told her. "No need to zoom through everything so fast. I suggest you make a real effort to slow down, Savannah. People are starting to wind down for Christmas, not taking off like a rocket."

"Slow down," repeated Savannah, sounding like a robot. She nodded at her boss. "Moms do this all the time. It's second nature for us, multi-tasking and whizzing through things fast. I guess I haven't fully switched off from mom mode."

"How come you're doing temp work?"

Savannah gave her a smile. "I moved to New York a few months ago. It's hard finding full-time work and I have a little boy to take care of. I wanted the flexibility that a temp contract offers." She felt more at ease working here now. Briony was friendly and Savannah hadn't had the misfortune of running into Tobias Stone or his ice-maiden PA again. The fact that Briony had given her extra work to do gave her hope that there might be more work further down the line if she played her cards right.

"I'll say it again. You're a good worker, and I don't say that lightly. I know how hard it is to find a good temp these days."

"Thanks," replied Savannah. "Do you think there's enough for me to do until you break for Christmas?"

"We're only here for two days next week," Briony told her. "If you still want to work right up until Christmas Eve—which is what your agency has you booked here until—it will help us out. You would only be covering the office, taking phone calls and checking emails. I can find you little jobs to do, if you're really desperate to do something."

"It won't be a problem." Savannah told her.

"Great. I'll run you through a few things, but it's going to be dead quiet here. I'm not even sure if Tobias will be around. He usually takes off and goes somewhere hot for Christmas, Mustique or North Island. He doesn't *do* Christmas."

"No?"

Briony shook her head. "He's a workaholic."

"I didn't know," murmured Savannah, even though the man annoyed her, he still intrigued her. She'd noticed the way the others in the office sometimes spoke about him, in revered tones, as if they had a thing for him. Yet the talk was never disrespectful. It was what the women *didn't* say that made her more curious.

Savannah fixed Briony with a curious stare. She'd heard them talking about the office Christmas party next week and caught a few excited giggles about Tobias's attendance there. She leaned in towards Briony and asked her. "I get the feeling that most of these women have the hots for him."

"Can you blame them?" Briony whispered back. "The man's disgustingly rich; some think he's good-looking, though I can't see it myself."

Savannah frowned. For someone who claimed to have not much interest in the man, Briony was doing an awful lot of talking about him.

"What?" Briony cried, then made a face at Savannah's unspoken accusation. "Oh, puh-lease! I don't have time for men. Though I can see why people see him as a babe magnet."

Laughter rang out as the others shared a joke but it was cut short as sudden silence swept across the room. Both she and Briony turned to see Tobias staring at them, wearing a displeased expression. His blue eyes glittered with anger.

There was pin-drop silence.

Savannah wondered how much of their conversation he'd heard.

"Briony, in my office, now."

Savannah jumped, hearing the anger in his voice. Yet she sensed that he was, at some level, questioning her presence in Briony's office.

"And bring her too," he said, his eyes not once leaving Savannah's face. Almost at once, she felt the heat scorching her cheeks. She swallowed, unsure of the reason for his anger and what it had to do with her. He turned and left the room.

Briony stood quickly and glanced at her. "I don't know what

this is about," she said, as if answering the question that Savannah had. "Hurry. Grab a notebook and pencil."

Savannah did as asked and followed Briony to Tobias's office.

"Sit down," he ordered, his back turned to them as he stood, a tall and imposing figure, staring out of the window behind his desk. It wasn't so much a window as a whole wall of glass. From top to bottom. Even though the nearest building opposite was a distance away, Savannah wondered if he was ever worried about someone being able to see right into his office.

"The Dalton file is missing."

The Dalton file? Savannah tried to remember. She didn't know what Tobias was talking about. Briony looked at her first, then looked at him. "Missing from the system or the hard—"

"Both. We have old records. But it hasn't been updated. Candace can't find the folder either." His voice was cold.

Briony turned to Savannah. "Do you remember a Dalton file?"

She'd worked through a lot of files, but she didn't recall that name, although the reason her memory had gone to mush right now was because this man appeared to be blaming her for it.

"I made a note of all the files I scanned. I write them down in my notebook as I worked through them. Let me go get it."

"Don't you have it there?" Tobias asked gruffly, nodding his head at the thin green notebook she gripped in her hands.

"I had another one, a notepad. It's on my desk. I'll go get it." Her voice wavered and she was fearful that she'd messed up.

"Please go check," Briony told her and Savannah made her escape. Her heart pounded beneath her ribcage. Tobias Stone was furious and she didn't understand the level of his anger which was disproportionate to what had happened. It was only a file. Someone else most likely had it, and she was sure it would soon turn up. They weren't working on the latest cure for cancer and people weren't going to die because a file had gone missing.

She hadn't paid much notice to the papers she had been scanning, and had no idea what they pertained to. She'd done her job exactly as she'd been told, and she was conscientious. It hadn't helped when the boxes had tumbled down and the papers had fallen to the floor like confetti at a wedding. But she was thorough, and diligent, and fast, and she'd soon reorganized everything back again.

Ignoring the sympathetic looks from the other girls as soon as she walked in, she grabbed her notepad and rushed back out again.

But as she neared Tobias's office, she heard his raised voice.

"How do you know? She's a temp. Someone you hired last minute, you told me yourself. She could be *anyone*."

She thought she heard Briony laugh in surprise. "She's a good worker, Tobias. She's honest and I trust her. She's not a spy."

A spy?

Savannah's nerves bristled at the suggestion of it. This man thought she was *spying*? She couldn't believe her ears. His level of anger and his accusation suddenly made sense—in a strange and surreal way.

Before she walked in, she scanned through her notes and checked. There was no record of the Dalton file here.

What, she wondered, would he make of that?

She knocked on the door hard, her anger spilling over into her fist. She clenched her jaw when he opened the door.

"I don't have Dalton on my list. See for yourself." She handed her notebook to him. "These are the files I scanned."

Tobias pushed the notepad back at her, barely glancing at it. "So where is it?" His expression hardened as he hurled his accusation at her.

"Perhaps it was never in the boxes in the first place," replied Savannah calmly.

"We have the files for your top one hundred clients, Tobias, Just as you asked. Matthias or one of the other board members, might have it. Have you checked?" Briony suggested.

He walked towards the window, rubbing his forehead with his hand. "Candace told me she had checked."

"You could double-check with Candace," Savannah suggested icily. "Because I haven't stolen it or sold it to one of your competitors."

She remained standing, looking at him as if she wanted to throw the notebook at him. From her peripheral vision, she could make out Briony looking at her as she absorbed the cool look Tobias Stone now gave her.

"Briony, could you go check with Candace again?"

Savannah spoke up. "Can we please check—because I hate being accused of something I haven't done." Her body was rigid with anger, the same way she felt when Jacob told her about children who laughed at him because of his inhaler. That same spirit now shot forth, even though the situation was different. She was answering back to a man who had the power to take her job away with a snap of his fingers.

She gritted her teeth together.

"Let's check." Briony replied, giving her a you'd-better-get-the-hell-out-of-here look. Savannah turned to follow Briony out of the door.

"Not you," said Tobias, looking at Savannah. "You sit." Briony threw her an apologetic look and rushed out.

Savannah didn't like the way this man had ordered her to sit, as if she were a dog, but she thought better of standing up to him, and instead forced herself to work on calming her temper.

"What agency are you with?"

"Lakestar Recruitment."

"And what did you do before?" He walked towards her slowly with his hands in his pockets.

"I don't see how this is relevant."

"Answer the question."

"I moved here in the summer. This is my first proper office job in the city."

"Proper?"

"I was working at the supermarket in Sunnyside." She felt embarrassed telling him this as if the work she'd done prior might take away from her work credentials.

"Interesting." He watched her like a hawk. She felt as though he was about to pounce on her any moment if she gave him the wrong answer.

"And before that?"

Before that? Why did he need to know what she had done before? She swallowed, doubly surprised that he was asking her such questions, taking her back to that place inside her she'd tried hard to bury; a place filled with black memories.

"Why would you need to know what I did before?"

"Do you want to keep your contract?"

Was that a threat? What she wanted to do was to tell him what she *really* thought of him. And after that, she wanted to tell him to shove his contract up his ass. But she needed this job badly, and so she said nothing. Working for this asshole meant that she and Jacob would get to have a good Christmas.

"I lived with my aunt in Pennsylvania."

"Your aunt?"

Savannah closed her eyes. "I don't see the..." But a knock on the door silenced him.

"Come in," he said, curtly. His eyes narrowed as Briony walked in with a file. It was green—like the others she'd been working with and she prayed it was the Dalton file.

"Matthias had it. He apologizes."

Savannah turned her attention and stared at the man before her with hatred spilling out of every ounce of her body. She was curious to see what he would do now.

"Matthias?" His lips moved together in a tight line, and the muscles in his face hardened. He stared at Briony. "Thank you. That will be all." He nodded at them both.

"I think an apology is in order," demanded Savannah, as she sat waiting expectantly in her chair.

"We should go." She heard Briony's voice behind her but it was Tobias's gaze that kept her pinned to her seat.

"You may leave, Briony. It seems that Ms. Page has something to say." She heard the door close and didn't need to turn to see that it was now only the two of them in the office. She was so drenched in anger that she could barely speak.

"Where is it?" she asked him, trying to control the pitch of her voice. She hated bullies. First Colt, then the children from school. Now this man.

"Where's what?"

"My apology."

His right eyebrow lifted slightly; the movement was so subtle that she'd have missed it if she'd blinked. She got up slowly. "The word doesn't exist in your vocabulary, does it?"

He stood with his arms folded over his chest, watching her but his nonreaction fueled her rage further. "You're a bully, Mr. Stone. An arrogant, self-centered, big bully. I teach my son to stand up to people like you. It's the sort of behavior I expect to see in a school playground, not in a grown man's office, and certainly not in the office of a so-called billionaire. But maybe a country girl like me expects the good in most people. I was mistaken for thinking you might know better."

She walked towards the door, knowing that he wasn't going to apologize.

"I haven't dismissed you."

She turned around, incredulous. "Unbelievable," she muttered, shaking her head.

"You can leave this employment any time you wish, if you don't like my leadership."

"Your leadership leaves a lot to be desired," she shot back. Not only had she done a good job, she'd worked hard, finished her tasks quicker than she'd needed to. Briony was more than happy with her. "I would leave if I didn't need this job so badly."

"Well?"

"Well what?" She kept her hand on the door handle. They stared at one another, gazes locked as she felt a flush creep along her cheeks, knowing that she had overstepped her boundary. It was obvious that a man like Tobias Stone wasn't used to being spoken to in this way.

Colt had been like this, and worse. And his hadn't only been words. He'd talked with his fists too.

She was no longer going to take this shit from anyone—billionaire or not. Did she need this job that much?

Her pride spoke first. "I'll leave right away." She opened the door, ready to walk out, but he was behind her in a flash, and placed his hand on the door to prevent it from opening further. Through the half-open door, Candace stared at them, a surprised look on her face.

Tobias closed the door and she felt his body close behind hers. Not touching hers, but she still felt the heat of his closeness. And it sent shockwaves deep inside her.

"I'd rather not talk to the back of your head, Ms. Page."

He wanted her to turn around now?

Butterflies danced in her stomach and anger gave way to excitement. And she had no idea why. She turned around slowly, just as he backed away. Her heart raced.

"You don't have to leave."

This was his version of an apology?

Her lips twisted, and she was determined not to speak. After all, she wasn't going to thank him for anything because she'd done nothing wrong. Yet despite her best efforts to appear calm and unfazed, her gaze fell to his lips, full and perfect, as his hooded eyes bore into hers.

"I need to get back," she replied, trying hard not to get caught up in the intense look he gave her.

She crept out of his office, staring right past Candace's still surprised face.

CHAPTER NINE

Briony was waiting for her outside her office and she beckoned her into room 222.

"What happened back there?" She looked anxious.

"I *almost* lost my job."

"What?" Briony's eyes widened.

"But it's okay. I'm not going anywhere."

"That's a relief," sighed Briony. "He's not normally so wound up. He's known for his mood swings, and I know there have been problems with a recent business deal."

"It's not right. That was ridiculous, accusing me of taking that file."

Briony threw her arms into the air. "I didn't say he wasn't a jerk occasionally. The guy has more money than you and I could ever dream of. I guess that's how those people live, in constant fear and paranoia that they'll lose everything they have."

"It still doesn't give him an excuse to behave like that. I don't care how rich or successful he is."

Briony shook her head. "Hon, this is New York, not some

farm out in Idaho. This is how people roll in the big city. You have to toughen up a little."

"I'm no softie," Savannah assured her.

"I can see that. The way you spoke to him, not just now but that first time too, when you stood up for me when the boxes fell on you. Nobody says boo to him. Except for Candace."

"You stand up to him," said Savannah. "You're not a complete pussycat with him, either."

"Sometimes," Briony agreed. "But you're something else. Sometimes I'd like to take that man down a peg or two, but I don't have your balls."

"I'm only a temp. Maybe that's why I have more balls than most."

"I'm glad you're here. Oh, I wanted to tell you, on a completely different note, that I got a ticket for you to the Christmas party next week."

"It's a ticketed event?"

"Because you're a temp and the parties only extend to permanent employees, I had to get permission. So, I have a place for you. Can you make it? It's a big fancy affair, a nice meal, plenty to drink. It's not too bad as far as work parties go."

Savannah thought about it. She could do with a night out. Had it really been over a year since she'd left Jacob with her parents to watch a movie with her friends?

"A Christmas party?" She'd have to think about it.

"It's a dressy event too and it's at the Plaza Hotel." This extra information had Savannah reconsidering. The food and drink and talking to Briony part of it appealed but she had no dressy clothes.

"Is Mr. Stone coming?"

"Not you too," Briony groaned.

"What?" She felt the heat pinch her cheeks.

"It's bad enough that the women around here get all excited

wondering if they'll run into him. I thought you were better than that."

"I'd rather not run into him again," said Savannah, dismissing Briony's assumption.

"Then come," Briony pleaded. "We can hang out together while everyone else tries to suck up to Tobias. Not that he will stay for long. He doesn't stick around much and usually takes off on his jet to some exotic location."

"Mr. Stone has a private jet?"

Briony frowned. "That man can buy anything he wants. And puh-lease stop calling him Mr. Stone. You're on the twenty-first floor, which, if you hadn't realized by now, is where the board members have their offices."

"They do?"

Briony rolled her eyes. "Behind the elevator bank, off the corridor near Tobias's office. Luckily, all the high-end administrative staff and managers are down this end." She wiped her brow in mock exaggeration. "It means we don't run into them much."

Now that they were talking so freely, it gave Savannah the courage to ask what had been preying on her mind. "Do you know when I get paid?" She hadn't been too sure if it would be before Christmas or after.

Briony made a sad face and shook her head. "You don't get paid until next month. Sorry."

"*Next month?* In January?" Savannah jolted upright.

"Why, is it a problem?"

Goddamn it, yes. It was a huge problem and it meant she would have to dip into her small reserve of savings. Otherwise, there was no other way to make the kind of Christmas she'd been envisioning come to life. "No," Savannah lied, her hopes free-falling to the ground.

The worry had already started. She'd been so excited for

Jacob, thinking of the money she'd earned, and this latest news was like a bullet through her soul.

"Try to come," said Briony. "It might do you some good, getting out for a change."

"I'll think about it." Savannah promised. But she wasn't so sure anymore.

CHAPTER TEN

He wasn't a bully and the fact that she'd called him one rankled Tobias for the entire day. Something about the new temp made him curious.

The way she'd looked at him, full of disgust, bothered him. Obviously, with hindsight, he knew he'd been hasty to jump to the wrong conclusion. How was he to know that Matthias had the file? Candace had told him that she'd already checked.

He trusted no one, least of all a temp who'd only started a few weeks ago. How was he to know that she wasn't a spy for his competitors who hated that someone as young as him had turned his company into such a stellar success?

A man in his shoes, in his position of power and extreme wealth, could trust no one. As far as he was concerned, he'd done nothing wrong and had merely acted in the best interests of the company.

"You're quiet, more so than usual," commented Naomi, slipping her bra back on. Tobias stared at her as he zipped up his pants. He shrugged.

"You were rough today," she purred, seemingly unperturbed by his silence.

"Sorry. Did I hurt you?"

"Don't be sorry." She slipped him a smile. "The harder, the better. You know how I like it."

He knew how she liked it and what she did for him.

"What's wrong?" Now she was asking too many questions and he preferred not to answer. "Are you still sore about that business deal?" She walked up to him and stroked his cheek, pressing her body up against him.

"It didn't work out," he said, moving away.

"Ooooh," she said. "That explains it. I could...stay a while... if you want?"

"No," he replied quickly, before she started getting any ideas that this was anything other than a strict transaction. When he wanted sex, he called Naomi. It was as simple as that.

"Thanks," she said, picking up the white envelope that he always left by the dresser. "I'll be waiting for your call." He nodded and knew that she would see herself out.

It was late; almost midnight. He'd had problems sleeping again. It always happened when he felt extremely tense. He'd needed this deal, not because he needed the money but because in his world, a deal was a deal. It showed strength and power, which he liked, but he also liked the chase, of going after something that everyone else wanted, and winning it.

But with the highs came the lows and when he'd been tossing and turning, even after a two-hour session in the boxing ring with his trainer, and a run through the streets at eleven, he'd had to resort to calling Naomi. He paid her well and she cost more because he didn't share her with anyone else. She was a high-class call girl just for him. It would cost him far less to have a regular girlfriend, but then he'd need to be there emotionally, make conversation, be nice, smile, pretend to listen. And Tobias Stone did not like to do any of those things. He didn't do relationships. Period.

The love that he'd experienced, the depth of emotion he'd felt and the connection they had shared had died with Ivy. His friends and family told him he was still in shock and that time would heal everything, even wounds this deep. But four years had passed and Tobias still didn't feel a thing.

He had no interest, wanted no commitment, no soulmate, no partner.

Sex? Yes.

A meaningful relationship? Never.

As his thoughts meandered, he came to the realization that he had acted badly in regards to Savannah Page. At the very least, he needed to apologize to her. For some reason, it mattered to him that she'd called him a bully and he wanted to put her straight.

It wasn't his style to own up to his weaknesses or his wrongdoings, but in this instance, he felt compelled to admit that he'd been wrong.

The Christmas party next week would be an occasion where he could do just that.

CHAPTER ELEVEN

Tobias Stone gazed out of his window as he was driven home. He needed to be at the Plaza Hotel around eight o'clock.

He normally didn't like these events but it was the annual Christmas party and he had to make an appearance. He threw an extravagant party for over a thousand of his employees that were based at Stone Enterprises, the head office.

It was an event that was often mentioned in the press due to the huge expense, but to him the cost was irrelevant.

For most of his employees, it was the highlight of December, probably for the year. Most would never have ventured into the Plaza in Manhattan, otherwise.

Tonight, it was his intention to show his face for an hour, spend a little time mingling with the managers and making small talk. It was common for him to show up and then slip away in his private jet somewhere hot. Someplace away from Christmas festivities and crowds.

This year, Christmas was going to be a quiet affair in New York. Naomi was pissed. She'd loved going to North Island last year and now he regretted mentioning a few months ago that they might slip away to Mustique this year. It was a given that she would accompany him. Naomi was sex on tap and he needed her to help him unwind.

He shifted in his seat. The idea of Christmas in New York was not easy for him, because it was filled with too many bad memories that even Naomi couldn't extinguish. With the deal having fallen through, his mood had soured and he had now decided to stay at home during these holidays.

As he sat in the car in heavy rush hour traffic, he felt irritated. Not only was he *not* going away, but the uneasiness he felt about having to apologize to Savannah Page niggled him further.

Tobias didn't like things that niggled him.

He liked everything to be in order.

He liked his world to be calm and orderly.

It had taken years for him to reach that stage and whiskey was still his best friend when things got really bad.

He would go to his apartment, shower and change and then head out to the party later that evening. He would talk to Savannah Page, make his peace and be done with it. But as the car stopped at the traffic light, Tobias did a double take as he stared out of the tinted windows.

It couldn't be.

It was.

He squinted, trying to get a closer look. There, standing in a long line of people, was Savannah Page.

The car slowly started to move off. "Wait!" Tobias shouted to his driver.

"I can't, sir. The traffic's moving."

"Pull over."

The driver parked the car a few yards down and Tobias sat in the car, hidden behind the dark tinted windows, waiting for Savannah to pass by.

What was she doing here? Shouldn't she have been making her way to the party? He looked ahead and saw a mass of people further along the street but he couldn't see what they were lining up for.

"What is this place?" he asked.

"I believe it's a food bank."

"A food bank?" What was Savannah Page doing at a food bank? He waited and watched, curious to see, knowing that any moment now she would pass by as the line shuffled along. Being able to see her without her knowing that he was watching her gave him a secret thrill.

As the line slowly moved forward, she was almost level with his line of sight and he took a good look at her face. She looked anxious and tired, but most of all she looked worried.

But why was she here?

Tobias swallowed. He remembered the desperation in her eyes a few days ago when she'd told him what she thought of him and he'd suggested she could leave.

"I would if I didn't need this job so badly."

He'd thrown something at her that had hurt deep, that would have worried her, and now he understood.

"You can drive on now, Morris."

"Yes, sir."

CHAPTER TWELVE

After much convincing from Rosalee, Savannah had decided to go to the Christmas party. "You're young, you're beautiful and you must go. You cannot sit inside your entire life. I will look after Jacob at my house. He can play with my grandson." The woman had been so insistent that Savannah felt she'd had no choice but to go.

The women in the office had been giggling like schoolgirls all afternoon and from the sounds of it, not much work was being done after lunch. The pre-party buzz filled the air; adrenaline surged, and hopes and wishes floated around the office like fairy dust as the women wondered who would be at the party tonight.

Only Savannah and Briony managed to keep their heads down and work.

Everyone had hung up their dresses on the coat rack in the corner, and one look at the short and showy red and black dresses convinced Savannah that the plain black dress she'd worn to a funeral once was better off neatly folded in her bag. She would rather risk wearing it creased up than hang it up for everyone to see.

But when Rosalee called her later, rather apologetically, to tell her that her grandson had run a fever and her son was taking her back to Brooklyn tonight instead of on Christmas Eve, Savannah was almost relieved to have an excuse not to attend.

"Just come for an hour. Have something to eat and a few drinks and then leave." Briony had done her best to convince her to go, but Savannah had pushed that idea to the back of her mind. Briony wouldn't understand. She had no children, and it sounded as if she and her partner, Max, had a carefree lifestyle; no kids, no worries, no debt. Aside from working for an a-hole like Tobias Stone, Savannah considered Briony to have the perfect life. But Savannah considered herself to be extremely lucky, despite the hardships she'd endured. She could never imagine a life without Jacob. She loved her son with all of her being and knew her life was all the richer for having this little guy be part of it.

"I can't," she told her disappointed friend and in the end she left the office and the excitement of the party behind her.

Since she had left a little earlier, she decided to pass by the food bank before she caught the subway home. Her worries about not getting paid this month had put her into panic mode. She was looking for ways to make her money last longer and at the last moment had visited the food bank where she'd picked up powdered donuts, packaged cookies and canned goods in an effort to make the food last over the holidays.

She picked up Jacob from Rosalee's place and was grateful that she had fed him. Having Rosalee close by, treating her and Jacob almost like family, meant that she didn't feel completely alone in this big, and at times unforgiving, city.

When she arrived back home, she fixed herself a sandwich and tried to stop wondering what Briony and the others would be doing at the Christmas party. She tried not to get too disheartened about missing out on an evening at the fancy hotel she'd often seen in movies. It would have been something to have seen what it looked like from inside.

Of course Tobias Stone would be there and it was better that she was at home, away from the danger of running into him.

"Can I play for a while? Please, Mommy."

"Half an hour and then bedtime. Tomorrow you're going to have to come to work with me."

Jacob's face glowed with excitement. "To work? With you? Really?"

"Yes, *really*."

He ran off, super excited. With Rosalee's grandson getting sick and her going to stay at her son's two days earlier than planned, it now meant that she had two days without childcare. She had no option but to take Jacob to work.

But she was worried too, especially knowing that Briony and the other women were away now until the new year. She hoped she wouldn't run into Tobias Stone—not now, with him being so mad at her. She needed all the work she could get and while it hurt her, the delay in receiving payment, she knew next month would be sweeter for it. She'd dipped into her savings and bought the Christmas gift that Jacob had coveted, as well as a few other little things she knew he would like, and she couldn't wait to see his face when she gave them to him.

She wanted to make this Christmas special and hoped that it would herald a new beginning for them both.

Tomorrow, she had the pressure of getting Jacob into the building. She had decided to leave early in the morning, before the masses showed up for work, and then she had the tricky task of keeping him hidden in the office. Thankfully, it would be empty.

She only had two days left at work and then she would need a Christmas miracle to save her from more debt worries.

CHAPTER THIRTEEN

Tobias Stone walked around the foyer outside the grand ballroom of the hotel and had already lost the enthusiasm to attend his own Christmas party. He had been on a mission to speak to Savannah Page—to make himself feel better—and to have her see that he wasn't always a hard-nosed bastard.

Her name had been on the list of attendees from the twenty-first floor. He'd purposely asked for that list from Candace for this very reason. But she obviously wasn't coming. He looked around for Briony, hoping that she might give him a clue as to why.

He was about to walk up to her when Candace rushed to his side. Dressed in a bright red cocktail dress, she was impossible to miss. She'd been here all day overseeing the plans for this evening.

"Tobias," she trilled, flashing him an ultra-bright smile that made him wince. "Nice of you to attend your own Christmas party."

"I thought I'd show my face."

"I hope you're staying for dinner after your usual annual address, since you're not jetting off this time."

"I'll stay for dinner." Or maybe not. Maybe he would disappear after the appetizers.

"How did Naomi take it? The news about you staying in New York?" Everyone, even Candace, believed that Naomi was his girlfriend and he liked to keep it that way. He paid Naomi enough for her to keep her mouth shut.

He shrugged. Naomi had no opinion. He didn't pay her for her opinion. But it hadn't stopped her from whining or making the occasional remark when she'd found out that he wasn't going away this Christmas. She was onto a good deal, and the girl was smart, she knew it wasn't in her best interests to piss him off.

"You're not very talkative this evening, are you?" Candace was the only other person who spoke to him on an even level, like that Page woman. But sometimes Candace's overfamiliarity grated on him. He clenched his jaw. "Let me get you a drink," she suggested, hooking her attention onto a poor, unsuspecting waiter. "It might loosen you up."

"No," he shook his head.

"You need to lighten up, Tobias." She grabbed a drink for him nonetheless.

"I don't pay you to disregard my orders." Taking the glass of champagne from her, he saw the mischief in her eyes and guessed that she'd had more than a couple of drinks by now.

"Sometimes you need to be told, Tobias."

"There are boundaries, Candace. Don't forget them," he said, before she made a comment that would make them both uncomfortable. She was excellent at her job but sometimes she crossed the line. If she had any illusions about ever becoming something more, he wasn't going to risk her getting any ideas.

"You're sitting with the board of directors at table one," she informed him, sobering up immediately.

"Another night of fun," he muttered under his breath as he

looked around the huge foyer. Just a walkway away there was the Centennial foyer filled to the brim with more employees. Food was served, buffet style, and people were spread out all over the hotel, mixing, flirting and enjoying themselves. Even if Savannah Page had been here, it would have been hard to find her.

Scanning his gaze around, he caught sight of the shock of auburn hair and recognized Briony talking with her friends, all with glasses of champagne in their hands.

"Excuse me," he said, and without even looking at Candace, he left, and cut his way across the packed room to where Briony stood. People greeted him as he moved past them, so that it took longer than it should have to get to her. She turned to him in surprise. "Tobias?" They both knew he wasn't one to seek out others, not in social situations. He usually preferred to watch from a distance, and keep his distance too.

"Is something wrong?" Briony asked.

"No," he replied, wondering if he instilled the fear of God into everyone. The other two women smiled and looked into their glasses, but he remained silent, and they soon disappeared, as if on cue.

"I got it wrong with the Dalton file," he said finally.

For a moment, Briony looked puzzled. "Oh, that." She threw her head back slightly and he knew she considered it odd for him to bring that up now. "Yes, you did."

"I haven't had a chance to talk to you since that day. I wanted to clear up a few things." He found himself in the awkward position of having to explain himself for he knew that whatever he said stood a chance of getting back to that Page woman. For some reason, which he didn't even understand himself, he'd been thinking about her lately and seeing her earlier in the line at the food bank had made him more curious.

"Clear up a few things?"

"It was remiss of me to assume that your temp had taken the file."

Briony was quick to nod her head. "Savannah wouldn't do anything like that. She's a hard worker, and she's honest and reliable. She finished the original job I hired her for within two weeks. We'd taken her on for three. She could have taken her time, but she didn't."

"You're not easily impressed," said Tobias.

"That should tell you something. She's the best temp I've ever hired."

Tobias lifted his face and stared across the room. "She's not here."

"I know she didn't like the accusation you made but she was planning to attend. I think she decided against it at the last minute."

Tobias nodded his head. Maybe she was still mad. He knew he would be if someone had accused him of something he hadn't done.

"Just out of curiosity," he said, trying to sound casual. "When do temps get paid?" This was uneasy territory for him, not just making small talk, but because of the type of information he was after—and it had nothing to with hedge fund transactions.

"Not until January," Briony replied. "Apparently, it's how the agency works."

Tobias narrowed his eyes. So that was why. The bastards. He was certain the agency had most likely already invoiced his company for the bill.

"That's a shame. Some people need the money before Christmas. I pay my employees before Christmas and I'm sure it would help her."

"Now that you mention it, I think it would. She seemed a little shocked when I told her."

"Are you in the office tomorrow?"

Briony shook her head. "No," she replied. Then after a moment, "You're not inhumane after all, Tobias. It seems as if the Christmas spirit has touched you, too."

"Don't push it," he warned but couldn't help letting a smile slide onto his lips.

"Tobias." Matthias approached him with a firm handshake. "Sorry for the mix-up with the files."

"So you should be," replied Tobias coldly. He was reminded about Savannah Page again. The image of her lining up to get food from that place troubled him. It had been hard enough when he was growing up, but his parents had never had to go to a food bank. He tried to imagine what that felt like, especially with a young son to look after. He noted she didn't wear a wedding band. Where was the boy's father?

One thing he did know was that a woman in her position didn't need any more aggravation from a man like him.

CHAPTER FOURTEEN

It was an hour earlier than usual and Jacob was still bleary-eyed by the time they made it into the sprawling office building.

Savannah felt a touch of sadness that after tomorrow she would no longer be coming here. Or have a job. Briony hadn't said anything about whether her contract would be extended further or not and she assumed that it would end tomorrow.

Most of the talk yesterday had been about the Christmas party.

She had no proper work to do, having finished the last task Briony had given her and these next two days would be easy enough. She only needed to rearrange the files in Briony's work area and keep an eye on the phone and email messages. She anticipated an easy time, with the only difficulty arising from having to sneak her son into the office and then to make sure he stayed there. She knew it was too much to ask of a six-year-old, especially being cooped up in a confined space for a long time.

"You can't bring him in," said the security guard, barring her way to the elevator. The trying-to-walk-in-casually-with-a-child approach had failed at the first hurdle.

Jacob hid behind her legs, as she knew he would. She could sense her son was scared of the large hulk of a man and that his unfriendly tone would scare Jacob. It always did.

Remnants of life with Colt.

But she wasn't going to give up. She couldn't *not* work and she couldn't leave Jacob anywhere. The lobby was decidedly quieter and she hoped it was due to the fact that a lot of people had already started their holiday vacations. Hopefully Tobias Stone had, too.

"You can check with Mr. Stone. He's fine with this. But I'd think twice if I were you, about challenging his decision. I work on the same floor as him," she pointed to her security tag, and tried to sound as if she didn't care. But her nonchalance was only skin deep. Inside she was a quivering mess. After the recent run-in with Tobias and the Dalton file fiasco, she didn't want to give him a good reason to throw her out. That man seemed to take pleasure in making people suffer. Maybe she should have dialed her response down slightly. But she'd been that other type of woman when she'd been with Colt and it hadn't served her well. She wasn't going to become that person again.

She prayed that the guard wouldn't check, and then she also prayed that Tobias Stone wouldn't be in, just in case he did. The guard eyed her warily and picked up the phone. Savannah's heart thundered as if she was getting ready to race a hundred miles.

This was definitely dismissal. Her lying, and Tobias finding out. But the man appeared to reconsider and put the phone down. "If Mr. Stone okayed it, then it's not a problem. Go ahead."

"Thanks," she beamed, closing her eyes and silently thanking the universe.

"Have a good, day, ma'am."

"You too," she said, rushing towards the elevator.

"This is a big place, Mommy." Jacob looked around excitedly as she ushered him in. "This is Tobias's company?"

"Yes, honey. And it's Mr. Stone to you."

"Can I go see Mr. Stone?"

The elevator doors closed.

"No, Jacob." She crouched and looked at him level in the eyes. "He doesn't know you're here, Jacob. He won't like it if he found out. And he will throw me out."

"He'll be nasty to you, like daddy was?"

Oh, god. He still remembered every terrible thing.

"No, honey. He's not nasty. It's just that children aren't allowed in here. So you have to be very quiet. Okay? Do you remember Harry Potter's invisibility cloak?"

"I don't like Harry Potter. It's too scary. I like Iron Man. You should know that, Mommy."

She let out a groan and didn't see how being Iron Man would help. But she nodded, conscious that the doors would open any minute. "I don't think Iron Man can become invisible, can he? He only shoots off into space and I don't see how that—"

"He *can* be invisible if he has the stealth suit."

"Okay, then pretend you have one of those." She rushed out of the elevators and pushed her son into the safety of the office, relieved to have seen nobody on their way up. At this quiet time of year she knew the chances were slim that someone would see them. As long as that someone wasn't Candace or Tobias, then she was fine.

Once inside, Savannah looked around. She couldn't very well ask Jacob to hide under the table for the whole day. Nor could she lock the office door. But she could block the entrance to it by putting a chair with some heavy files on it in front of it.

"We're going to play a game, Jacob."

"A game?" Excitement spread all over his face.

"If someone comes into this room, and you hear the door handle move, you have to take your things—your books, your toys, your coloring pencils, and hide under that table." She pointed to the table that was on the right of the door. It would give him some time to hide even if someone had managed to wedge the door open a little. "And you can't come out again until I come and tell you. Do you understand?"

"It doesn't sound like much fun. What's the prize?"

"Prize?"

"There's always a prize in a game."

She let out an uneasy laugh. "Santa knows you're helping Mommy, and he knows you've been a really good boy this year. And I think he's going to get you something really amazing this year."

"You mean like the new Iron Man things in that shop?"

She nodded.

"Okay," he said. "Now it sounds like fun."

She settled down and powered up the computer, checked through the emails and saw that Jacob seemed to be keeping himself entertained. When the phone rang again, she answered it quickly, eager to have something to do. She preferred being busy to doing nothing; at least it made the day fly by.

"Ms. Page, please come see me." The sound of his voice made the hairs on her arms stand up.

Tobias Stone.

Her worst nightmare was not only in but he wanted to see her. He couldn't have found out about Jacob already, could he? She looked around the room for CCTV cameras.

"I'll be right there."

She put the phone down and wondered what Tobias Stone wanted with her. She wished Briony was here. At least then she could have also found out about the Christmas party last night. She stared at Jacob and tried to muster a smile. "I have to go to a meeting, Jacob. You have to stay here and be quiet. Promise me?"

"Are you going to see Tobias? Can I come too?"

She didn't like that her son was so informal about her boss. "It's Mr. Stone, honey. And yes, I am going to see him, but no, you can't come along." Her son gave her one of his cutest and most endearing looks.

"It's not going to work, Jacob. 'No' means 'no'. Stay put and be good, otherwise I'll have to take you home." She smoothed a hand through her hair and wished she'd shampooed it last night. It was limp and hung like wet spaghetti.

Just get this over with.

She knocked on his door and was surprised when Tobias opened it himself instead of ordering her in as he usually did.

"When were you going to tell me?" he asked as she walked in, her mind running wild with fear.

Tell him what?

She tried not to look as nervous as she felt but there they were again, the butterflies dancing in the pit of her stomach. Feeling ever more anxious, especially with the way he hovered around her, she took the bold step of sitting down.

"Did I tell you to sit down?" he asked.

She frowned. *Was he being serious?* She turned to stare at him.

"I didn't realize we were in a military academy." She wished this man, always so stiff and so cold, would pull that steel rod out of his ass. "If you think I'm going to stand back up again and wait for your permission, you can think again."

She thought she saw the faintest wisp of a smile on his lips.

"You've got some spunk."

"Excuse me?" She leaned forward, taken aback by his word choice.

"Bravado. I like it. You're not afraid to speak your mind." It had cost her dearly when she hadn't. She'd only learned recently that the best way to fight bullies was to stand up to them. Not cower from them.

"It seems to me that most people are afraid to tell you what they think."

"Why do you think that is?"

"You really want to know?"

"I really want to know." His gaze was cool, magnetic, and she could not look away if she tried.

"Because you have money and power, and people want to please you."

"People want to please me," he said, slowly repeating her words. He walked over to his side of the desk and sat down. "Do *you* want to please me?" He clasped his hands together and placed them on the desk.

"I want to work. I don't look at it in terms of whether it pleases you or not. You don't factor into my equation."

He nodded, and placed his elbows on the table, lifting his hands so that his chin rested on them. He said nothing for a few moments, and she was left with a mouth that had suddenly gone dry.

He stared at her, as if awaiting an explanation, and she, remembering the way he had interrogated her the other day, chose to remain silent. Finally he spoke. "I'm sorry." It sounded as if it pained him to say the words.

"*You're* sorry?"

"It's not a trait that is alien to me."

She drew her eyebrows together.

He continued. "I'm sorry for implying that you had taken the Dalton file."

Now she remembered. "For thinking I was a spy, you mean?"

"I have enemies everywhere, Savannah. I can't let my guard down, or trust anyone."

"What a sad way to live." The words slipped out before she'd had a chance to put them through her internal filter.

"It's not for everyone." He adjusted the cuff of his sleeve and she wondered if he was buying himself more time or thinking of something else to say.

"Was there anything else?" She was anxious to return to Jacob. This whole exchange with Tobias had taken her by surprise and she knew she would analyze their conversation later. In a place of safety, away from him.

"No. Please close the door on your way out."

She was more than relieved to leave his office and escape to the safety of hers. Walking back into her office and seeing Jacob's smiling face made her forget the awkwardness of meeting with Tobias.

The rest of the morning went smoothly enough. Nobody had tried to come in. The phone had rung a few times, but it was things that could wait until Briony got back. She responded to all emails as soon as she received them, otherwise she continued to tidy up Briony's network folders.

Then Jacob spoke. "I'm hungry, Mommy." He'd been a good boy all morning, quietly playing with his Spider-Man figurine and doing some drawing. But now he wanted food and she had forgotten to make lunch. She usually brought sandwiches to eat but with both of them leaving so early today, she'd clean forgotten. It meant that she now had to go out to get their lunch. There was no way around it. She had to leave the office and leave Jacob unattended—something she hated to do. Yet to take him out of the office during the busy lunchtime risked her getting caught.

The building had no restaurant, except for vending machines on a few floors and she wasn't going to feed her boy snacks for lunch. She had no option but to sprint out of here, across the road, run into the sandwich shop and sprint back.

It would be better to go now, before the stores got too busy, than run the risk of taking more time later, when the lines built up.

"Jacob, listen to me." She walked over to his desk and bent down. "I'm going out very quickly to get some lunch."

"Can I come?"

"No, you have to stay here."

"You're leaving me?" Fear walked in his eyes.

"It's just across the road. It will take me ten minutes. I promise."

"Don't leave me, Mommy." The begging in his voice clutched at her heart strings. Nowhere else would she leave him alone, but she was caught between a rock and a hard place. He would be safe here if he did as she told him, and it wasn't as if she was leaving him in a public place. She hated doing this, but she had no choice and she would be back quickly.

She forced a brave face knowing that Jacob would sense her fear and feel scared himself, and she never wanted him to be scared ever again. "Ten minutes, Jacob. I promise." This wouldn't happen tomorrow. She would make sure to bring lunch with her.

"We can do this, champ. Do you think you can turn on your super powers?"

"Like Iron Man?"

"Like Iron Man."

The fear vanished as he became the superhero. "Go, Mommy. Ten minutes, you promised."

She rushed out, her thoughts on Jacob the whole time as she dove into the elevator and tried to still her beating heart as the elevator descended painfully and slowly, stopping at different floors along the way. She was more frightened by the idea of leaving him alone, knowing she had left him willingly, than by him being found. When she reached the ground floor, she sprinted out.

And almost crashed straight into Candace who was on her way in.

"In a rush?" Candace asked her.

"Yes," she said, and gave her a quick smile before rushing out of the door.

CHAPTER FIFTEEN

Tobias arrived back from his meeting with the chief finance officer simmering with anger as he stepped back into his office. It had taken two hours to discuss what should have taken no more than forty minutes.

No sooner had he sat down than Candace knocked.

"You're back," she said cheerily.

"I've been in meetings all morning."

"Yesterday was a great success, by all accounts," she said, sounding her own trumpet.

"Good," he replied, hoping she would move on quickly. He had emails that needed his attention as well as the pressing matter which refused to leave his thoughts. "Anything else?"

She seemed surprised by his directness. "Are you in a bad mood, Tobias?"

"Candace, I'm really busy. Did you want something?"

"No. I'm only in for half a day today and tomorrow. Is there anything you need me to do before I go? Do you need anything?"

"No, I can cope." He gave her half a smile. "I'm not completely useless without you."

She smiled at him. "I noticed that temp is still here."

"And what of it?"

"I thought she'd finished."

"Briony asked her to stay on. Why?"

"No reason. I saw her just now and she seemed to be in a huge rush. She almost knocked me over when she got out of the elevator."

It made him wonder, but he remained silent.

"What are you up to this Christmas?" she asked, refusing to budge. But her gaze soon fell upon the Tiffany box on his desk.

"Oooooh," she purred, her beady little eyes honing in on the blue and white box. He knew exactly what she was thinking. "Naomi will be happy."

Tobias felt his jaw clench. He badly needed Candace to disappear, not only because his nerves were already frayed, but he had so many things he needed to figure out. In an effort to get rid of her, he remembered something. Ignoring her comment about the gift, he instructed her. "Call Herman in accounting and get him to make sure that Ms. Page gets her wages paid into her account before she leaves work tomorrow."

"Temps don't get paid until the following month."

"I'm well aware of that." But it hadn't been anything he'd concerned himself with before.

"But I can't do anything. It's up to the agency—"

"I don't think you heard me, Candace. Make sure Ms. Page gets paid tomorrow. Tell Herman to charge it to the company if he has to. And in case you're in any doubt, I own this company, and I can damn well do as I please."

His PA narrowed her eyes as she stared at him. "I'll do it right away. Anything else?"

He shook his head. "Candace," he said slowly, his expression tight. "Sometimes your attitude borders on unprofessional. Let me remind you that you're an assistant and this means that you follow my orders."

"Understood," she said, and he could tell by the look on her face that he'd crushed her.

Candace left Tobias's office in a jumble of emotions. What was wrong with the man all of a sudden?

He thought she was *unprofessional*?

Tensed up with anger, she flexed her fists, and marched into her office. Throwing down her bag, she picked up the phone to call Herman and made the necessary arrangements.

She sat simmering in her seat for a while, then, feeling restless and edgy, she got up. It was time to pay that little minx a visit. Find out what was really going on. She should have been back by now.

She knocked on the door to the office where Briony usually sat, but there was no reply. She knocked again. This time she wrestled with the handle and tried to open the door but it wouldn't open easily. "Savannah?"

Still no answer.

She pushed it slowly and saw that a chair had been wedged up behind it and on the chair was a box full of files. But the office was empty. The other desks looked unoccupied, too. Were they all away? Was it only that bitch in here?

She looked around and saw a toy lying on the tabletop. Curious, she walked over, picked it up and examined it. It was only then that she heard a shuffling noise underneath the desk.

She bent down and discovered a small boy huddled up, sitting on the floor with his knees drawn into his chest. Large, shiny eyes full of fear stared back at her.

"And who are you?" she asked, a slow smile spreading across her face.

CHAPTER SIXTEEN

The day wasn't going particularly well for Tobias. Maybe going away could still be an option for him. Just to get away from everything.

When Candace knocked on the door again, he was about to lose his patience again but the sight of a small boy, a boy who looked completely scared as he stood next to her, immediately stopped him.

"Look what I found." Candace beamed as if she'd caught a prize. Tobias looked at the boy and saw the fear in his eyes. He got up slowly and walked over to him.

"Hey, Jacob." His voice was soft as he bent down so that their faces were at the same level.

"Hey, Mr. Stone." The boy's lips trembled and Tobias smiled at him. "It's okay. You don't have to be scared."

"Please don't throw my Mommy out. Please."

"Throw her out? Of course not, Jacob. Why would you think that?"

Jacob shook his head and clutched his Spider-Man figurine to his chest. "She said you would throw her out if you found out I was here."

Tobias shook his head gently. "No," he said. "I would never do that."

"She didn't know where to send me and Rosalee has gone away for Christmas and—"

"Jacob!" Footsteps sounded outside the office and Savannah rushed in, then seeing Jacob, she flew forward and hugged him tightly. "Oh, thank god. Oh, baby. I was worried sick." She held him tightly, oblivious to everything and everyone else.

"This is against regulations, you can't bring—" Candace started.

"Enough." Tobias stood up.

"This isn't a daycare center—"

"Enough, Candace. Leave."

His PA opened her mouth to protest but he didn't give her a chance to say anything. "Go now, or else," he barked, moved to close the door behind her. Savannah's sandwich bag lay on the floor beside her handbag. Tobias picked them both up and put them on his desk.

"What happened?" he heard Savannah ask her son.

"I was hiding underneath the table and that lady came in. I'm sorry, Mommy. Mr. Stone said he wouldn't throw you out."

Savannah stood up and, with her arm protectively around her son's shoulder, she faced Tobias. Her frightened eyes searched his. "I'm sorry. I didn't know what else to do."

"It's not a problem." He could see her fear, could sense her worry, and didn't like to see her crumble like this. She looked so much more vulnerable when she was around her son.

Don't throw her out, please, Mr. Stone.

He wanted to know what would make a child think that.

"I'm only here for two more days and if I could just—"

"I already told you. It's not a problem."

But she looked at him as if she didn't believe him.

"I insist, however, that Jacob sits at a table, and not

underneath it." He looked at Jacob. "You don't want to sit underneath a table, do you, Jacob?"

The boy smiled back at him. "It was just a game Mommy told me to play."

Tobias looked at Savannah again, and it was as if he was seeing her with new eyes, with her guard down. The other Savannah would have given him a piece of her mind by now.

"Thank you," she said. "It's a huge help. I had childcare lined up but my sitter was called away and I have no backup." He didn't imagine it was easy for her, and from the sounds of it, she appeared to be alone.

She picked up her sandwich bag and handbag and, holding Jacob's hand, left his office.

Tobias was left wondering what he could do to make things easier for her. The thing he didn't want to confront just yet was why he cared so much in the first place.

CHAPTER SEVENTEEN

"He's nice, Mommy." Jacob yawned as he settled underneath his 'Avengers Assemble' bedsheets that Kay had bought for him.

"Who?" Savannah asked absentmindedly while trying to figure out her future plans.

Time was marching on. Once Christmas and New Year's were over, she was looking at something like six months. Kay would be back in the summer and Savannah had until then to turn her life around. A decent job that paid enough so that she could afford to rent in a safe area. She'd have to say goodbye to New York and the good money and try to find a job as a secretary or a PA somewhere in the suburbs, in a place near a good school. That was her plan.

"Mr. Stone."

"You like him?"

"Yeah." Jacob yawned again, and she could see how the long day had tired him out. "Do you like him?" her son asked.

Savannah got up and kissed him on the cheek. "I have to like him, honey. I work for him. He owns the company."

"It's so big! He owns *all* of that?" The tiredness slipped

away as his eyelids flew wide open. She nodded and for the first time considered his wealth.

"Wow!"

"Bedtime! We have another early start tomorrow, honey."

"I can't wait."

"For what?"

"To go to work."

She had to laugh because the words sounded so funny coming from his mouth. "One day, you will go to work. Just make sure you find something that you love doing. Then it won't feel so much like work."

"Okay." He turned to his side and closed his eyes.

"Love you, honey. Sweet dreams."

"Love you too, Mommy."

She closed the door, leaving it ajar just in case he needed anything. This was a luxury—them having separate bedrooms. When she'd been at her aunt's, she had shared with Jacob and had loved every moment of having her little boy snuggle up against her but she had often lain awake at night and wondered if things would ever get any better or whether she was destined to struggle for the rest of her life.

With a child to take care of, it was harder to get a job and work the hours she needed when she had Jacob to think about. School pickups and childcare always had to be the number one priority for her. Jacob was her priority. Colt didn't have a care in the world. He might even have remarried by now. Her parents never told her even if they knew. He was out of her life now and she was grateful for that.

She'd been the first of her friends to get married and had Jacob just before she turned twenty-three; while her friends were still childless and enjoying life with their boyfriends. Colt had won her over easily and the first three years had been bliss.

It was only when he lost his job that his spiral into depression hit home and they struggled to keep it together.

She cleared up her dishes, her mind already thinking ahead to the new year and all the agencies she would have to visit. Working these past few weeks had given her a happier and more positive outlook. It was strange how that happened when money was coming in. Being able to return to the toy store and pick up presents for Jacob had put a smile on her face.

The only thing to cast a dampener on her mood was the fact that tomorrow was her last day at Stone Enterprises.

CHAPTER EIGHTEEN

There was a buzz around New York, especially on Christmas Eve. Sparkly decorations and bright lights lit up the night sky but more than that there was expectation in the air.

Unlike her son, Savannah loved the lead-up to Christmas Day and for her, the magic of Christmas peaked on Christmas Eve.

She felt happier today, uplifted and the sad thought of this being her last earning day soon melted away. And since Tobias now knew about Jacob being in the office, she didn't need to worry on that front either.

"Hey, Jacob."

"Hey, Mr. Stone." Jacob stopped his coloring and looked up. Savannah turned around to see Tobias walk in with his hands in his pockets. She noticed that he'd dressed down today. No formal business suit; just dark slacks and a dark shirt. He looked devastatingly handsome and the dark colors showed off his sandy-colored hair and deep blue eyes even more than usual. Heat scorched her cheeks as she gave him a slight nod and turned away. The file she was about to return to the filing cabinet would have to stay put for now because returning it meant having to walk past Tobias. And for some reason, she suddenly felt extremely self-conscious.

She opened her emails again, even though she'd only looked through them less than a few minutes ago. What she couldn't do was turn and face Tobias. She heard him talking to Jacob, asking him about his Spider-Man figurine, and it was plainly evident from Tobias's conversation that he didn't have much knowledge about these characters. She heard Jacob tell him about the new Iron Man model and the Age of Ultron armor and voice changer mask.

As they spoke, she started to wonder what Tobias's wife was like and it got her thinking about whether he had children. If he did, they'd be pretty young, she guessed, otherwise he would know about superheroes.

Her son lived and breathed them.

She kept her attention firmly on her computer screen, even though her ears were listening carefully to their conversation. She wondered what type of Christmas Tobias Stone would have. She imagined a big, fancy mansion somewhere in the city; a house decorated with beautiful golden lights and with a large tree sprinkled with decorations dainty and colorful, from one of the big department stores. She imagined beautifully wrapped Christmas presents in sparkling gift wrap tied with white satin ribbons lying underneath the tree.

A knock at the door burst through her daydreams and then Candace's shrill voice rang out. "Tobias." Candace stood at the open doorway, surveying the scene with displeasure. "I've been looking for you everywhere." She glanced at Savannah and gave her a fake smile. Tobias turned around. "And now you've found me. What is it?"

Candace's lips twitched as if she was about to say something. "I'm leaving; I was only here for half a day."

"I know. You told me yesterday. Have a good Christmas, and happy New Year."

"You too," she replied. Savannah saw the look on the PA's face as she appraised the scene before her. Something in her countenance told Savannah that the woman didn't like what she saw.

"Have a merry Christmas," said Savannah, eager to part on good terms.

Candace beamed her a false smile. "Nice to have met you and good luck."

"Thanks," Savannah replied.

It was just the three of them once more and Savannah was conscious that she hadn't yet said anything to Tobias. She was conscious that ever since he'd found out about Jacob, she'd been wary and quiet, and she'd avoided facing him. And she still had no idea why.

"As much as I'd like to hear more about your toys, Jacob, I have to go do some work."

"Bye, Mr. Stone."

She felt the heat of his gaze first. "Savannah, would you come by my office before you leave? Most people are going home after a half-day."

"I told Briony I'd work the full day."

He nodded.

"I'll be here until late. Come by before you leave."

She swallowed. "Is something wrong?"

"No," he shook his head calmly. "Should it be?"

"Should it be wrong? No." But she was worried, all the same.

"I'm hungry, Mommy," Jacob whined.

Despite her best intentions, she'd forgotten to make sandwiches again. "Shall we go out and get some lunch, Jacob?"

"Can't I play with Mr. Stone and you go out?"

"No," she said, her voice harsher than she'd intended.

"Why?"

"Because Mr. Stone doesn't play," she replied in a tight voice.

"That's not quite true," Tobias stepped in. "I can watch him," he offered.

"Why?" She sensed that he pitied her on some level, the way most people did once they got to know her. Many went out of their way to help her. Like Kay, like Rosalee, like Briony. She didn't like that Tobias Stone was also pitying her.

"Because you'll worry when you're out."

"You have a company to run, Mr. Stone. I'm sure you have other things to do."

"On the contrary, it's Christmas Eve and I don't have much to do today."

Then why the hell are you here? she wondered.

"Thank you, but I'll take him with me. He's been cooped up in here all morning." She reached for her coat. "Jacob, put your coat on. We're going out." The boy made a sad face.

"Bye, Mr. Stone."

"Bye, Jacob."

Tobias left the room and when he was out of sight, Savannah scolded her son. "Jacob, you have to stop talking to him like that."

"Like what?"

"Like he's your...friend."

"He *is* my friend."

"He's not your friend."

"He is, too."

"He's my *boss*, Jacob, and you can't be that friendly, talking to him like he's one of your friends from school."

"You always told me to be nice to people. I was being nice, Mommy."

She didn't know how to answer that. "Come on," she said, taking his hand. "Let's get you some hot soup."

CHAPTER NINETEEN

This was it. Goodbye.

She looked at the office, with the files organized and rearranged to perfection, and felt sad to be leaving.

She glanced at her watch. It was time to leave. "Get your things together, Jacob." There was only one thing left to do. "Stay here. I'll be back quickly—I'm just going to see Mr. Stone."

"Okay," he said, rearranging Spider-Man's limbs.

She knocked on the door which Tobias opened even though he was on the phone. "We've been through this before, Naomi. I don't want to discuss it."

She sat down and tried to be discreet, but it was impossible not to listen to the conversation. Instead, she surveyed his clean desk and her eyes rested on the blue Tiffany box.

So, his wife was named Naomi.

"No. Don't. I'll call you. I have to go, someone's waiting for me." He put down the phone and walked over to his chair, but he didn't sit down.

"You said you wanted to see me?" She had no idea what this was about. Maybe he was going to have stern words with her now that she was leaving, and he hadn't done so because Jacob had been in the room.

"How have you found it? Working here?" His question immediately threw her.

"It's...been...interesting," she replied slowly, unsure as to what he was after.

"Interesting? How?" He folded his hands together. Big, manly and soft hands, and she swallowed, seeing the ring on his finger. A sudden and unexpected bout of envy stabbed her and her gaze rested once more on the gift box.

His voice was as smooth as melted chocolate and she at once felt shy and vulnerable. "It was..." She struggled for the words. How could she tell him that she was grateful for having a job? Not only *a* job, but *this* job. Of being in this huge skyscraper that reeked of success and money and power, and how she felt independent, after leaving Jacob at school and taking a subway to the city, of how she once more felt free, a young woman in a big city, and how wonderful it felt walking around the streets of New York, breezing through the silver revolving doors and coming to work *here*.

This man could not possibly understand. He had no idea of the difference that three weeks of working here had made to her short-term livelihood. She tried not to stare at his smooth face or his high forehead. Tried not to stare too long at the way he wore his clothes, at his immaculate hands, soft and clean.

She looked away. They might as well have been from different galaxies. "I've had a great time working here. Briony has been wonderful and I've enjoyed the work." She hesitated for a moment, then decided to thank him, too. "Thank you for being so accommodating."

"Accommodating?"

"For letting Jacob stay in the office."

"I wasn't going to throw him out." His gaze pierced right

through her. "He was worried that I might throw you out. Why would he think that?"

"I don't know. He has a very active imagination." She stared at her hands and cleared her throat, avoiding eye contact. "But thank you for your kindness."

"Anything to help."

She hated those words. All too often people used those words when they sensed her desperation. No matter how hard she tried to hide it; that she was dirt poor and that she had no savings, that she lived from paycheck to paycheck, that she'd had to go to a food bank just to make food for Christmas last that much longer.

It had almost made her cry with happiness when she'd paid for the few toys she'd bought for Jacob. Those three words, 'Anything to help' only reminded her that she was in a desperate place and that people could see right through her.

"I was just doing my job, Tobias."

"Briony spoke very highly of you."

She smiled at the thought.

"She spoke so highly of you, in fact, that she's extended your contract."

Savannah gulped. "She did?" Briony hadn't said a word to her.

"Unless you have a better offer from elsewhere?" She didn't miss the fire that flashed in his eyes as he asked that question. Frightened by the thought of being without a job in the new year, she had emailed her resume to a few agencies. Worries about her financial situation had made her look elsewhere as a backup.

"I don't," she replied quickly. "This is wonderful news. It's—it's—it's..." It was the best Christmas gift she could have asked for.

Tobias nodded. "Hasn't she emailed you?"

Savannah shook her head.

His lips pressed together. “She was supposed to. Apparently no one’s covering the office next week, between Christmas and New Year.”

This was new.

“If you can’t that’s fine. I know it’s short notice and I’m surprised she didn’t let you know in advance.”

“I can do it.” Savannah insisted. Rosalee would be back by then.

“If you can come in, and if you still don’t have childcare—”

“I have childcare, or I will have,” she said quickly. “It’ll be fine.”

He scratched the back of his neck. “I guess it’s better for Jacob not to be cooped up in the office.”

“Yes,” replied Savannah. Thank goodness for Rosalee.

“It’s double pay, too.”

Even better.

“I’ve signed off the necessary paperwork.” He coughed lightly. “You’ll also find that your wages will be paid into your account today.”

She wrinkled her brow. “But I thought...” She hadn’t expected to see that money until January. Tobias looked away with cool nonchalance, and flicked through his planner. “She mentioned something about the agency not paying until next month, but...well. It *is* Christmas.”

The money in her account today? She couldn’t help but smile. “That was so thoughtful of her.”

“Wasn’t it?” Tobias commented.

“It’s the best news...” She closed her mouth before she said too much.

“I’m happy to hear it. Hopefully, you and Jacob can enjoy the holidays.”

"Thank you. You too." She sat in her chair, waiting for him to say something.

"That will be all." He dismissed her, and she got up slowly, feeling a lightness seep into her body as she almost floated to the door.

"One more thing," Tobias said, just as she reached for the door handle. "You weren't at the Christmas party."

She gave him a puzzled look. It seemed so far away, and her thoughts were still on her recent contract.

"No." She replied. *Why was he asking?*

"Was it because of what happened with the Dalton file?"

"I didn't attend that night because I had no childcare. It wasn't because of your accusation."

"How naive of me to assume otherwise."

"Merry Christmas, Tobias."

"Merry Christmas."

She rushed out and as she walked down the hallway to Briony's office, Savannah felt as though she were floating on air. She walked into the office smiling from ear to ear. Her son stared up at her.

"You look happy, Mommy."

She felt overwhelmed with happiness because her contract had been extended and it had suddenly changed her outlook on life. All because Briony had given her the perfect Christmas gift.

"I am, honey. I'm very happy. Let's go home."

A man like Tobias Stone had women dropping at his feet like flies. This woman, not particularly glamorous, nor sophisticated, nor worldly wise, still had him thinking about her. He would bet good money that if he put her in a five-thousand-dollar Dior dress, with that attitude, she'd own the dress and the room.

His interest in Savannah Page had suddenly tripled.

He had lost interest in women years ago and he considered himself in no danger of falling for any woman, much less an employee, but the mere idea that he had been thinking of Savannah Page intrigued him.

That he'd had any interest in anyone at all was cause for speculation in itself and he found himself thinking about her long after she had left his office.

She was a temp, and even though she wasn't directly an employee of his, it still made her off limits. He never, ever dated women who worked for him, permanent or temporary.

He had Naomi.

But still.

The thrill was in the chase.

Savannah Page tickled his interest in a way that no woman had, not since Ivy. And that fact alone made him curious. And whenever Tobias Stone was curious about something, he went after it.

THE GIFT, BOOK 2

The Billionaire's Love Story (#2)

CHAPTER ONE

"Merry Christmas, Ms. Page." Arnold's gravelly voice came through the intercom.

"Merry Christmas, Arnold. How come you're working today? I thought you told me you had the day off."

The affable elderly concierge greeted Savannah daily. Having an apartment to look after in New York was one thing, but having a concierge as well seemed like an extra luxury. Arnold was an elderly man and had taken a particular liking to her and Jacob. She'd become used to seeing his rumpled and leathery face as she left each morning.

"Don't tell anyone, but I went out with some friends last night and it was too cold and too late to go home. I ended up sleeping here instead."

She laughed. "You couldn't have slept very well, but don't worry, I won't tell a soul."

"It's lucky I did come in because someone delivered two packages for you. One of them looks good enough to eat."

Packages for her? Surely there had been a mistake? "Are you sure they're for me, Arnold?"

"Savannah Page and Jacob, it says here on the labels."

Colt? The thought gripped her tightly, stealing her breath away. It couldn't be. They were divorced now and there was no reason for him to come looking for her, or Jacob. "Who delivered them?"

"The delivery man," replied Arnold, telling her nothing.

"I'm coming down."

A delivery on Christmas Day? She didn't recall any stores making deliveries on Christmas day.

She closed and set aside the book which she had been reading, snuggled up on the sofa while Jacob played with his new toys. He was still in his PJs but she'd been dressed hours ago, even if she was only lounging around in her leggings and big, fluffy cardigan.

Only her parents and her aunt, Sylvie, Kay's mom, knew she lived here and neither of them had ever sent her anything before; she didn't see why they would do so now. Besides, her parents had already sent her money in their Christmas card which she'd received a few weeks ago. Her dad's chest infection had kept them at home this Christmas, and they'd promised to visit her in the new year.

"Where are you going?" Jacob asked. She could clearly see the dark shadows under his excited eyes. He'd been up early, sometime around six in the morning, and had crept into her bed. Typical. On school mornings, he could barely get up yet this morning he'd woken up without any intervention from her.

She'd woken as soon as he'd slipped in, to find him staring at her, smiling and waiting for her to say the word. She'd held him in her arms and loved the feel of him as happiness engulfed her. But she couldn't hold him back much longer—his excitement making him fidgety and restless.

Less than a quarter of an hour later, Jacob had opened all of his presents. She told him to open the presents from her first. He'd ripped the wrapping paper and given them a quick glance before leaving a gooey kiss on her cheek. The coloring pencils and coloring books from her, along with a coat and clothes he badly needed—all the sensible and boring presents—quickly lost their appeal. His attention was fixed on Santa's presents which she'd carefully wrapped in different gift wrap, securing the myth of Santa for another year at least. Jacob's eyes had lit up the moment he'd opened them and then the worth of her gifts was quickly forgotten as Santa became his new hero.

She so badly wanted this to be a great start to their new life and she had gone a little overboard this Christmas—fueled by the promise of an extra week's work and at double pay. As a result, an enormous pile of presents lay underneath their small Christmas tree this year.

She had no gifts to open for herself, and this had upset Jacob but he soon cheered up when she told him she would buy herself something with the money Grandma and Grandpa had sent.

His eyes sparkled and gleamed. Santa had given him the whole collection of superheroes he loved; he had his favorite at last—Iron Man—but there were also Venom and Wolverine and Captain America figures. He also had an Iron Man mask and glove which he could wear to turn into his favorite superhero, and Santa had given him an Iron Man alarm clock and night light.

Sometimes Jacob still woke up in the middle of the night feeling scared, even though the arguments and screaming had stopped.

Back then, when she'd lived that nightmare, she'd been so busy trying to survive that she hadn't considered how much her young boy had absorbed, even though she'd tried her best for him not to see or hear things. She had always tried to soothe Colt, tried to temper down his anger, tried not to cry out if she'd been unsuccessful and his rage flared out of control.

Now it was slowly coming out, little snippets of something Jacob would say told her that he had seen and heard more than any child should have. As a mother, she felt she'd failed him and her focus now was on making it up to him and giving him the best life she possibly could.

"Arnold says we have a delivery," she said, slipping on her shoes. "I'll be back in a minute. Don't open the door to anyone." Not that anyone would come in but she was always extra careful when it came to Jacob. As she took the elevator down the four floors, she wondered who might have sent her something on Christmas day.

"Santa did pay you a visit," exclaimed Arnold, holding out his hand at the large and beautifully decorated Christmas gift basket that graced his workspace.

She stared at him in surprise. There had to have been some mistake. "But I'm not expecting anything," she murmured, stepping towards the table, her gaze fixed on the gift basket that was so big she wasn't sure she'd be able to carry it back easily. And then she saw the second gift, wrapped up in gold wrapping paper with white snowmen dotted all over it.

"Who would...?" Her words trailed away as she searched for gift tags. This wasn't Colt's doing, she knew that much, even though he kept telling her parents, at every opportunity, that he was now a changed man.

She had changed too, and she knew that there was no future for them together; he had never expressed much interest in wanting to keep in touch with either her or Jacob.

"They're for you, my dear. There's no mistaking it."

"But..." She examined the gift tags; the one on the luxury gift basket said, 'Savannah Page' and the one on the giftwrapped present said, "Merry Christmas, Jacob." It didn't make sense. Who would have sent them? And then she guessed.

Kay. She laughed, more from relief than anything else. Her cousin, Kay. *How thoughtful of her.* "That woman," murmured Savannah, all smiles and joy.

"You know who it's from?"

"My cousin."

Arnold nodded his head. Kay hadn't even known his name, much less given him the time of day but she and Jacob had come to see him as a friend and often stopped for a few moments each day to talk to him. "At least it'll put a sparkle on your face and your boy's too."

She felt a tingling in her bones as she cast her eyes over the jars and boxes and bottles inside it.

"You're not spending Christmas day here, are you, Arnold?"

"No," he replied, closing his craggy eyes as if she'd said something horrid to him. "I'm going to my daughter's house for the day. I'd better go home and freshen up first, I think."

"I think it would be a good idea, Arnold." Savannah smiled, feeling happy that he wouldn't be alone on a day like this.

"That looks mighty fine," he said, eyeing the huge gift basket.

"Doesn't it?" she agreed, "What would you like?"

He shrank away. "Oh, no, no, no. You and Jacob enjoy your feast."

"We can't possibly eat all of this," she protested. "Don't be shy, Arnold. I insist. What would you like?"

"Nothing at all, my dear, but thank you for asking." He shook his head stubbornly. "You're going to need help carrying that, Ms. Page. It's mighty heavy." She tried to carry it in her arms; he was right, she would have trouble taking this back to her apartment alone.

"We'll both carry it," she suggested. And they each took one end of the basket and carried it slowly towards the elevator. They hauled it to her apartment, where Savannah knocked on the door with her foot and told Jacob to open. His eyes opened wide when he saw them.

"Is that ours?" he asked, his eager eyes taking in the gift basket.

"It is," Arnold replied. "Merry Christmas, Jacob."

"Merry Christmas, Arnold!"

"This way," said Savannah and guided Arnold towards the kitchen where they finally set it down on the kitchen table.

"Is that from you, Arnold?" Jacob asked.

The elderly man shook his head. "No, it isn't, son. And there's more." He winked at him. "I'd best go back down," he said to Savannah and quickly left.

"I'll be down in a minute," she told him.

"Is there really something for me, Mommy?" Jacob asked.

"Apparently so. I'll go get it in a moment," she told him. "First, I think we should share this with Arnold, what do you say?" He nodded happily. The gift basket was decorated with ribbons and covered with cellophane wrap. She cut a slit into one end and took a few things out that she thought Arnold might like and put them into an empty bag. "I'll be back," she promised Jacob.

She raced back to the lobby. "Merry Christmas, Arnold." She handed him the bag of goodies. His eyes glossed over and he looked away. "That's awful kind of you, Ms. Page." Despite the number of times she'd told him to call her Savannah, he stubbornly refused and kept his old-fashioned manners.

"Please," she insisted. "There's only so much that Jacob and I can eat and I hate to waste food. It would make me happy if you would share it with me."

"If you put it like that," he said, bowing his head and accepting her gift. "Thank you. God bless you both and Merry Christmas."

"Merry Christmas, Arnold. I hope you have a lovely time

with your family." She picked up the second gift. Unlike the gift basket, it was light and easy to carry.

"I reckon that'll make the little fella happy," commented Arnold.

"He's already happy and I think this is definitely going to be the best Christmas we've ever had."

She rushed back into the elevator, eager to call Kay and to thank her.

The chill crept around him like layers of ice stealing through the wide open doors.

In the early hours of Christmas day morning, so early that he hadn't yet gone to bed, Tobias stood staring out at the darkness.

There was no Christmas tree in sight, no decorations, no lights. Not even Christmas cards.

He was too young to be wearing the plush velvet robe and the slippers he had on, but he'd been lounging around, lost in his own private hell and this old man's garb kept him warm.

What was the time?

He glanced over his shoulder. The clock said 3:37 a.m. He lifted the glass of whiskey to his lips and took a big gulp. It warmed him as he stood looking out at the murky darkness that had swallowed up the landscape outside; a part of him wished that it would swallow him up and make him disappear, too.

It had taken the wrong person. Why hadn't it been him instead? Now he was left alone in a place he very much didn't want to be in, nor deserve to be.

He hated Christmas and everything that went with it. But drinking his way through bottles of whiskey and screwing Naomi for hours was a way of forgetting. Naomi hadn't said it, she knew better than to do that, but her transparency was a dead giveaway; she'd been bitterly disappointed that he hadn't gone away this Christmas, because it would have meant she'd have been able to get away with him. Instead, she'd been texting him and her messages were starting to irritate him, like nails clawing the surface of a blackboard. She was desperate to know when he wanted her to come over.

Except Tobias wasn't in the mood for sex lately. Drinking into the early hours of the morning was infinitely more appealing.

CHAPTER TWO

"You have a present, Mommy. It's got your name on it." Jacob beamed at her as she walked back in. She'd told him that Santa only brought gifts for little children.

"I know. It's exciting isn't it?" She gave him the box. "This is for you."

His mouth dropped open and he looked at her like a shocked fish. "For me?"

"For you."

He examined the gift tag. "Can I open it?"

"Of course you can," said Savannah, picking up the phone. She called Kay as she settled back down on her sofa. When her cousin answered, it sounded as though she was at a circus from the raucous laughter that screeched out of the phone.

"Thank you for the presents," she said, raising her voice.

"What presents? Hang on." She heard some static and then the background noise dimmed. "That's better. What presents?"

"The Christmas gift basket and Jacob's present," replied Savannah.

"I didn't send you anything."

"You didn't?" Savannah got up and walked back into the

kitchen to double-check. The gift tag bore only her name and there was no other information indicating who the sender was. She cast her eyes over the chutney jars, cheeses, meats and boxes of crackers and chocolates.

"Look, Mommy!" Jacob whispered excitedly, knowing she was on the phone but unable to contain his delight. He'd unwrapped but hadn't opened the box which he was trying to hold while still also clutching two superhero figures in his chubby hands. The box contained an Iron Man figurine with an aircraft.

More Iron Man.

"You didn't?" asked Savannah, doubly confused.

"I wish I had sent you something, now that you mention it." Kay sounded a little tipsy. Savannah tried to think. Would Briony have sent this? It didn't seem likely. She and Briony weren't friendly enough to be exchanging gifts and she was certain that Briony didn't even know what her son was named let alone what toys he liked best.

"Someone sent you a gift basket?" Kay shrieked.

"Where are you?" Savannah asked as Jacob looked excitedly at her. Surely his eyes could open no wider? He mouthed a 'Can I open it?' but she shook her head and put her finger to her lips. He nodded then placed the box on the floor and continued to play with his other toys.

"In a restaurant. With...with...uh. I forgot his name."

Savannah shook her head. She knew her cousin well. Kay was all for having a good time. She worked hard, but she played even harder. *Good-time Kay,* her friends called her, and the name didn't come without a reason.

"Merry Christmas," she said, trying hard to think who else might be the mysterious benefactor.

"Stop it!" She heard her cousin's coquettish voice. "I'm on the phone..."

"It sounds busy where you are. Who were you talking to?" Savannah scratched her eyebrow. The suspense of finding out who her gift donor was made her antsy.

"Dessert."

"Dessert?"

Kay giggled and Savannah could have sworn she heard Kay ask, "Your place or mine?"

"You got to the third course and you don't remember his name?"

Kay squealed and Savannah heard her tell someone to go. "Sorry," said Kay, her voice loud on the phone again.

"Are you talking to me now, or having a conversation with *Dessert*?" Savannah asked her.

"I'm talking to you."

"I'm afraid to ask where you are and what you're up to," Savannah confessed.

"We're at a restaurant that is serving Christmas dinner. Except that it's like a dating kind of thing. We change seats with every course." Pride rang out from her voice, as if she'd scaled a high mountain.

Savannah gasped, horrified by the prospect of such an event. She didn't mind being single, in fact she loved not having anyone to answer to. Yet she knew that Kay found it tough and took every opportunity to get hooked up. This Christmas day dating event sounded like a nightmare and Savannah shook her head in despair at her cousin's never-ending quest to find a partner.

"Didn't you consider having dinner at home with friends?"

"This *is* dinner with friends, or at least some of them will become friends. It's mostly expats. I'm trying to settle in, Sav. It's not easy. Everyone here just works all the time and I'm lonely, you know what it's like."

"Horny, more like," said Savannah.

"That, too," sniggered Kay. "Don't *you* ever get lonely?"

No. She was never lonely, but then she had Jacob. She'd been so relieved when her divorce had come through that the idea of having a relationship was so far from her mind so as to be nonexistent.

"I'm going to have to go soon, it looks like my next course is being served," Kay announced, and Savannah didn't know if she was referring to food or eye candy. "Isn't there a card on the gifts to say who they're from?" Kay asked, as the noise in the background turned louder.

"No," replied Savannah. "And nobody aside from you, your mom and my parents know that I'm living here."

"Maybe it's a secret admirer."

"I don't have a secret admirer."

"It sounds as if you do," Kay insisted, emphasizing her words with a sexy voice.

Savannah ignored her. "I was worried that Colt might have found us."

Kay hooted with cruel laughter. "As if that loser would ever spend a dime on you and Jacob. A sorry but true fact."

"I know," said Savannah quietly.

"I'm excited for you, Sav!" Kay giggled as the noise in the background turned louder. "Promise you'll call and tell me as soon as you find out."

"I will."

"Merry Christmas and give my love to Jacob."

"Thanks, I will. Merry Christmas."

"It sure is looking that way," laughed Kay. As soon as she hung up, Jacob raced into the kitchen. "I know who sent this!" he cried.

"Who?"

Happiness streamed from his face. "Mr. Stone!"

Savannah sprang back in surprise.

Tobias Stone?

"How do you know?"

"That day when we went to the toy store, he told me to pick something."

"Did you?"

Jacob shook his head. "He asked me what I wanted and I told him coloring books but I was playing with this." He stared down at the box in his hands.

Tobias Stone had sent this?

But why would he? What possible reason could there have been?

Anything to help. Those had been his very words to her a few days ago. He'd obviously taken more pity on her. She stared at the Christmas gift basket which contained enough food to feed an army.

"Aw, Mommy. He's so nice, and he gave you a present too."

"Tobias Stone," she murmured. Of all the people she thought might have sent this, it made perfect sense that Stone would be the main contender. Well, she couldn't accept this. Definitely not. And then she remembered that she'd already opened the gift basket and had given Arnold a few items from it.

"Jacob, honey," she hesitated, knowing that he hadn't rushed to open his gift, that on some level her son could sense her own hesitation.

"Can I open it?" His green eyes sparkled with hope and she gulped, torn between letting him have it, and giving in to Tobias Stone, or holding onto her dignity and making her son suffer. "I'm not sure we should accept this, Jacob."

"Why not?"

"Because Santa already bought you lots of gifts and I think he sent this to the wrong address."

"But it isn't from Santa. It's from Mr. Stone and it has my name on it!" She'd forgotten what a bright spark her son was and it killed her to refuse him when he was so obviously desperate to play with his gift.

"Honey, we can't keep it because..." She was flailing helplessly in deep water. *Because the man who gave this only did so because he feels sorry for us.* "You know, we weren't supposed to be there that night—the night we went to the toy store."

Jacob's face crumpled. "Do you think this is for someone else?"

"No, I—"

"Because it's got my name on it and the basket has your name on it." She sighed and clenched her stomach, thinking about her wages which had been paid into her account before Christmas. She hadn't thought too much about it before, but now that she was forced to consider it, even that could not have been Briony's doing. Briony couldn't change how or when she got paid. Only Tobias Stone had that power and she had the worrisome feeling that it had been his idea.

Did she really look that desperate? Were her clothes and shoes such a dead giveaway? Because it seemed that he'd seen right through her.

"We didn't give him anything," she replied in a dull voice. *Stop asking so many questions, Jacob.* "I think it's only right that we give this back."

She couldn't accept it and now, knowing what she did, she didn't want to accept any of it. But the damage had been done. She'd already opened the gift basket. At least they would eat well, not only today but for the coming days too, and she would have plenty of things to give to Rosalee.

"But won't that make Mr. Stone sad if we tell him we don't want his presents?" Jacob's face fell and she hurried to soothe him, hating herself at the same time but knowing she would hate herself more if she accepted both gifts.

She opened her mouth, but no words came out.

"It's okay, Mommy. You can give this back. I've got enough toys, anyway." She nodded, because she couldn't find her voice. "But can we keep that?" He pointed to the gift basket, his eyes, she felt sure, had already glimpsed the boxes of cookies, crackers and chocolates. "It's *your* present."

"It's not my present. This was intended for both of us."

"Is that a turkey? Wouldn't it be nice to have turkey?" Jacob said, looking closely at the gift basket. She hadn't bought turkey because it would have been too big for the two of them. Now she stifled the sadness that rose in her throat on hearing Jacob's simple request.

Accepting the gift basket meant they could have a truly extravagant Christmas feast. It would make a change from the small roast chicken dinner she'd planned, and she could freeze the chicken she'd already bought. She pulled the decorative festive gold and green ribbon and peeled the cellophane completely away. "Look, honey. There's ham as well. You like ham, don't you?" So much wonderful food. His eyes sparkled with happiness again and the gift was forgotten. "Thanks, Mommy. I can't wait!" He kissed her on the cheek.

No, she thought, her eyes misting over as he scrambled away with his Marvel toys. *Thank you, Jacob.*

She took the contents out one by one. There was a spiral sliced turkey breast glazed with honey, and a ham, and smoked salmon, roasted vegetables and scalloped potatoes, all cooked; they only needed to be heated. And there was sourdough bread, and relish, lots of types of cheeses, chocolate truffles, mixed nuts, and cherry and walnut slab cake and so many other little jars and boxes. She could almost see the extra inches adding to her waist and hips during the coming days. And there were bottles of red and white wine, and Champagne.

Warmth radiated all over her body at the thought that

someone had gone to the trouble of putting this together. That Tobias Stone had done this. Of course, *he* didn't put this together and had probably just called the store, or asked Candace to. But still, the thought had been there. A caring intention, even if she still couldn't reconcile the action with the personality of the man as she had come to know him.

Yet it was because of his actions that she and Jacob really would have the best Christmas ever.

Two years ago, she would never have dreamed that she would be spending Christmas in New York, yet here she was and now not only did she have a beautiful apartment, not hers, but still... and a job, one that was temporary, but still...and a magnificent Christmas feast, not bought by her, but still... things were so different.

The decision was made.

She would keep the gift basket and return the toy. After all, there was only so much charity she would accept, even from Tobias Stone.

CHAPTER THREE

Their sumptuous two-day feast kept their overstretched stomachs deliciously full all of Christmas Day and the day after.

Yet Savannah wasn't sure how she felt about the matter. At first, she was annoyed, then she was grateful, and then she alternated between the two emotions as she tried to analyze the reasons behind Tobias Stone's act of goodwill.

Charity. That's all it was, she kept reminding herself.

Jacob's contented sighs, as he had double helpings of turkey and ham, convinced her that she had done the right thing in keeping the gift basket at least.

She would deal with Tobias Stone when she next saw him but she wasn't sure when that would be. If he didn't come in next week then she would never see him again and she wouldn't get the chance to thank him for his gifts.

According to Briony, he wasn't jetting off on vacation this Christmas, but she could hardly imagine that a man like Stone would come into the office during this time of year.

He probably had better things to do and was most likely having the kind of Christmas she could only dream about.

Her return to work a few days later was made all the more painful because she had loved spending time with Jacob, playing games and reading, watching endless amounts of TV and eating. She wasn't looking forward to heading back to work, even though she was grateful for having a job.

With slight trepidation, she walked into the Stone building and made her way to the twenty-first floor. She carried the toy gift and went straight to Tobias Stone's door, and after knocking and not getting an answer, she placed it on the floor outside his door.

Feeling as though a heavy burden had been lifted from her shoulders, she walked back to Briony's office, hoping that these next few days would be quiet and easy. She wasn't sure if she was expected to work a full day on New Year's Eve but hoped so. The extra hours would help.

But when she opened the door, she jumped back in fright. The sight of Briony's spiky, auburn hair confronted her. Her mouth fell open. "Briony?"

Her friend turned around. "Hey," she nodded cheerfully. "How are you?"

"I thought you were on vacation?"

"I am supposed to be but I remembered a few things I had to do."

"So, you've come in on your day off?" Savannah set down her handbag on the desk and stared at her.

"I had some things I had to sort out."

"And they couldn't wait?" asked Savannah.

"Not if Tobias Stone has asked for them." Briony ran her slender fingers through her short hair and got up from her chair.

"Like what?"

"The files to be scanned and filed, I remembered that there were some more boxes in the basement."

"Is it urgent?"

"Urgent as in I should have authorized maintenance to get them from the basement before I went away. It's a pain in the ass to find anyone to do anything during the holiday period. The place is like a morgue. Do you think you can continue with what you did last time, scanning and saving the files?"

"Sure," replied Savannah, feeling happier that she would have some proper work to do instead of waiting for the phone to ring, or checking email.

"You'll be doing exactly the same thing. You remember, don't you, or shall I show you again?"

"I remember," replied Savannah. It was a simple enough task. She started to remove her scarf and hat. "He called you in to do that?"

"Who? Tobias?" Briony collected her sheets of paper and lined up her pens neatly. "He didn't have to call me in. I should have gotten this done a few weeks ago. When Tobias tells you to do something, you'd better do it."

Savannah blushed, then held on to her scarf and hat. "Shall I go back to my old office?"

"Your old office," Briony grinned. "Yes, please. You're in there for the rest of this week. I'm guessing it will take you up until New Year's Eve to work through the extra boxes, even with you working at your crazy speed."

Savannah grabbed her handbag. "By the way, thanks for extending my contract."

"See, that's another thing I should have spoken to you about before I left but what with the Christmas party and Max having last-minute problems at work and everything else...I don't know where my head was last week but I forgot so many things."

"Don't worry about it," Savannah reassured her. "Tobias

told me." She was reminded to ask Briony about her wages being paid into her account early.

"At least with you being here, I can enjoy my few days off without having to worry too much about what goes on here," said Briony, tidying away her things.

"Are you leaving already?" asked Savannah, disappointed. She'd been looking forward to having more conversation and finding out how the Christmas party had gone.

"Max is waiting for me downstairs."

"What are you up to?" asked Savannah, "anything nice?"

"We're going skiing in Lake Tahoe."

"That sounds exciting." Savannah had never skied before. It seemed like one of those experiences that she would never have, like eating oysters, or deep-sea diving, or lying in one of those so-called cabanas on the beach, getting a massage. She'd seen it in holiday magazines.

"Getting away from work is always exciting," said Briony. "I can't wait to get out on the slopes." She paused. "Did you have a good Christmas?"

"It was wonderful," said Savannah, sighing at the memory of the lazy few days she had had. "How about you?"

Briony crinkled her nose. "My parents for Christmas Day, then Max's parents the day after, and now we're all parented-out and we just want to go away and be by ourselves." Her face radiated excitement. It made Savannah think for one miniscule second what that might feel like, to go away somewhere exciting with someone worth going away with.

"Have a great time," she said, sensing that Briony was anxious to leave. "And thanks for arranging to have my wages paid in advance before Christmas."

"He managed to figure that out, did he?" asked Briony, zipping up her handbag. Savannah stared at her in silence.

"He?"

"Tobias mentioned it at the party."

"He mentioned it to you?" asked Savannah breathlessly.

Briony nodded, hovering at the door. "I'm glad he figured it out."

"Was that your idea?"

"No, we don't usually get involved. The agency handles all of that. I'm glad you got paid before Christmas. I hope it came in handy."

So, it had been Tobias's doing?

"It did," Savannah murmured.

"That man must finally be growing a conscience," Briony remarked as she walked out of the door.

"Imagine that," replied Savannah slowly.

"I've rerouted all the calls from this office to 218 but I don't expect you to be too busy on that front," said Briony. Savannah followed her but was lost in deep thought. "He's grown a conscience," she repeated, hoping to prompt Briony.

"He doesn't care what happens at the lower level," said Briony as they stood in the corridor. "Tobias doesn't concern himself with these things."

"He also apologized," said Savannah, hoping to elicit more information that might help her to put together the complex jigsaw puzzle that was Tobias Stone.

"He apologized?" Briony stared at her. "To you?"

Savannah nodded. "Is that unheard of?"

"Tobias Stone wouldn't apologize to his mother. What for?"

"The Dalton file saga."

Briony blew out a whistle. "There's hope for that man yet."

Briony's obvious shock at the news convinced Savannah to keep the information about her Christmas day deliveries all to herself, for now.

"I'm outta here!" Briony seemed suddenly energized. "Don't work too long on New Year's Eve. Most people leave early and you should too. There aren't many people in between now and New Year's Eve, and I don't expect that you'll see the likes of Tobias, Candace or Matthias around."

"Nobody from management will be in?" Savannah felt a little disappointed.

"Tobias for sure won't be coming in," announced Briony. "Even though he's here this year. I don't know why he's not going away because he usually does. I bet she's pissed."

"Who?"

"Naomi," replied Briony, matter-of-factly as she wrapped her scarf around her neck.

"Have you met her?"

"A couple of times. Take it easy and try to chill. I'm sorry to give you the extra work, otherwise you could have had a lazy week."

"Was that your idea or Tobias's?" Savannah asked quickly, hoping she wouldn't blush because she felt her cheeks heating up.

"I must go. Max is waiting," said Briony, frowning at her cell phone which had just beeped. "It was my idea. I know how much you like keeping busy but don't rush to get it all done, okay?"

"Okay," said Savannah, feeling somewhat relieved.

"Be good!"

No chance of me being anything but, thought Savannah, feeling sorry for herself.

CHAPTER FOUR

Savannah worked uninterrupted the entire day and the phone had only rung once. No emails had come in and she was doubly grateful that Briony had given her proper work to do, otherwise she would have sat around twiddling her thumbs all day long with time passing by at a slug's pace.

The next day when she came in, Savannah peeked by Tobias's door and sure enough, Jacob's gift still lay on the floor outside. If he didn't come in during the next few days then she would have to take it home with her before she left. She didn't want the likes of Candace to see it and ask too many questions. Savannah had a feeling that Tobias wouldn't want that either.

She and Jacob were still working their way through the gift basket, even though she had shared it with Rosalee and given her some of the savory crackers, cheese and chutneys to take home with her. There was still plenty left over for them.

With New Year's Day approaching and the promise of another public holiday, she wondered if she could afford the small luxury of taking Jacob ice skating. It was all very well going out to work and earning money, and she was thankful that

Rosalee was able to look after Jacob, but he would be back at school next week, and she now felt the double-pronged sword of guilt, wondering and worrying that she hadn't spent enough time with him.

But at least she was at a place now where she was starting to feel happy with her life. Things hadn't always been easy for her but lately they were starting to look up. She walked back into room 218 and wondered what it would be like if this was her permanent workplace.

Sometimes she routinely indulged herself with these notions in order to make herself feel better, but in fact, the future *was* starting to look a heck of a lot brighter than it had in earlier years. Having been at Stone Enterprises for almost a month now, this room felt familiar and comfortable and even though it was smaller than Briony's office, she liked the snugness of it. It felt more 'hers', and this, coupled with the fact that she was the only one on the twenty-first floor during this time, made for a pleasant, albeit solitary, working environment.

Hard-working as ever, she continued with her work happily; she'd never been the type to ease off and take things easy. It wasn't in her blood. Secretly, she was pleased that Briony had found something for her to do but she had been hoping that Briony might have mentioned there being more work for her in the new year.

She was aiming to work through the boxes fast enough so that by New Year's Eve, she would be able to go home early. As the day neared to an end, she was halfway through the boxes and she still hadn't seen a soul on the twenty-first floor. She didn't mind the solitude and as she left for the day, she walked past the elevator bank and peered at Tobias's door, expecting to see the toy gift still there.

But it was gone.

"Looking for something?" Goosebumps sprang up along the

base of her neck at the sound of his voice behind her. Tobias Stone walked past, giving her a cursory glance as he stood outside his door, ready to enter. He looked disheveled, dressed down in casual clothes, a pair of jeans and a white shirt, with stubble dusting his jawline. He stared at her, and she remained frozen, rooted to the spot like an iceberg.

"Hi," she said, startled by the way he had appeared out of nowhere. "I didn't know you were in," she managed to say.

"I can see that."

Time seemed to expand and silence hovered between them as she waited for him to say something. It seemed that he was waiting for the same thing from her.

"I wanted to thank you for–"

"Come in," he ordered brusquely, opening his door. He hadn't given her a chance to finish and his interruption surprised her. She braced herself for another Tobias-type encounter.

He took a few steps towards her so that they stood in the middle of his office facing one another. She didn't dare to sit down and instead folded her arms, trying to steel herself and stand firm. He seemed at ease, with his thumbs hooked into his jeans, yet when he spoke, his voice said otherwise. "You returned Jacob's present," he asked tightly. "Why?"

She felt waves of displeasure spreading outwards from him, like shockwaves as he stared at her coldly.

"I–" she began, and promptly forgot the exact reason for her return. She'd had it all prepared–her words, her defense, her reason, but she had forgotten it all now that he'd sprung upon her and left her feeling edgy once more.

"It was for Jacob," he said smoothly, clearly not at all interested in hearing her reasons. "I made him a promise that day he came into the toy store."

"You shouldn't have. We crashed your charity night and walked in by accident."

"Nevertheless, I bought presents for all the children there and I told Jacob to pick one for himself."

"But we weren't supposed to be there."

"But since you were..."

"Can I ask why?"

"Why what?"

"Why did you send the gifts?"

"All of my employees get a gift. The Christmas party is an end of year 'thank you' and some—those who deserve it—get a bonus."

"Is that what it is? A bonus?"

"You can call it what you want. Briony seemed pleased with your performance." *Then why had Briony not mentioned anything to her?* She looked down at her hands. "I still don't feel right about accepting—"

"The toy was a gift for Jacob, not you. As for the gift basket, consider it a Christmas bonus, if you really feel the need to justify it to yourself." She flinched at his words, delivered in a cold voice, devoid of any warmth, and looked at him sharply.

"We don't need your charity, Mr. Stone."

His mouth hardened into a straight line. "Who said anything about charity, Ms. Page?"

She wasn't going to allow him to feel sorry for her. "The Christmas gift basket was..." She swallowed, realizing that between her, Jacob and Rosalee, they had worked their way quite happily, and easily, through that particular gift of charity. "It was a kind gesture."

"Kindness had nothing to do with it." His words cut into her skin more sharply than a knife would have and she dared to stare up at him, unsure as to why he seemed so tense. She hadn't intended for their conversation to be so tightly wrought and yet all of her interactions with this man seemed like hard work. Surely her refusal to accept the gift couldn't solely be responsible for his surly mood now?

Did she look so much like a walking train wreck that he seemed to think she had 'welfare' written all over her? She had wanted to ask him about the reason for having her wages paid ahead of time but she reconsidered the idea in view of the thunderous look on his face. She was in no mood to take on further discussion with this man and as she looked into his eyes, she saw that they were no longer as blue but the color of granite, and as hard and cold.

He took a few steps towards her and she fought the desire to move back. If invading her personal space was his way of trying to get her to back down, she wasn't having it.

She'd stood up to worse before.

"Despite what you say, Mr. Stone, it *was* very kind of you."

"And yet you think it's fair to return Jacob's present but okay to keep the gift basket?"

When he put it like that, she wished more fervently than ever that she had returned that too. "I—uh ...," she stammered, trying to explain her reasons behind her decision. "The goods in it were fresh and I couldn't carry both things back—and..." She didn't want to admit that she'd already opened it and shared the contents. "Jacob liked the cookies." Ashamed of pinning the blame solely on her son, her guilt deepened and she heard the sound of blood pounding in her ears.

Why did this man always invoke the fight or flight response in her? She felt defensive around him, as though she'd done something wrong.

"You made good use of it then?" His eyes glinted as he spoke and she was vaguely aware that his hands were in his pockets and that he stood too close to her; close enough for her to sense a prickling energy radiating between them. Like static; something invisible but strong in the space that separated them.

She nodded guiltily. "We had a wonderful Christmas dinner, and for days afterwards. We're still..." Her words petered away. *Anything to help.* Despite what he said, she knew his act of kindness, no matter how he chose to label it, was because he'd felt sorry for her. Bringing Jacob to work with her before Christmas would have shown her desperation a million times more clearly than the state of her clothes.

Thank heavens he would never know that she'd gone to a food bank just to make ends meet.

His presence always reduced her to a helpless state; it was something she didn't like because it left her feeling inferior, even as she tried to stand her ground—something she had learned to do out of necessity. But when others took pity on her, she felt embarrassed and humiliated. As she did now.

He angled his head as if studying her reaction and even though he remained silent, the telltale tightness around his eyes indicated that this conversation was as uncomfortable for him as it was for her. She blinked quickly then looked away and her gaze fell on the Tiffany box which still lay on his desk. Christmas was over and she wondered why he hadn't taken the gift home yet.

"Thank you," she whispered, in a faraway voice.

"I insist you give Jacob the gift I promised him. In fact," he lifted his head and stared out of the window, "I'll only take it back if Jacob doesn't want it."

She remembered her son's face and the way it had shone when he'd opened the wrapping paper. "He wanted it," she said softly, recalling the moment.

"Then you must make sure he gets it." He nodded towards the corner where the gift lay on the black leather couch. She gritted her teeth, accepting defeat this time. She only had to put up with this man for a few more days. Maybe it wasn't a bad thing that Briony didn't need her any longer.

She walked over to the couch and picked it up. Holding the toy in her hands, she silently wondered how she was going to carry it back on the subway with the shopping bags full of clothes she'd picked up for Jacob in the sales during the lunch hour.

"I need to get going," he said, more to himself than to her. She turned around as he pulled his jacket from the chair and slipped it on. Her throat dried up as she watched him slip his arms through the sleeves of the dark gray jacket; his shoulders were wide, his arms thick. He was a fine figure of a man and Savannah looked away, feeling guilty for even staring at him.

Being single for a few years had made her awkward around men. She'd never paid them much attention, nor had she been interested in pursuing anything after Colt. But this man made her feel uncomfortable, and interested, and edgy all at once. He pushed her away with his harshness and pulled her towards him with his kindness. It was the fact that he invoked a reaction in her at all—and not just because he wore a ring on his finger—that she found most disturbing. He was out of bounds, and she felt guilty for having any thoughts about him at all, but he was also so far out of her league that he might as well have been an alien.

"Is anyone else in?" she asked, her voice feeble as she tried not to stare at his muscular arms. The combination of his white shirt and dark gray jacket made his blue eyes look so dark that she couldn't drag her gaze away even if she tried.

"I don't know," he replied, indifferent. She got the impression that he hadn't come in to do any work and was only passing through. He snatched the Tiffany box from the desk and she was tempted to ask him about it but moved towards the door, sensing that he was in a hurry.

"Happy New Year," she said, in a last attempt to be friendly.

"You, too." He barely glanced at her.

CHAPTER FIVE

The only reason he'd gone to the office was to pick up the gift, but he'd been shocked to find something lying on the floor outside his office door. Closer examination showed it to be the present he'd bought for the boy, unwrapped, but unopened.

She had returned it.

She had just this moment left his office but the idea of Savannah Page returning a gift that hadn't been intended for her in the first place had sorely pissed him off.

If his mother had come to learn of this—if he'd been stupid enough to tell her about his private life—she would have concluded that he was obsessed by the idea of Jacob, especially at this time of the year, when the past was all the more poignant. Maybe he was, maybe he wasn't. Maybe the kid reminded him of himself, maybe he didn't. Maybe Jacob showed him what the future might have held, or maybe these were mere stories he tortured himself with. Maybe he just felt sorry for the boy and his mother and the idea of her scrounging for extra food had made him feel something.

Now *that* was a rarity.

We don't need your charity. She'd tossed those words at him carelessly. His jaw would have dropped but he'd learned to control his feelings and his reactions.

But, sweetheart, you do need my fucking charity.

He'd been tempted to tell her just how much he knew she needed it, but something had stopped him. Maybe it was the sight of her standing in front of him and looking vulnerable, something that was unlike her. He had expected more of a fight from her and yet she'd looked almost helpless, as if she was unsure of something. So he had refrained from telling her that he'd sent the gift basket because the sight of her lining up to get food had seeped into his consciousness. He felt sorry for her.

Ordinarily, he felt sure that she would have crucified him because she had that kind of temper on her.

If he was being honest with himself, it made him secretly happy to know that he might have made her Christmas easier, even if he didn't believe in the season of goodwill anymore.

Now he was left staring at the Tiffany box, debating what to do with it. *Return it,* his instinct told him. *And move on.*

The beep of his cell phone momentarily distracted him and he pulled it out of his pocket. Naomi was hounding him again. Her actions surprised him because she should have known better but he knew what drove this: she was worried that he was losing interest in her. He hadn't gone away and he hadn't called to see her either. She'd been waiting for him; waiting for the booty call.

He briefly considered the idea of asking her to come over tonight. If anyone knew how to relieve him, it was Naomi. Hours of sex with her drained him, leaving him too tired to remember and sleep would come quickly.

But he wasn't in the mood for sex, or her.

He grabbed his car keys and knew what he had to do. He'd given his driver the week off, starting on Christmas Day, right after he'd asked Morris to drop the gifts off at Savannah Page's address. It had surprised him, where she lived, because it was an up-and-coming neighborhood with newly built apartments. Not the type of area he expected someone to live in if they had to visit a food bank. The woman certainly had an intriguing set of circumstances and his interest had been more than roused.

But he'd never expected her to return the gift, and she'd come in at a time when he was least prepared for it. This recent exchange with her had left him feeling restless. He decided to stay off the whiskey tonight. Maybe he'd hit the boxing ring and go a few rounds with his trainer instead.

The coming year was going to be a big one, and he needed to be fighting fit and ready.

The thought inspired him and he locked his office and headed out, ignoring Naomi's text completely. But Savannah Page was waiting for the elevator. He stopped, ready to retreat but it was too late because she'd already seen him. She appeared just as painfully surprised to see him. A forced smile crawled from her lips, a smile which he returned just as begrudgingly.

They waited in awkward silence for the elevator and, once inside, they suffered even more discomfort with only the two of them and twenty-one floors to descend.

She finally spoke. "I don't want you to think that I was being ungrateful about returning the gift. Jacob was over the moon when he unwrapped it." She already looked weighed down by the toy box and the shopping bags in each hand and he was half tempted to call her a cab. For a brief second, he even contemplated offering her a lift but convinced himself that she would only regard it as further charity.

"Which is why it surprises me that you were so adamant to return it," he replied, settling his back against the elevator wall.

The elevator stopped at the thirteenth floor and someone got in. Savannah moved closer to him. "It's a nice thing you do—for those children from the adoption centers," she said and he noticed that her gaze fell on the Tiffany box in his hands. An unasked question lurked in her eyes.

He nodded in return but said nothing.

"Did you have a good Christmas?" she asked, obviously trying hard to make conversation. Under normal circumstances he felt sure she would not have bothered. Had he, by giving her the gifts, made her feel indebted towards him? He didn't like the thought of that. She was doing what most people did. She was making an effort because of who he was: Tobias the Great, rich and successful.

It was an imbalance most would covet, yet it made him uncomfortable. He was certain that if he were an average nobody, she wouldn't have bothered.

With a third person in the elevator, Tobias felt even more guarded. He wasn't in the mood to make conversation with anyone right now, not even Savannah Page. Having something to say implied interest, it implied wanting to find out more about the other person, it implied a level of interest he did not feel. And yet he felt something for her. Only, he wasn't sure what it was—pity or something else? But he knew one thing; it had been the first time since Ivy's death that he'd been interested in another woman in this way.

"Did you?" she asked, frowning at him, when he didn't reply.

"Christmas is Christmas," he replied, fully aware that his answer told her nothing. Silence fell again and he stared straight ahead at the door and hoped that this woman wasn't exchanging pleasantries just because she felt obligated towards him.

Mercifully, she remained quiet and when the elevator doors opened at the ground floor, she murmured a quick, "Have a good evening," and rushed off. He watched her struggle to get through the revolving doors, loaded down as she was with her bags and the moment she slipped out of sight, he wished he'd made more of an effort and not done that cold distance thing he did with most people.

"I want to return it," Tobias insisted.

"If you're sure, sir."

"I am." Tobias was anxious to leave because this place had too many memories. He had bought her many items of jewelry from here over the years.

The manager nodded his head. "Would you like to exchange it for something else, perhaps a—" He was about to open the window of the display cabinet behind him but Tobias stopped him. "Don't."

"As you wish, sir, but it is a large amount of—"

"I don't want anything. Don't you fucking understand?"

"Of course, sir. Certainly. One moment, sir." The man disappeared behind closed doors, leaving the other two salesclerks glancing at him nervously. One attempted a half-assed smile.

He'd bought the gift in a moment of drunken madness. Even then, the salesclerks had hovered around him like fleas the moment he'd stepped into the esteemed Tiffany store.

People always hovered around him. They were always too eager to please and to do his bidding. He hated it.

That day had been especially bleak for him and he'd given in. Whatever he did, however much he drank, however much he used Naomi's body for his own satisfaction, or no matter how hard he drove his business negotiations, he always felt the void—the one *she* had left behind.

He missed her. He missed her with all his heart and soul, but as time went on, the memories and feelings he'd treasured had slowly started to slip away. It wasn't that he was beginning to forget her, but more that the vividness of his memories had started to fade. Her essence still lingered around him, but not as strongly as before. He could still see her smile, hear her voice, feel her skin, but only for a few seconds before the imprint of her image slipped through his fingers like water.

People told him that it was high time he moved on but the stain of his misery wrapped itself around his soul and refused to leave him completely. It lingered around him, dragging him to the cellars of darkness whenever he tried to come up for air.

But something strange had happened this morning. He'd woken up feeling better than he had these past few days. Consecutive nights of not sleeping much, coupled with heavy drinking and spending Christmas alone, had left him in a sour mood for the most part. Yet he'd woken up alert and refreshed, and ready to take on the world.

Maybe he had needed time away by himself. No board members to bother him, no business meetings to attend, no Candace, no Naomi. Not even his parents or his brother, Xavier.

This morning, he had decided that it was time to return the gift. Buying a gift for Ivy was as sick as it got.

Coming to the office today had been a way of getting back into the world. Of leaving his place that reeked of alcohol and dirt. He had loped around in his PJs, looking like a sixty-year-old has-been. At least he'd successfully managed to dodge his parents' pleas to join them for Christmas in Aspen. He'd even ignored Xavier's calls.

Another salesclerk, one who carried an inflated air of self-importance, appeared before him. "I'm sorry to have caused you some distress, Mr. Stone. The transaction has been reversed and your account will be credited shortly. However, due to the holidays—"

Tobias waved his hand at the man and turned to leave. "It's not a problem."

"Have a good day, sir. We will be updating our designs in time for Valentine's Day, should you be interes—"

His body tensed as his heart rate skyrocketed. "My wife is dead. She won't need a fucking Valentine's gift any more than she needed the—" The words stuck in his throat like thorns on a rosebush. Any more than she would have worn the necklace and earrings he'd bought for her.

Imbeciles.

He raged silently as he walked out, wishing he had never set foot in this damned place.

CHAPTER SIX

"Another present for Jacob?" Arnold's gappy smile greeted her as she walked through the door which he held open.

"Oh, yes," she replied, "one more gift for Jacob." Relief swept over her as soon as she entered the lobby. The bags had weighed her down, becoming heavier towards the end of her almost hour-long commute and she was anxious to be relieved of them.

"Jacob will be very happy," Arnold continued.

"I expect he will be."

Rosalee gave her a perplexed look the moment she walked into the apartment. "Didn't you take that to work with you a few days ago?"

"It was a present for Jacob."

"What happened?"

Savannah set the box down and busied herself by taking her coat off; she was reluctant to explain.

"Well?" persisted Rosalee, folding her arms.

"It was from someone at work and it didn't seem right to accept it."

"Someone at work showed a kindness to your son at Christmas, and still you say no?"

Savannah shrugged. "I brought it back. He can have it now."

"The gift basket?" Rosalee placed her hands on her thick, wide hips. "Was that from work too?"

Savannah nodded.

"Your work people seem to appreciate you. That's a good thing."

"Hmmm," she replied casually, not wanting to encourage too many questions from her highly observant sitter.

"You make sure you stay there for life," advised Rosalee, taking off her apron. "I made dinner and now I must leave you."

Savannah sniffed the air. "Thanks Rosalee. It smells delicious but you didn't have to go to the trouble of cooking."

"I have to eat," the older woman replied. "And your gift basket is still full of good things."

"Thank you, and take whatever you want," Savannah encouraged.

"I already did." Rosalee smiled, her face worn out like old material.

"Has Jacob been good?"

"Your boy?" The elderly woman gave her a surprised look as she put on her coat. "He is an angel. Bye, Jacob," she shouted over her shoulder. "We will meet again tomorrow."

Savannah knew he was an angel. Somewhere from the depths of his room, she heard Jacob shout out to Rosalee.

"Thanks, Rosalee," said Savannah, opening the door. "See you tomorrow."

She walked towards Jacob's room carrying the toy in her hands, and he shuffled back a step and then yelped with delight when he saw it. "But I thought you said...?"

She walked over and sat by his bed, narrowly missing two of

his superhero figures which lay facing one another. "Mr. Stone insisted you keep it."

"You mean it, Mommy? I can keep it and play with it?" he asked again, as if she might change her mind at any moment. She nodded and two seconds later the box was opened and empty and a second Iron Man was flying around on something that looked like a spaceship.

"Will you tell Mr. Stone I said 'thank you'?"

"I already did."

"Yeah, but will you say it again?" Jacob's eyes twinkled as he asked her.

"Okay," she replied, feeling apprehensive at the thought of meeting the man again.

"I told you he was nice."

Tobias Stone's sainthood had been sealed in Jacob's eyes. Savannah tucked her hair behind her ears and said nothing.

CHAPTER SEVEN

She was hoping for an easy and nonconfrontational day at work today, and had high hopes of having the twenty-first floor to herself.

She prayed for a Tobias-Stone-free day and hoped it was highly unlikely that he would be in again since she got the impression that his visit to the office yesterday had been a flying one.

Keeping her word to Jacob, she emailed Tobias as soon as she got in, thanking him for the present on her son's behalf. Email seemed the safer option, whether he was in or not.

Then she got to work driven by the need to finish the task she had been given by tomorrow, New Year's Eve. Since it was so deathly quiet, she put a Taylor Swift playlist on YouTube to break the silence. It wasn't too loud but loud enough for her to get caught up in the songs which she and Jacob often danced to, and she soon forgot where she was.

Therefore it wasn't all that surprising that she was blissfully unaware of Tobias standing at the door watching her get her groove on. It was only when she turned all the way around, with a file in her hand, jiggling her hips suggestively from side to side that she caught him looking at her. She almost tripped forward in shock.

What the hell was he doing here?

And was that amusement that flickered across his eyes and the hint of a smile that kissed his lips—or was he trying hard not to laugh at her?

Her body turned rigid except for the furious movement of her chest as it rose and fell sharply. For a few long, distressing seconds, time seemed to have stopped and she was lost for words. A silent prayer for the earth to shift and swallow her up went unanswered as she stood frozen, trying not to analyze how ridiculous she must have looked.

"Do you know how to modify a Word template?" he asked coolly.

A Word template? His words made logical sense but she was still drenched from head to toe in embarrassment and it took her a few seconds to answer. She nodded, then managed a "Yes."

"I need you to fix something for me right away. I have a document which I need to send out in half an hour."

"Yes," she said, in a robotic tone. "I mean, okay." Relieved that he'd chosen to completely ignore her dancing, she followed him like a lamb to the slaughter, back to his office. She walked slowly, dropping back slightly so that she walked more behind him than beside him.

He strode into his office and walked over to his computer. "I need it to look like this one." He showed her a document on the screen. "I don't understand why this one looks such a goddamn mess." He opened up a second document. Standing beside him, her chest pounding, she stared at the screen and forced herself to concentrate.

"I can fix that," she said easily and with relief because she knew she could.

"Sit," he told her, and then stayed where he was, standing

and watching over her shoulder. He stood so close that she recognized the heady wood and spice mix of his aftershave and was immediately transported back to that day in the elevator when she'd gone to the thirtieth floor by mistake.

Fix his problem, she told herself, and kept her eyes glued to the screen. Why was her heart banging against her ribcage so loudly?

Could he hear it?

She didn't like that he watched her like a hawk or that he stood so close behind her that she could feel the heat of his stare on her back. Something about him set her on edge and made her feel self-conscious, and her reaction to him both puzzled and disturbed her. She couldn't work like this.

"Do you mind?" She turned her head to the side and stared up at him.

"Do I mind what?"

"Do you mind moving away?"

He lifted his shoulder in a half-shrug and walked away.

"Just this one?" she asked, tidying up his template and fixing the document he had given her.

"Yes."

After a few minutes her task was done. "Here you go."

"Already?"

"It doesn't take long," she said, getting up from the chair. He was by her side quickly and she stepped away.

"Wait," he said, ordering her to stay as he looked over the document carefully. She caught the fading scent of his aftershave, but there was something else, something less sensory, something imperceptible, almost like an invisible web in which she felt herself entangled.

Did he feel it too?

Or had it been so long since she had been around someone

who wasn't Jacob, or a woman friend, that her body no longer knew how to react?

Tobias Stone made her nervous, not like Colt, but another type of nervous. A type she hadn't encountered before. She wasn't even sure if what she felt was a sign of nervousness or something else.

"It looks fine," he said.

No 'Thank you'?

And instantly she dismissed her naiveté in expecting one.

"I have some more." He fixed his gaze on her and sent her insides into free-fall. "Could you fix them?"

"Now?"

"It doesn't take long," he said, echoing her words. "I'll keep myself busy seeing that you feel so uncomfortable with me hovering around."

"You don't make me uncomfortable," she lied, narrowing her eyes at him, even though her heart rate had gone up in the last few minutes. She had yet to figure out whether she hated him because he was such a cold and arrogant bastard, or because his very aloofness was something she had come to see as a challenge.

"No?" he asked, his mouth twisting.

"No." She looked away and pretended to look carefully at the documents he'd opened up for her.

Get through these as fast as you can and get the hell out.

He walked over to the leather sofa and started to go through some paperwork while she worked quickly, going through the documents one by one and fixing them all. A couple of times when she glanced at him, she'd catch him staring, and he would look away sharply, and then she would return her gaze, and her attention, back to the computer screen.

She noticed that he didn't look so harsh today. He was still all hard angles but there was something softer about him, compared to yesterday when he'd looked more wound up. She knew all about that tortured look in a man. She had suffered for it by being with Colt. Towards the end, he'd started to take his anger out on her more often but the slapping and punching stopped hurting as Jacob got older. She had developed the ability to mask her pain so that her son didn't have to hear her cries.

Yes, she knew about tortured souls and today Tobias Stone looked less like one of them.

"All done," she said, getting up quickly, and hoping that he wouldn't come over to check every document.

"Briony said you were quick."

She managed a smile at that. "Do you want to check?"

"Do I need to?" He smiled at her. It was a rare event and it completely surprised her.

"A control freak like you?" Her tongue had loosened and with only one more day left, she didn't need to watch what she said to him. He walked towards her with his hands in his pockets.

"A control freak?" His face was neither hard nor soft. "Nobody has ever had the balls to say that to me before."

"I can see why."

"But you," he said, standing by her side, "you have no filter."

She felt braver today; maybe it was because he'd needed something from her and the act of him asking had given her strength. In any case, she felt less indebted. "Maybe the people around you are too scared to tell you the truth."

"Is that what you think?"

"That you frighten people? Perhaps."

"You don't frighten easily."

Not anymore. "No," she replied, stepping away from the desk as he glanced at the screen.

"I trust that these will be fine, but if not, I know where to find you."

She edged towards the door.

"I received your email this morning," he said, just as she reached the door. She turned around.

"I emailed you because I didn't think you would be in today. Jacob loved your present and he wanted me to say 'Thank you' to you."

"He liked it?" Tobias asked.

She nodded.

"I'm glad to hear that."

"He played with it for hours last night, if you really want to know. Your gift has even superseded mine and Santa's."

He gave her an appreciative nod. "It wasn't my intention to do that."

"It's not a problem," she said breezily, leaning into the conversation, which for once bordered on being almost polite. "You know what children are like. In a few days' time, he'll find another favorite toy and your gift will be cast aside." But even as she said this, she knew it wasn't completely true. Jacob had been faithfully loyal to his tattered and battered Spider-Man for years, but he was now obsessed by Iron Man and she knew that even with the other toys she'd bought him, Iron Man and Wolverine would be his new accomplices for the next few years. Until the next superhero emerged.

"Children..." he said, uttering the word so low that she wasn't sure she'd heard right.

"Christmas is for them," she said, and wanted to ask him if he had any children but his face hardened in that instant and the softness was gone. She decided not to risk it. "You know where I am if you need anything else," she said, making a getaway before he responded with something hurtful and ruined the moment.

CHAPTER EIGHT

He lay in bed thinking about Savannah Page and their conversation, until another text from Naomi interrupted his thoughts. She wanted to know how he was—with the veiled underlying question being why he hadn't called.

It was enough to get him to go into the office again in order to keep his mind busy. And really, he had no pressing urge to fuck her right now.

He'd managed to get a lot done yesterday with it being so quiet and with nobody around. Nobody, that is, apart from Savannah Page.

He showered and dressed and was at his office by 7:00 a.m. and within an hour he had managed to power through the itty-bitty tasks he'd been putting off all year, things he didn't want Candace to deal with. Thank-you and follow-up emails to clients, business friends and acquaintances.

With the documents that Savannah had fixed, he was able to work on his strategy for the coming year, refining the finer details of the plans which he had been putting together for a few months. These he would share with the board members in the first meeting of the year once everyone returned to work.

While he valued the opinion of the board members, and they were important to him and to the company, it was Matthias he relied on the most. Matthias was his right-hand man and had been instrumental in the success of his company. Of course, he was highly rewarded too. The man was as astute and shrewd as Tobias and understood him and his vision for where he wanted to take Stone Enterprises in the future.

It was a shame, or perhaps it was really a blessing, that Xavier had shown no interest in joining the company. Having his brother on board would have been interesting, mused Tobias. But they were polar opposites.

In his office, with no Candace to bother him and no meetings to attend, Tobias was able to get through a lot of things that had been on his 'to-do' list. He'd been surprised at how quickly the time had flown as he'd diligently worked away uninterrupted, and when his cell phone rang, he answered it without looking.

"I'm here. Upstairs, waiting for you." Naomi's seductive voice had the opposite effect than what she'd probably intended. He bared his teeth, enraged by her cunning, and slammed down his cell phone.

What did she hope to achieve?

She'd breached his most fundamental of rules: To be available when *he* needed her.

Bolting out of his chair, he raced out of his office, his anger inflamed at the woman's imposition. He stabbed the elevator button repeatedly, driven by his haste to reach the penthouse and put her straight.

"That was fast." The look of surprised satisfaction quickly vanished from Naomi's face as Tobias glared at her. The sheer white shirt she had on didn't hide the lacy bra she wore, and her pencil skirt had a slit all the way up her right thigh. He'd never thought of her in terms of a high-class hooker before, but her dress code today screamed 'fuck me' and he looked away in disgust.

"I didn't call you," he said slowly, gritting his teeth together.

"I missed you," she countered, walking towards him and putting her arms around his waist. "A whole week has passed, and you never called, not even during Christ—"

"We had a deal." He moved her hands away.

"I know," she said, sounding unsure for the first time. He stared down at her perfectly shaped lips now painted burgundy. With her wavy blonde hair and brown eyes and eyebrows, she looked like a cross between a newbie movie star and a rock princess. "I was worried about you, Tobias. What's changed? You don't call. I haven't seen you for a while, and you've been distant lately."

"This was never supposed to be a relationship. I made that very clear from the start. You do understand that, *don't you*?"

Her forehead puckered. "I know that. I know the deal we have—"

"Then you must know I pay for your services as and when I need them."

She placed her hands around his waist once more. "I understand, Tobias. But I've been waiting for you and I miss you." She leaned in and slipped a kiss on the side of his face, but he moved his face away quickly and stepped back.

"I will call you when I want to fuck you. Do you understand?" He threw his words at her like cold water over her feelings. Her eyes glistened.

"I'm sorry. It won't happen again."

"Why did it happen this time?"

"I was worried about you. You never returned any of my texts. It's not like you, Tobias."

He stared at her, at the open invitation that she was, leaving nothing to the imagination. He could screw her right now, and she'd be fine with whatever he did to her. A man's dream, and here she was, ready and waiting for him; only, he'd lost his appetite lately. Naomi was too easy. Not that it had ever been about the thrill of the chase with her. She was a sure thing. He got what he paid for.

Savannah Page, on the other hand, was something else. She offered more in the way of mental stimulation and she managed to do it in her sensible shoes and clothes that clearly looked as though they'd seen better days. He couldn't figure it out—his interest in her—but knew only that she had something that piqued it.

Mistaking his silent contemplation as a sign of his weakness, Naomi started to unbutton her shirt.

"Don't," he warned.

"I'm here now."

He gripped her wrist to stop her from undoing the last few buttons. "I said, '*Don't.*' "

"You want me, Tobias. I can see it in your eyes." He clenched his jaw tightly, allowing his mind to drift to the thoughts of what she could do. She was a great lay. Sensational.

"Let me," she reached down to unzip him, but he grabbed her wrist.

"Get dressed and leave."

"Is there someone else? Is that it?" She challenged him. Then softening, "You can still have me. I'm discreet. You know I am."

"You broke our agreement."

"I'm sorry," she whined, the pleading in her voice grating on him. "Don't do this."

"Are you telling me what to do?"

She stepped back and quickly regained her composure. "No. No, I—" she started to button up her shirt.

"Never break my rules again."

"I won't. I promise. It won't happen again, Tobias." She slipped on her jacket and grabbed her handbag, following him to the door. He said nothing as they got into the elevator, but he could tell that she was anxious. She was probably worried that she had messed things up.

He had nothing to say, not even to put her out of that wretched misery he could see so clearly on her perfectly made-up face. They weren't so different after all, he decided. Her and Candace. Naomi fixed him when it came to sex and Candace fixed him when it came to office duties.

In between the two was a wide-open void in which he floundered, lost and bitter. When the elevator stopped at the twenty-first floor, he turned to give Naomi a final parting nod.

"I'll wait for you to call me," she said quietly.

He stepped out and almost walked into Savannah Page.

CHAPTER NINE

"Hi," said Savannah when she saw Tobias getting out of the elevator. But the smile on her face soon slid to the floor when her gaze fell on the woman who remained in the elevator.

"I'll wait for you to call me," Savannah heard the woman say.

Tobias rushed out without replying and Savannah caught a glimpse of the faint tell-tale lipstick stain on the side of his face.

This was his wife?

And they'd both been in the penthouse.

She smiled at the woman and said, 'Hi.' The woman smiled back but said nothing and then looked away as though she didn't want to talk.

Savannah settled back against the elevator wall and stared. She had often wondered what Tobias Stone's wife was like and here she was with a clear view of the other woman's side profile. The woman stared at the door, her face was turned away, but Savannah's quiet observation took in her attire from top to bottom. She was professionally dressed, smart and sexy, and she was pretty, too. When a few more people got in at subsequent floors, she was able to observe without it being so obvious.

She felt a twinge of something. Disappointment, or was it jealousy? Self-conscious, she smoothed her hair down and stared at the sensible pumps she had on before stealing a gaze at the woman's shiny blood-red slingbacks. They had tiny pencil-tip heels, and her shoes matched her handbag.

Savannah shuffled her feet together and clung tighter to her tattered dark brown handbag. The inside seam was ripped and sometimes her possessions would disappear in the space between the lining and the cheap leather, making it hard for her to find her keys or cell phone which always seemed to slip into that gap.

Maybe she would treat herself to a pair of shoes at some point, even though she couldn't compete with this glamorous woman. Savannah ground down on her teeth. Why was she even thinking of competing? Tobias Stone's wife had no worries in life and she probably had a daily routine that was so very different from hers.

The elevator emptied at the ground level and Savannah watched as the woman left the elevator first. She followed closely a few steps behind, but once the woman went through the revolving doors, Savannah soon lost sight of her.

She crossed the street and headed towards the coffee shop. During the entire week, she hadn't brought sandwiches with her to work. Instead she'd given into the luxury of buying her lunch, feeling at last as though she finally belonged in this city that never slept. Now if only she could secure a permanent job, her plan for this year would be well underway.

After lunch, she had half a box of files left which she worked through half-heartedly. She'd lost her enthusiasm. Feeling a little lonely, she emailed Briony to give her an update and was surprised to receive an instant reply from her:

"You didn't take my advice and slow down, did you?"

Savannah replied:

"I don't know what 'slow down' means. Speed is built into my DNA."

She was still smiling to herself when Briony's reply came through:

"If you're done for the day, then you might as well leave. I'll see you next week."

At that moment, her phone rang, and she answered it without thinking. The sound of Tobias's voice made her jump, not because he was loud, but because she had convinced herself that he wouldn't be in anymore.

"I have another document that needs fixing. Could you come and do your magic?"

She closed her email. "I'll be right over," she replied, her stomach quivering already. *Better to get it over and done with.*

Seeing that the door to Tobias's office was already open, she walked in to find him sitting on the couch with files strewn open beside him.

"The document's open on the screen," he told her.

"Are you doing an end-of-year clean-up?" she asked, noting that his office had never looked messier. His desk was strewn with more paperwork. He attempted a smile but the skin around his eyes was tight, and he looked irritated.

"Something like that."

She sat down and started to work. "It's easy enough to fix."

"What is?"

"The template. I could show you how to, if you want."

He shook his head in irritation. "You can show Candace when she's back. I don't need to know."

She was about to tell him that she would be leaving tomorrow but judging from his previous reply, she decided not to say anything. *Tobias doesn't concern himself with such lowly matters*. Briony had said something like that. Savannah glanced over at him and watched briefly as he flicked through his papers. Tension hung low and heavy in the room and she wasn't sure what had happened, but he seemed to have closed up again.

She got up. "It's done. Was there anything else?" He continued to scribble away, looking busy with his paperwork. She stared at the faint lipstick mark on his face as she walked past. "You have a slight—"

He looked up and she coughed lightly, pointing vaguely at her own cheek. "A lipstick mark on your cheek."

At first he frowned then, understanding, he scrubbed his face roughly.

"It's gone," she offered, wanting to be helpful. Something about the way he avoided eye contact with her gave her the courage to push forward when her gut instinct warned her to back off. But she'd already seen his wife and she felt it was only polite to ask. Her curiosity was getting the better of her. "Did she like it? The gift?"

"What gift?"

"The blue gift box? Did your wife like it?" Savannah asked.

His face hardened at her words and she sensed that she had pried too far into his life.

"My wife?" he asked quietly. "You think she's my wife?" She knew in that instant that she'd made a mistake.

"I'm sorry, I assumed ..." But it was too late to take back her words. She left quickly, without saying another word.

Back in the safety of her office, she collapsed in her chair and stared at the screen in despair.

And then it came to her, and she wondered why she hadn't done this before. She started to search online for information on Tobias Stone.

And what she found made her heart sink. She stared at the screen, her insides feeling cold as she reread the article. Not content, she searched some more and clicked on every single link to do with him. It all pointed to the same thing. How the clever boy from Queens had built his empire, and how he'd lost his young wife in a tragic car accident years ago.

There was no mention of Naomi anywhere and though he appeared on many lists—in the hot, young bachelors list, the most desired men in NY list, and in the wealthiest young men lists—there was hardly any coverage of him with women.

After a while of perusing through the information on Tobias Stone, Savannah held her head in her hands and contemplated the man's reaction. It hadn't been so bad, given his circumstances.

The poor man.

CHAPTER TEN

Mistaking Naomi for his wife was the worst insult to Ivy's memory. Tobias threw down his pen and got up as soon as Savannah had left.

It was bad enough that Naomi had pissed him off this morning, but now this. He stared at the papers strewn everywhere. This was what happened when his mind was in disarray.

If Savannah Page didn't know that his wife had died, she must have been one of the few women in New York to be ignorant of the fact.

The press intrusion into his life at that time had been merciless. He had proved their accusations of a cover-up to be false, and he had told them everything. He hadn't held anything back. But he was bait, a billionaire who had fallen down and one whom many wanted to see stay down.

It had taken him a year to get through the outcome of what had happened, and to walk away from it and attempt to carry on with his life. Despite the verdict, he still blamed himself. Nobody could take that away from him.

He had managed to successfully avoid being connected to

any one woman since then. Truth was, he wasn't interested in anyone. His single-minded focus had done wonders for his business, taking him to wealth beyond his wildest dreams. But personally, and emotionally, he was a broken man who hid his emotions, or tried to.

He got through his days with the sole focus of building his business and taking it to newer heights. Men of his position and power never sat back on their laurels. It was like an addiction, wanting more, being the best, amassing more wealth. Becoming more successful and killing off the competition. It was far easier than going through the pain of falling in love and then having it all ripped out of his hands.

Being left behind was brutal.

But now this temp had managed to wriggle under his skin and asked questions that nobody else had dared, mostly through ignorance, but she also stood up to him. Each time he spoke to her, she seemed to have a knack for unsettling him. And yet he was drawn to her out of curiosity.

When his cell phone rang and Xavier's name blinked at him, he was forced to dispense with his thoughts and he took the call reluctantly, knowing that if he didn't, his mom and his brother would spend all of the next day bugging him.

"He answers," Xavier muttered.

"What is it?"

"Great to hear from you too, Bro."

Tobias hung his head. "What do you want, Xavier?"

"It's New Year's Eve tomorrow."

"And?" He had managed to avoid his family over Christmas and hoped to do the same over New Year's. Seeing them for Thanksgiving had been enough. They didn't normally badger him but because he was in New York this year, they seemed to think he would be especially lonely for their company.

"How about we get together? We haven't seen you, not even for Christmas. Mom was really mad."

"I know." He'd have to fix that at some point. His father didn't hound him but his mother more than made up for it.

"She's worried about you, that's all."

"I'm fine."

"Are you?" Xavier asked.

Tobias made a gruff noise and scratched his forehead. "Yes." He wished they would leave him alone. He *was* fine. He hadn't fallen to pieces, his company was booming and the share price of his stock was increasing. What more proof did they want?

"Come out tomorrow evening. I'm arranging something with some of the guys. You should come along instead of sitting around on your own doing nothing."

Tobias closed his eyes, trying to find an excuse. He preferred his own company and wanted to see the new year in alone, with only a bottle of whiskey for comfort and company.

They all worried about him, but he wasn't an alcoholic. He'd seen the lives that had been destroyed by one drunk and he wasn't about to make the same mistake. If anything, he was a control freak; wasn't that what Savannah Page had called him? Control freaks like Tobias Stone would not allow themselves to drink themselves to death.

"What do you say?" Xavier asked as a knock at the door, hard and insistent, clamored for Tobias's attention.

"Sure, why not?" he replied, hoping to get rid of Xavier quickly. He'd find a suitable excuse later.

"I'll swing by tomorrow," Xavier threatened.

Tobias slid the cell phone onto his desk and answered his door. Savannah Page stood outside twisting her fingers nervously, and he was curious to find out why.

"I'm sorry."

"For what?"

"For earlier. I'm sorry. I didn't know about your wife." Her face turned red and the muscles in his body tightened.

She'd only just found out?

"I had no idea," she warbled on, speaking in the silence that hung between them when he declined to answer. "I'm sorry for mistaking Naomi for your wife."

Enough.

He wasn't used to talking to anyone about Ivy. The court case had been hard enough and he didn't want memories of that time to be ruffled up again. Now this woman who barely knew him and knew nothing about Ivy was bringing it up again. He stepped forward and grabbed her wrist.

"Don't. Ever. Say. Anything. About. My. Wife. Again." Quickly realizing that he had gripped her tightly, he quickly loosened his hold. "And don't ever make the mistake of thinking Naomi is her."

Her brows pinched together and she seemed to crumple before his eyes. Pulling her hand free, she rubbed her wrist as she stumbled backwards, lowering her head, but not before he saw the look of anguish in her eyes. And then she rushed away.

He'd gone too far and he knew it.

CHAPTER ELEVEN

Shock dulled her brain as she stumbled back to her office, reeling from Tobias's actions.

Savannah was glad she hadn't spoken to Briony about extra work—she'd be glad to see the last of Stone Enterprises and the tyrant of a man who ran the company. Turning off her PC, she left the office an hour before it was time to go home.

Her mood blackened further as she sat on the subway, her thoughts a firestorm of chaos as she recounted what had happened. Every interaction with Tobias Stone left her feeling as though she'd been stamped and trodden on.

"What happened to you?" Rosalee asked, when she returned home later that evening.

"Nothing," replied Savannah, bravely trying to muster a smile. She kissed Jacob who'd come running to her but he raced off again before she had a chance to speak to him.

"Nothing?" Rosalee stared at her closely. "That face does not suit you." Savannah loved Rosalee's expressions, and this one made her smile. "That one I like," said the elderly woman, approving. "Are you working tomorrow?"

That didn't sound too good. "I am," she replied slowly. "Is it a problem?"

"No problem at all. My son and his family are visiting tomorrow, and I can look after Jacob at my place."

She felt as if she'd given Rosalee no choice in the matter. If her son and his family were coming over tomorrow, then Jacob would only get in the way. She considered the possibility of taking a day off sick and after the sort of day she'd had, she didn't want to risk running into Tobias again. Of course being a temp, she wouldn't get paid for it, but she didn't want to take Jacob into work either. Getting too lax about things at Stone Enterprises, as she'd recently found out, bit her where it hurt.

What had come over him? It was as if he'd ignited as soon as she'd opened her mouth. She had only come to apologize because she felt genuinely sorry for what she'd said but his reaction had hurt her and left her feeling angry and humiliated.

Tobias Stone was unpredictable and his moods were mercurial. He was like a stick of dynamite and she never knew when his fuse had been lit.

"Tell me," said the older woman, gently touching her arm. "What is wrong?"

Savannah tried to lighten up. "I'm wondering whether to play hooky tomorrow."

Rosalee made a face signifying that she didn't understand. "Hooky?"

"I might stay at home."

"You are sick?"

"I could pretend to be sick."

"Why would you do that?"

So that I don't have to go to work and risk seeing that man again. "It would be nice for you to spend the day with your family, and I could spend the day with Jacob." That too.

Rosalee frowned. "But your work people are so nice and

they gave you such lovely gifts at Christmas." Jacob breezed past at that moment with Iron Man and Venom in combat.

"Mr. Stone did that, Rosalee. Mommy's boss. He wanted us to have a nice Christmas." And just as quickly, he ran off again with Iron Man leading the way.

"Your boss?" Rosalee's eyes opened wide, as if she'd discovered the secret to eternal youth. "This boss of yours—is he single?"

Savannah expressed horror at what Rosalee was driving at. "Stop it, Rosalee. It's nothing like that. He's not a..." She wanted to say he wasn't a nice man, in contrast to Jacob's defiant mantra about him but Jacob seemed to adore the man and she didn't want to ruin that. "He has a girlfriend."

"Hmmmmpph." Rosalee gave her one of those knowing snorts. This-isn't-the-end-of-this-conversation type of snorts. Before she headed out of the door, she gave Savannah a last look. "You leave Jacob with me tomorrow. He is no trouble; he is like a grandson to me. You make sure you go to work."

Armed with that directive, Savannah could hardly back out.

She returned the next day but soon wished she had stayed at home with Jacob.

At lunchtime, she'd taken the hour and sat in a coffee shop eating her sandwich and reading a magazine, looking through the latest fashions and wondering what she would buy if she had lots of money.

She would go insane, of course, and buy dresses of all lengths, and skirts, and boots, tight jeans, well-cut suits and jackets, with sweaters and blouses and accessories to match.

A girl could dream.

Kay had often commented on her slender figure. "Not fair!"

she had cried, "You've had a baby too." She wasn't tall, but she was tall enough, and because she was slim, it helped make more of the height she had.

She turned the page and stared at the beautiful selection of underwear; the shiny, silky and lacy lingerie that looked nothing like the off-white and unsexy cotton pieces she always wore.

A girl could dream indeed.

She enjoyed her hour out of the office, not just because she could turn her mind to things that weren't related to work or Jacob but because it was a way of avoiding Tobias Stone. He had come in today; she knew this because she'd checked on her computer to see who else had logged onto the network. It was an easy way of finding out who was around. Tobias Stone had been in the entire morning and she had been lucky not to run into him so far.

It had been an odd week, nothing like the easygoing post-Christmas spell she'd imagined. Though it would have been, had Tobias Stone not been around.

Maybe she was partly to blame? Had she become too familiar, too brash with him? He'd seen her dancing around and then she'd helped him. It hadn't been like a 'normal' week at work. Yet she'd tripped a boundary somewhere along the way by asking him about his family. Was it really so off limits given that he'd sent her those Christmas gifts?

The bitter chill nipped at her ears as she rushed towards the Stone building having had her lunch.

My last time, she told herself as she rushed through the revolving doors and went inside.

She had finished working through the last of the boxes and now there was nothing left for her to do. Bored, she decided to reply to Briony's email from yesterday.

It's my final few hours here and I wanted to wish you a happy New Year! I hope you're having fun, skiing or otherwise.

I'm bored to death, so if you have anything to do to keep me busy for the afternoon, just let me know. You know how much I hate sitting around trying to look busy.

The phone rang and she answered it instantly.

"You have nothing to do?" Briony's cool, glacial voice cheered her up and she realized how much she missed having another person around; a normal person with a normal temperament, unlike Tobias.

"I finished the work you gave me."

"I hoped it would last you until the first week back, while I put together a list of things for you to work on in the coming month."

"What?"

"I have lots of things in mind; I just have to prioritize them."

"You want me back?"

"I told you that."

"When? I thought this was my last day."

Briony let out a long groan. "So that's what you meant in your email. I thought you meant this was your last day before the holiday."

"I didn't think you needed me anymore."

"Sorry," Briony sounded flustered. "I told you my memory had gone to pot. I extended your contract and the agency already knows. I thought you said Tobias had already told you?"

"He said I'd be providing cover for this week."

"Well, I've extended your contract until the end of January and I'm sure I can keep on extending because there is plenty to do. It was one of the reasons I wanted you to get these files out of the way now."

"You can keep extending?" She was hopeful once more.

"Easily. You really are something else, Savannah Page, and I have more work than I can handle." Savannah felt as though the sun had burst through the dark, gray clouds outside. A lightness settled over her chest.

"Thanks, Briony. You don't know what this means to me."

"Hon, you don't know what this means to *me*. I'm sorry I messed things up. Did you really think you were leaving today?"

"Yes."

"I'm usually not this disorganized—it should tell you just how swamped I am at the moment that I seem to have forgotten so many little details. Let me find the necessary paperwork and I'll email it to you. But first, let me check—are you happy to extend?"

In recent days, the shine had started to wear off this temp assignment but she loved working for Briony. Once things resumed to normal and everyone returned after the holidays, there would be no need for her to have any contact with the cause of her unease: Tobias Stone. She would report directly to Briony and it was guaranteed work for another month, at least. How could she turn it down? If she worked hard and made a good impression, there was a strong possibility it would continue. This could be the lucky break she'd been hoping for. "Of course I am. Thanks, Briony."

"I think I might even turn 218 into *your* office."

Savannah laughed. "How's skiing?" she asked, feeling happier.

"Amazing! I'm a speed junkie, and I can't get enough of it."

"I wouldn't know. I'm more a Miss Play-It-Safe."

Briony laughed. "Why don't you do something daring and go home early today, like now. It's, what, four o'clock?"

"Do you think I could?" Savannah asked.

Briony mocked her outrage. "Why not, Miss Diligence? You can *so* go home early especially since it's New Year's Eve. Loosen up, Savannah. It's not like you're embezzling funds from Stone Enterprises."

"I know—" She'd gone home early yesterday after that painful encounter with Tobias.

"I'm sure your son would like to see you home early for a change. I don't have anything for you to do so it seems to be a waste of your time. I can vouch for you if anyone asks. It's not as if anyone's in to keep an eye on you."

"Actually, Tobias has been in most days."

"Tobias?"

"Yes."

"Most days?" Briony sounded surprised.

"Yes."

"That's weird."

You're telling me, thought Savannah. "And I ran into Naomi."

"Where?"

"In the elevator going down."

"Interesting. The mystery deepens."

"What mystery?"

"Oh, nothing," replied Briony breezily. "I wonder why Tobias came into the office. Come to think of it, why did *she*?"

Savannah had questions of her own and decided to come clean. Perhaps Briony would have a better perspective on matters. "I asked Tobias about his wife."

"You did *what?*"

Savannah shrank further into her seat. "I thought Naomi was his wife. I didn't know."

"You didn't know about his wife or the accident?"

"I had no idea."

Briony made a low groaning noise in her throat. "I'd forgotten. You didn't even know who he was when you first started here."

Savannah blushed, remembering that time. "I thought he

was still married because he still wears that ring and so I naturally assumed that ..."

"Holy shit. What did he say?"

She didn't want to tell Briony everything that had happened because even though she felt she could trust her, she hadn't known her that long and didn't want to take a chance.

"He didn't say much."

She decided not to tell her that she had later apologized to Tobias and gotten in even more trouble.

"He's a man of few words and a real hard nut to crack," Briony confessed. A knock at the door stole Savannah's attention and she panicked at the idea that Tobias had been lurking at the other side; ready to piss her off again.

"I have to go. Someone's at the door."

"You mean to say Tobias is in today as well?"

Savannah jumped up and whispered. "I think so." Though it was not like him to knock. He usually strode right in.

"Happy New Year, hon. Go home. Even if Tobias is there. I can shoot him an email if—"

"No!" Savannah hissed. She didn't want any favors from the man and no special requests from Briony either. "I have to go." She hung up, her throat suddenly dry as she stood up and rushed to open the door, wondering why the person was still knocking.

She found herself staring at someone she hadn't met before and the relief that it wasn't Tobias made her smile wider. The man who now stood looking at her had a softer face and longish hair.

"You must be Savannah?" he asked, smiling at her.

"I am. And you are?"

"Matthias Rust," he said, holding out his hand. "Mind if I come in?"

So *this* was Matthias? She'd heard his name many times.

He'd been the one who'd had the file that Tobias had wrongly assumed she had taken.

She opened the door wider and stepped aside. "I work alongside Tobias," he told her. Savannah smiled and at the same time wondered what he wanted from her.

"Is there anything I can help you with?"

"Not a thing," he replied good-naturedly. It made a refreshing change to have a normal conversation with someone who wasn't going to jump down on her. "I only came by to see who else was in. Tobias said you were working in here so I came over to introduce myself. So, this is where you've been hiding?"

"I've hardly been hiding."

"I'm only joking," he replied, his eyes twinkling with merriment.

Loosen up, Savannah.

"I've been quietly keeping myself busy," she said, moving back to her desk and leaning against it. "And I've finished everything I had to do."

"You've been here through the holidays?"

"Every day aside from Christmas Day and the day after."

"Tobias let you go home for a few days, did he?" Mischief lit up the man's eyes.

"He couldn't have kept me here," she replied defensively, "no matter how much he likes to think he's king of the jungle." The bitter memory of yesterday infused her words with anger and made Matthias laugh.

"Someone who doesn't hide her true feelings about the man," he chuckled. "How long are you here for?"

"A month at least."

"A belated 'welcome' to you then."

"Thank you," she replied. "It's great to meet you at long last. I've heard your name a lot."

"I dread to think why." Matthias flicked his hair to the side and looked around at the boxes which she'd neatly lined up against the wall. "Is that what you've been working on?"

She nodded. "Scanning and filing. I just do as I'm told."

"Working for Tobias, I'm sure you do," he whispered conspiratorially. She cheered up even more and already felt as thick as thieves with him. "It's been good to meet you, Savannah," he said. "It's deathly quiet isn't it? I don't know why I bothered to come in to the office today."

"Why did you?"

"To pick up some paperwork. I hope you get to leave early. Don't stay imprisoned in here too long. It's New Year's Eve, don't forget."

"Imprisoned?" She laughed. "I'm planning on making my escape soon."

"What have you got planned for this evening?"

"I'm not exactly sure," she replied, folding her arms and thinking about it.

"It's New Year's Eve and you've got nothing planned?" he asked. And then they both turned to look as the door opened and Tobias walked in.

CHAPTER TWELVE

Savannah's heart thumped wildly and the carefree mood she'd been in vanished as her stomach tightened. She unfolded her arms slowly and resisted the urge to move over to her chair.

"Matthias." Tobias greeted his colleague with a slight nod then glanced her way. She'd avoided him since yesterday and had no desire to interact with him today. But now he had come looking for her. She was thankful that Matthias was here.

"I was making myself known to this delightful young lady," said Matthias.

"I'm sure she already knows who you are," said Tobias tightly.

"She'd heard of me, but who hasn't?" Matthias laughed. "I could do with her help, if Briony runs out of things for her to do."

"Briony has some projects in mind for her," Tobias replied coldly. The easygoing atmosphere in the room had turned to one of tension and unease ever since Tobias had entered.

"I see," said Matthias carefully and winked at Savannah,

who couldn't help but giggle back at him. Tobias heard the slight laugh that escaped from her and his face clouded over.

"Matthias and Tobias, we sound like a German DJ Duo, don't you think?" Matthias asked, giving her a wicked smile. "You can call me Matt—my friends do—but whatever you do," he leaned in towards her, "don't call him Toby." She clenched her stomach tightly to stop herself from collapsing into laughter because even though she couldn't see Tobias's face, she felt the heat of his stare and sensed his displeasure at Matthias's words.

The idea of such a nickname for Tobias was ridiculous. It implied a friendly nature that didn't belong to the man at all.

"I'll be sure to never make that mistake," she replied solemnly, staring at Tobias.

"Did you want something?" Tobias asked the man.

"Not particularly. Like I said, I came to introduce myself to Savannah. It's just as well since she's going to be with us for another month. Why didn't I see you at the Christmas party?" he asked her.

"Because I didn't go."

"You had a better offer, I suppose. It wouldn't be surprising. An evening at the Plaza Hotel with Tobias Stone or—"

"Weren't you leaving?" asked Tobias.

"I was," replied Matthias.

"I've left some paperwork on your desk," Tobias said. "You'll need to sign it and hand it back to me before you leave."

"I'd better do as I'm told, or else..." Matthias winked at her and headed towards the door. He turned to Tobias. "This young lady has finished all of her work so I hope you're going to let her go home early. I'm sure she has a celebration planned for tonight; not everyone sits around moping in misery." His words implied a small dig at Tobias but he didn't seem to be paying any attention.

His gaze was fixed on her and she didn't like the way he was staring at her.

Matthias walked towards the door. *Don't leave now,* she wanted to scream. *Let me shut down my computer and get my coat on.*

"Are you doing anything tonight?" Matthias asked him as Savannah rushed around packing her things away as fast as she could. If she left the office with Matthias, it would make for an easier, less awkward exit. She glanced at Tobias, curious to hear his response.

"No." His curt one-word reply was typical.

"And on that riveting note," said Matthias, throwing her a side glance, "I think I shall make my exit."

Desperate to stall him, she piped up. "Do you have any plans for tonight?"

"Now that you mention it, I'm going for a few drinks with some other poor souls who are lingering around in their offices on the pretense of doing some work. Why don't you come along?"

The out-of-the-blue invite took her by surprise. Although she wasn't sure what this man did or what his position was, she felt certain that he was high up and she didn't feel too comfortable about going out with him for a drink. Out of the corner of her eye, she saw Tobias's head turn in her direction and she sensed that he was waiting for her to reply.

Was he, or was she merely imagining it? She couldn't tell, but in that moment she wanted to spite him.

"Drinks?" she asked, waiting to see if Matthias's invitation was genuine. He dazzled her with his smile once more and despite the overt friendliness he had showered on her, the icy chill of Tobias's gaze settled over her, making her uneasy.

"Drinks, absolutely. Come along, the more the merrier, and that goes for alcohol as well as people. We're going to one of the finest watering holes this side of Manhattan. Come by my office in twenty minutes and you can leave with me. I'm four doors down from Tobias, on the right-hand side, hidden away around the corner in that godawful corridor."

The idea seemed tempting enough. She hadn't been out anywhere and perhaps this evening she could. One drink. It was New Year's Eve after all and it wasn't as if she had to rush back to relieve Rosalee. She could pick Jacob up at any time. Sensing that her response would tick Tobias off, for reasons she didn't understand, she agreed to it. "Thanks for the offer. I might just do that."

"I look forward to it," said Matthias, looking genuinely pleased. "And what about you?" he asked Tobias.

"I have things to do," said Tobias testily.

"Of course you do." Matthias gave her a mischievous roll of his eyes. "Twenty minutes," he said, and then left the room.

She had walked over to grab her coat, but this sudden invite from Matthias now left her at a loose end. She had twenty minutes to kill, and with just the two of them in the room once more, Savannah felt edgy. Tobias glared at her and she wished she hadn't agreed to wait around for Matthias.

"I need you to fix another Word document for me."

"You need me to do what?" she asked. Memories of yesterday made her blood simmer.

"Please." His voice had lost its harsh edge. "Would you take a look at my document?"

"Another one?" Her voice was weary, as if she was sick of hearing the same old request from him every time. "I thought I'd fixed all your documents."

"It's a new one I created earlier."

She frowned. "I'd fixed it so that your new documents would use that template." She didn't understand what he'd done; or how he'd managed to mess that up. How could this man run a billion-dollar business and have no idea of how to format a template? It made her wonder how much he relied on Candace.

"It won't take long," he said, as though he sensed her hesitation. "You can still run along to your date with Matthias."

She was surprised by his choice of words but decided against giving him a fitting reply. She didn't want to engage with him in conversation that would give him cause to be angry at her and since she was going to be here for another month at least, it made sense not to get on his bad side.

But she was secretly pleased that the idea of her going out with Matthias seemed to displease him. It was easy enough to tell. He was always so moody and miserable, and she was fast beginning to notice his moods; a skill she'd acquired and honed during her time with Colt. Back then it had been a survival skill because she'd needed to know what mood he was in when he came home. She had to be prepared for whatever he threw at her so that she could better protect herself and Jacob.

"Do you have time or not?" Tobias asked her.

"I can take a look," she replied, putting on her coat and grabbing her handbag. She followed him in silence back to his office. She noted that this time, instead of taking long, fast strides, he had slowed down, as if he wanted to say something to her.

Even if that were the case, she didn't want to hear it and she purposely slowed down even more.

She didn't want to talk to Tobias much less help him out.

CHAPTER THIRTEEN

Matthias Rust. The man could be a real asshole.

Asking a temp out for a drink; how desperate could he be?

Tobias felt the veins throbbing along his neck as he walked in silence along the corridor while Savannah Page trailed quietly behind him.

How easily she had agreed to go along with Matthias. The thought had pissed him off even more.

Tobias tried to walk alongside her, hoping to start a conversation—something that was alien to him—but all he wanted was to say his piece and be done with it. Yet the way she now stared at the floor, the way she so blatantly avoided eye contact with him, in such sharp contrast to the way she had joked and spoken to Matthias, made him even angrier.

He strode into his office and held the door open for her. She walked in and moved over to his side of the desk and stood staring at his computer, as though she was in a rush. "Where's the document?"

"I have to bring it up. Can you wait?" he asked, walking over to her. She stepped back, giving him easy access to his computer.

"Would you mind taking a seat?" He took control of the mouse. Word documents were the last thing he had on his mind. He had a document, something he'd been working on all morning, but this wasn't the real reason he'd asked her here. Their exchange yesterday had weighed on his mind and he knew he'd hurt her, not just her wrist and the way he'd grabbed it, but her feelings too. And it bothered him. He needed to explain and to apologize.

She moved past him and fluttered around the other side of the desk. "Sit," he said, and then it occurred to him that giving her an order wasn't the best way forward. "Please, if you don't mind," he added.

"I'm fine standing."

She was still annoyed with him, he could tell, and he didn't blame her one bit. "Is this going to take long?" She seemed especially eager to meet Matthias.

"I forgot," he sneered, "you're in a hurry." He stopped looking for the document. "I didn't know that you and Matthias knew one another."

"We don't, or rather we didn't. I only met him today."

"It didn't seem like it, the way the two of you were laughing."

"Some people are easier to get along with than others."

He tightened his jaw, studying her face and staring at the way her tousled hair fell around her shoulders. Thick and wild, and unruly. He imagined her lying in his bed covered only in his white sheets, with those hazel eyes staring up him. He shook his head from side to side in an attempt to shake away the vision that had suddenly stolen up on him.

"You're shaking your head; you don't agree?"

He agreed all right and he knew exactly what she was

referring to. Ordinarily he wouldn't care what other people thought of him but this woman was making him question his actions and his words. It was something he wasn't used to. But he didn't want to think about that yet. For now, he had to find a way of apologizing for yesterday without making a big drama of it.

The situation was awkward enough.

He drew in a breath. "About yesterday..." He began biting his teeth together. She folded her arms and stared back at him expectantly but a knock at the door soon interrupted the moment. He chose to ignore it. "About yesterday, what I said, when you asked about my wife—"

The door flung wide open.

"Bro!" Xavier, his lazy-ass brother, breezed in. Tobias glared at him. More interruption. At this rate, he'd never get to say what he needed.

"Whoa," Xavier stopped when he'd taken two strides into the room. "I didn't know you were busy."

"That's why I ignored the knock," Tobias replied tightly.

"Sorry. Am I interrupting something?" The expression on Xavier's face seemed to imply things of a seedier nature.

"Why don't you wait outside?" Tobias suggested.

"Hello there, I don't believe we've met." His brother extended his hand towards Savannah and stared at her as if he was going to eat her up. Tobias saw the look of apprehension on Savannah's face as she shook hands.

"No Naomi, then?" Xavier asked him.

"Shut the fuck up." Tobias scowled at his brother. "How much have you had to drink?"

"Not enough, that's for sure. It's after four and it's New Year's Eve," protested Xavier.

"What the hell are you doing here?" Tobias raised his voice.

"Ease up," his brother held out his hand in a calming

motion. "I came to get you. We're hitting a champagne bar first, some new rooftop club has just opened and then there's a private party at The Vault. It's members only...and we all know what that means." Xavier grinned as he walked over to his side then punched him lightly on his shoulder.

"Wait outside," Tobias ordered, flexing his fingers. If he'd been here alone, he would have thrown his brother out. As it was, Ms. Page already had a bad enough impression of him, and he wasn't going to embellish it further.

"I need to go. Matthias is waiting." Savannah's words pissed him off even more.

"You're not coming with us?" Xavier looked genuinely disappointed.

"She has a better offer." Tobias's fury built up.

"Can you show me the document?" she asked.

"It can wait," Tobias replied. This wasn't how he had imagined their exchange to go.

"Are you sure?"

"Yes," he replied, his mouth twisting.

"I'm back next week. I can fix it then or you can get Candace to look at it."

"You'll have to fix it," he said firmly. Whatever happened, he would have his moment, next week. He would wait until then. "You can go."

"Thanks. Have a great evening." She called out to them both, deliberately avoiding eye contact with him. He noticed it, just as he saw the way his brother turned to admire her.

"Have a good New Year's..." Xavier started to say, but she had already disappeared. "Nice piece of ass," he commented, giving an approving nod.

"Cut it out, you idiot," Tobias snarled.

"How long have you been screwing her?"

"Watch your mouth."

"You mean you're not?"

"She's a temp."

"As if that matters."

"I don't mix work with other pursuits."

"You don't have other pursuits. And that on-and-off girlfriend of yours..." Xavier still believed that Naomi was his girlfriend and that was the way Tobias liked it.

"But, seriously, Bro. You're not screwing her? What's her name?"

"Savannah."

"Savannah? Sounds like a piece of paradise. Did you not see the T & A on her?"

Tobias closed his eyes wanting to shut out Xavier's verbal vomit. "You've had too much to drink and maybe you should go home. You need to watch your mouth when you come here."

Xavier scratched his hair. "Sorry. I shouldn't have mentioned Naomi. It's just that she had her coat on and everything, I thought she was your new date or something."

"She's a temp who works here and she was going to look at a document for me."

"Whatever," said Xavier, rubbing his face. "I haven't had enough to drink and tonight we're going to par-tay! Hurry the hell up, will you?"

But Tobias was in no mood to go out, despite what he'd already told his brother yesterday, and especially now with things still weighing on him heavily and unresolved with Savannah. Why did it bother him so much? Was it because he was a hero in Jacob's eyes? Or because he kept doing the wrong thing when it came to the boy's mother? And even if that were the case, why did that matter at all? He'd never even noticed other temps before.

"Tell me you didn't drive here," he said sharply, turning his attention to his annoying brother.

"I didn't. I'm not stupid, Bro. I want to get trashed tonight. Come on, hurry it up, will you? There's plenty of pussy where we're going."

Tobias put his hands up as if to ward off any further discussion. "If that's all it is, I want out."

"Relax," said Xavier. "You're looking stressed out again."

"I'm warning you."

"It's nothing but a few drinks, I promise. There are plenty of women, but it's not *that* kind of party."

Tobias still wasn't convinced.

"Have a few drinks then you can go home and screw Naomi's brains out all night long, you horny bastard."

"Go to hell," said Tobias, already hating the idea of what tonight would bring.

CHAPTER FOURTEEN

Savannah left the office clutching to the only piece of good news she'd had all day—this wasn't her last day and she would be back in the new year.

The future looked promising and if all things went well, she might even be in a position to rent a small apartment for her and Jacob by summer, when Kay returned. By then, she would have enough experience with office work and could look elsewhere for a permanent job if the opportunity never arose at Stone Enterprises.

She wondered what it was that Tobias had wanted to say to her. Whatever it was, he'd looked angry when his brother had shown up. It had been the second time she'd been saved, first by Matthias and then by Xavier.

Being around him was like taking a roller-coaster ride in the dark and most of her interactions with the man often left her feeling drained. Yet as unpredictable as Tobias Stone was, she also felt for the man. Finding out about his past had opened her eyes and given her an insight into his hard personality. He'd suffered a devastating blow and she was secretly fascinated by his love for his wife, and to know that he still suffered for her loss.

He wasn't even her direct boss but in these few days with just the two of them in the office, he had managed to get into her head for all the wrong reasons. It was like being with Colt all over again except for the physical abuse.

But you aren't with Tobias Stone, she reminded herself. Naomi was. Men like Tobias and women like Naomi were perfect for one another. Savannah knew she would never feel comfortable being with someone that wealthy.

As if that would ever happen.

Why was she even thinking such crazy thoughts? Knowing he wasn't married changed nothing. Because as much as it piqued her curiosity and set her pulse racing, this thing between them was more hate-hate than a slow-burning interest in the man.

"Savannah!" She was about to push through the revolving doors when someone called out her name. She turned around.

"Didn't you hear me? I was right behind you," Matthias stated, his eyes glittering.

"Sorry. I was miles away."

"Tobias said you'd already left." He pushed her towards the revolving doors and they circled through to outside. She stepped back and faced him.

"I'm going to pass on the drinks. Thanks for the invite but I need to head home."

"Are you sure? It's New Year's Eve, Savannah. Have one drink at least, or has Tobias worked you so hard that you need to go home? That man can be a tyrant sometimes."

"I haven't been working for him," she explained. The wind blew her hair over her face and she brushed it away with her fingers. The noisy roar of cars speeding by made her raise her voice. "Besides, I have to pick up my son."

"You have a son?"

She nodded, smiling at the thought of Jacob and knew instantly that she wanted to go home and spend the evening with him.

"Surely your son won't mind you having a few drinks? It's not just me, in case you felt awkward, there are others coming along; those of us who have no inclination to rush home."

"Sorry, Matthias. I have an inclination to rush home. Another time perhaps."

"I'll hold you to that."

She laughed. "Have a great evening."

"Have a happy New Year." He moved in to kiss her on both cheeks, an act she found slightly forward given that she hardly knew him.

"Thanks. You too," she replied quickly, and forced a smile before walking away.

"Isn't that your temp?" Xavier asked as they came out of the elevator. Directly ahead of him Tobias saw Savannah walking through the revolving doors with Matthias.

"She's not my temp," Tobias snarled, keeping his gaze fixed on them as they stopped and talked outside. They seemed to be getting along very well.

As if he cared.

He didn't give a shit.

But in the next moment he saw Matthias kiss her on both cheeks and his jaw tightened.

"It looks to me like Matthias has an interest in her, wouldn't you say?" Xavier asked.

"Who cares?" growled Tobias, clenching his fists. "I need a goddamn drink."

THE GIFT, BOOK 3

The Billionaire's Love Story (#3)

CHAPTER ONE

Tobias scratched his jaw and looked away in disgust as girls in short, barely there dresses tittered around him. They primped their hair, touched their lips and cheeks, and batted their caked eyelashes. They leaned forward with their legs crossed, and their in-your-face breasts threatened to spill out of their Band-Aid designer couture, strips of fabric that teased and hinted at naked flesh.

Flirtation filled the air in the rooftop terrace of The Oasis.

Eager hopefuls, desperate to mingle with rich and moneyed young men, surrounded Xavier and his cronies, hopeful that they would get not only their drinks bought, but breakfast, lunch and dinner tomorrow. And more.

Tobias lifted his glass of whiskey and drank it in one go. *What the fuck was he doing here?*

His brother had raved on about the new twentieth-floor rooftop bar and restaurant, recently opened by one of his friends. The Oasis had a Moroccan-style influence, with its red drapes and jewel-toned fabrics draped over walls, its metallic hanging lanterns and amber-colored lamps, and comfy booths plumped up with oversized cushions. It was a welcome change from the cold grayness of winter in New York.

"Over here!" Xavier shouted to the pretty young waitress who had brought over a new tray of drinks. Tobias had lost count of the number of whiskey shots he'd had, preferring that to the champagne that Xavier had ordered so freely. The waitress put a glass down in front of him.

"Two more!" Tobias demanded, before grabbing the glass and downing it in one swig.

It wasn't the cold he felt as much as the desire to numb himself. He looked around the rooftop terrace; it was full, but not heaving. Full of perfect people, moneyed people and plenty of tits, ass and legs on full view no matter in which direction he stared.

They all looked happy; in a state of intoxication, high on seduction or drugs, or probably both.

He didn't belong. And he didn't want to be here. The disconnect he felt was easier to bear when whiskey was his partner. "It's new, hip, trendy, and hard to get into," Xavier had crowed when he'd first mentioned it to him. It probably was all of these things but none of them mattered to Tobias.

"Slow down," Xavier insisted, leaning close up behind his ear.

"I'm having a good time," Tobias replied. Unable to turn his head around completely to face his brother, he turned his head to the side instead and found himself staring at the woman seated next to him. He picked up another glass of whiskey.

"Why don't you talk to Larissa?" Xavier shouted into his ear. "She's the one you're staring at, in case you didn't know. She's been trying to get your attention for the last half hour." His younger brother patted him on the shoulder and disappeared with a skinny but buxom beauty dressed from head to toe in black.

Tobias stared at the long-haired vixen in a silver dress. The front of her dress was cut low, right down to her belly button, and for a second he was intrigued as to how she managed to keep the thing from falling to her waist. She stared back at him, shining in the glow of his attention and flashed an inviting smile.

"So, you're Xavier's brother?" She leaned towards him suggestively.

God, no. No conversation, or anything else. He didn't reply.

"I've heard a lot about you." She swept her hair onto one shoulder; it was a thick cascade of curls, strategically placed to reveal perfectly tanned shoulders. Savannah's hair was shorter, he recalled. Up to her shoulders, and it wasn't as shiny or as groomed.

And she was out with Matthias somewhere, right now.

He looked around for the waitress. Where was his second glass of whiskey? "Excuse me," he said and got up. The waitress had only given him one drink and he was in dire need of another. The woman beside him looked crestfallen.

"Do you want a drink?" he asked.

Her face instantly brightened. "I'll come with you." She got up quickly, the dress threatening to slip off her shoulders. His eyes weren't admiring the naked flesh on show, but more the manner in which she had managed to keep clothed despite the odds of her dress slipping off. *Glue?* he wondered, and was almost tempted to ask if that was how she managed to keep the dress up.

"I'll get it," he growled instead, eager to lose her fast. "What do you want?"

"What I need ... is to get some air," she drawled.

Sweetheart, we're sitting outside. He shrugged. Tobias hated places like this; it was the kind of place where people came to be seen. That was their idea of a good time. He swiftly cut through the medley of tables, heaters and beautiful people in his determination to get to the bar inside, not stopping to wait for the woman who seemed desperate to accompany him.

On the way, he was stopped by the waitress who had served their table. "Is there something I can get you, sir?" she asked, staring up at him, and giving him the kind of look that suggested she had more to offer than merely alcohol.

"Nothing I can't get myself," he replied calmly. It was then that he became aware of the woman who had followed him. She attempted to take hold of his hand but he pulled it away quickly and made his way to the bar.

Years ago, he and Ivy would have come to a place like this, for drinks and then dinner somewhere ridiculously overpriced and exclusive. Or even a KFC. He'd loved that about her. She'd never been the type to frequent an establishment just to be seen.

It was a shame that most of the women he met these days seemed more concerned with his money and his name. He had no interest in them, or any desire to start anything with them. They barely registered on his radar.

And yet Savannah Page had somehow wormed her way into his consciousness over the last few weeks without him even realizing, and these last few days she had stolen into his thoughts and stayed there. He would see to it that he had his time with her alone, next week when they returned to work.

He saw the bar area up ahead and noted that it was relatively empty. Just as he strode towards it, he noticed her, and he stopped to stare.

She was here?

Savannah.

Ahead of him, facing the bar, and surrounded by a group of people, stood a woman with the same brown tousled hair just below her shoulders. He scanned the crowd rapidly looking for Matthias and others he might recognize.

Turning around, he slipped a hundred-dollar bill to the

leech on his back. It was a small price to pay for freedom. "Get yourself a drink."

"But I—" She was silenced by the look he gave her, a half-pout starting to form on her Botoxed lips. But she snatched the bill and slunk away without a word.

He made his way over to the group and touched the woman's shoulder, wondering, at the same time, what he would say to her. She turned around and blue eyes—the wrong color—widened in appreciation.

"Hi," the woman smiled widely at him, probably thinking she'd been hit on.

"Sorry, I mistook you for someone else." His hopes vanished as fast as her smile.

"Tobias?"

A familiar voice behind rescued him from the awkwardness of the moment. He turned around when he felt a hand on his arm. It was Candace.

"What are you doing here?" she asked happily.

"The same thing as you, probably," he replied coolly.

She blinked at the woman he had mistaken for Savannah. "Are you together?" Candace asked, nodding her head towards the woman.

"No." He stepped away and headed towards the bar with Candace in tow.

"I didn't know you were coming here tonight. It's hardly your kind of place."

"It isn't. Xavier dragged me here."

A group of girls walked past, one almost brushing past him, and murmuring a suggestive, "Sorry," as she did so. Candace's face set like hard cement as Tobias ignored the intrusion which was a regular part of his life. A crowd of people at the nearby table laughed loudly among themselves while Beyonce's voice belted out one of her ballads.

"Where are you sitting?"

"Out there." He nodded towards the roof terrace.

"I'm with a group of friends over there." She nodded behind her shoulder, and he barely glanced in that direction.

"Did you come with Matthias?"

"Matthias?" She looked surprised. "Why would I? I haven't been at work since last week."

Tobias remembered. "I thought maybe..." He thought maybe he'd see *her* here. He stared at Candace and noticed for the first time that she looked different in her out-of-work clothes. Without the sophisticated suits, and wearing a slinky black sheath dress instead, she looked glamorous once she'd lost the executive office look. She caught him looking.

"Do you want to come over and say 'hi'?"

He shook his head quickly. Clearly, she had the wrong idea. "Since when do *I* do things like that?"

"Thought you'd gone home." Xavier snuck up behind him.

"Are you keeping an eye on me tonight?" Irritation masked Tobias's face.

"I'm making sure you're having a good time, Bro." Xavier acknowledged Candace. "Fancy running into you here."

"Fancy running into *you*." Candace eyed him appreciatively and ran her hand down the side of her dress. "The newest and hippest place in New York would be incomplete without Xavier Stone making an appearance," she cooed.

"You know it, babe." Xavier winked at her and gave her the once-over. "Are you moving on or staying here all night?"

"I could be persuaded to stay here," she replied, licking her lips. Tobias looked around and loosened the collar of his shirt, aware of being the third party in a twosome.

"We're going to the party in The Vault," Xavier announced. "Right after midnight. You game? I can get you both in."

"We're not together." Tobias set him straight.

"I know!" Xavier exclaimed. "But I can get you in."

Candace laughed proactively, tempted by the idea. "A private party?"

"Come along," Xavier encouraged her. "It's strictly members only, but don't worry about that, my friend owns this place." She stared at Tobias expectantly and he could see that she was up for it. Being seen with both the Stone brothers would raise her social profile.

No thanks.

"I'm not coming," he announced, desperate to leave. He'd been eyeing the bottle of whiskey behind the bar and in that moment decided he didn't have to drink it here.

"Why not?" Candace asked.

"I thought you were having a good time, Bro?" Xavier punched him lightly on his shoulder.

"I've *had* a good time." Tobias patted him on the shoulder. "Thanks. One step at a time, huh?"

His brother looked disappointed. "How are you going to get home?"

"I'll call a cab."

"I'll get Morris to come and get you," Candace offered.

"I can take care of myself," Tobias replied stiffly. He hated the way they all clamored to help him. Couldn't they leave him alone? "I'm outta here." He took off, waving a hand in the air as if to signal his goodbye.

CHAPTER TWO

"You mean it, Mommy? I can really stay up 'til midnight?"

"I don't see why not, honey. It's New Year's Eve." Savannah wiped down the countertops in the kitchen and was pleased that dinner and clean-up was over.

"It's like Christmas Eve but boring." Jacob sat with his head bent over his Marvel coloring book, rapidly coloring away.

"That's pretty." She stared at the colored-in pictures and noticed that he was getting better at coloring inside the lines. Jacob scrunched up his face.

"Don't say it's *pretty*, Mommy. That's a girlie word. Say it's *cool*."

"It's pretty cool," she replied, making him giggle. "You *have* been busy." He was almost halfway through the book and it was just as well that she'd bought a few of them. She considered the act of getting a book into his hands as progress. It was great that he used his imagination and played with his toys, and that he wasn't hooked on devices like so many other kids. She wouldn't have bought him a device even if she could afford one. Coloring books were good but getting him to read books of his own accord, instead of only when she or his teacher ordered him, would be next on her list of things to encourage.

Jacob was a good kid, and even when she was on her laptop —emailing or surfing the net—he didn't hassle her to go on it and play games.

She suddenly remembered that she wanted to reply to the email she'd received before dinner. She'd been surprised to hear back from anyone during the holidays but another agency had received her résumé and had asked about her availability for a temporary contract that was due to start around the beginning of February. It would last until the summer at least, and it paid more. This had been the deciding factor for her, because, as comfortable as she now felt at Stone Enterprises, and as nice as some of the people were, at the end of the day, money was money, and that was the main reason she worked. It was the only reason.

This new opportunity was too good to pass up. Even though her contract at Stone Enterprises had been extended for another month, there was no guarantee of work thereafter, even though Briony had hinted that she would keep on extending it. A hint wasn't enough of an incentive to convince Savannah to stay. She needed something more concrete.

The thought of returning to the office made her stomach churn. She wasn't sure how she would react when she saw Tobias Stone again. With everyone else back at work, there would be less opportunity for them both to interact, and she considered this to be a blessing.

"What do you want to do now?" she asked Jacob, having finished for the evening. "Do you want to read together?"

He scrunched his nose up. "Can I think about it?"

She grinned and ran her fingers through his hair. "Take your time." She picked up her laptop from the kitchen countertop and walked into the small living room. The kitchen and living room were connected without a door and she could still hear Jacob from behind the sofa where she now sat. "Why don't you come in here, honey?"

As Jacob sauntered in, she opened her email and quickly fired off a reply to the new agency indicating her interest in the position.

She stared at Jacob who now lay on his stomach with his elbows propping up his body. He had dispensed with the coloring book and now had his superhero toys out. There was some sort of elaborate setup going on with an empty shoebox, an empty egg carton and a few Christmas cards. He seemed content enough, so she turned the TV on and then, when she could find nothing interesting to watch, she aimlessly surfed online, and typed in the name 'Tobias Stone'.

A photo of him with his trademark solemn look, his strong face with those cool, steady eyes stared back at her. Her heart almost leapfrogged out of her mouth as she quickly skimmed over the text—it was information about him that she already knew, and there was nothing new. When her phone rang, she absentmindedly reached out for it.

"Happy New Year!" Kay's shrill voice pierced her ears. She was louder than usual and overexcited.

"Happy New Year," Savannah replied, still gazing at Tobias's face on the screen.

"I just got back," her cousin gushed.

"From where, or shouldn't I ask?"

"You know that dinner I went to? On Christmas day? Some of the people from there had a party which went on until three in the morning."

"What time is it?"

"Almost ten o'clock in the evening," Kay replied. *Of the next day,* Savannah reminded herself and found it difficult to reconcile the fact that there was such a long gap—thirteen hours

—between their time zones. She wondered what Kay had been up to for most of the day, if she'd only now gotten back. It was probably better not to know.

"Aren't you going out tonight?" Kay asked her.

"I was asked to go for drinks."

"Drinks?"

"With the people from work."

"Did you?"

"No." Savannah got up off the sofa and moved her laptop to the small wooden coffee table then walked into the kitchen, away from Jacob's prying ears. "It's not easy to go out when I don't have childcare," she whispered. Rosalee would have offered to look after Jacob, but Savannah didn't want to impose. Besides, she hadn't been so eager to go out with Matthias. This was nice, being at home, with just the two of them and no amount of drinking in a bar with people she barely knew would have made up for that.

"Oh!" Kay yelped, as if she'd been hit over the head. "Did you ever find out who your mysterious admirer was?"

"Huh?"

"The gift basket? Who sent it?"

"Work people." Savannah lowered her voice and looked over her shoulder to check if Jacob was listening.

"Uh-huh." Kay seemed to be giving her response careful consideration. "Your work people?" Kay questioned. "Is that a collective 'people' or someone in particular?"

Savannah didn't want to elaborate because she knew how vivid Kay's imagination could be. The less her cousin knew about Tobias Stone, the better.

"Oh, the department got together, you know," replied Savannah breezily, curling a lock of hair around her finger. "They wanted to say 'Thank you' for my efforts." Technically this wasn't a total lie. Stone Enterprises was a collective.

Suddenly, Tobias's face flashed into her mind and along with it memories of how he had grabbed her hand. She couldn't easily forget the tortured look on his face, and she had thought about it for days afterwards—about the grief that had hardened him. She didn't know what he had been like before but she had studied the photos of him with his wife and there was none of that hardness about him then. He must have loved her completely, to not ever have gotten over her death. "They're a nice bunch," she murmured.

"Hmmm," was Kay's response. She doubted whether her cousin would have believed her even if it had been true. Kay often embellished stories by adding romantic overtones to them.

"I'm there until the end of January," she said, hoping to fill the gap and prevent Kay from asking more questions. "But I might have a chance to start another contract elsewhere."

"That's great news, Sav. Things are looking up for you and about time, too."

"Thanks. How's it working out for you over there?"

"Hong Kong is crazy. They work ridiculously long hours here. I thought New York was bad but it's worse over here. To be honest with you, I can't wait to get back."

"Are you still coming back in the summer?"

"It's looking that way. I wish it were sooner."

Savannah wrapped her arm around her body, not so much because she was cold but because news of Kay's return always made her anxious. She loved her cousin, but Kay's return to New York meant that she and Jacob would have to leave and find a place of their own. If she couldn't stay here, near the city, she would have to move out further to the suburbs or, if she didn't get her finances in order by then, she'd have to return home to her parents. That would be the last resort and the worst-case scenario because returning to her small hometown in North Carolina would mean she'd failed on an epic scale. Her ex-husband still lived there and she didn't want to be within a ten-mile radius of that man ever again.

"It'll be nice to see you," murmured Savannah, hoping her life would be sorted by then. "Are you home alone tonight?" It sounded uncharacteristically quiet for a change, at Kay's end.

"I am home alone," Kay giggled. "I need a rest!"

Savannah didn't want to ask her what she needed a rest from, but she had a good enough idea. She turned around to see Jacob staring at her laptop screen. "You get some of that much needed rest. Jacob and I are going to wait up for the new year to roll in."

"Have a good one and give Jacob a big kiss from me."

Savannah hung up. "Aunty Kay says to give you a big kiss."

"His wife died," said Jacob, his voice flat. Savannah walked over to the coffee table and took the laptop from him.

Damn it. She'd left it on Tobias's page.

"Is it true, Mommy?"

She sat down on the couch and pulled Jacob onto her knees. "Yes, honey. Mr. Stone's wife died a few years ago."

"How?"

"She...she died in a car accident."

"Did he have any children?"

"No, honey."

"So he's all alone?"

"Uh—no, he has friends, Jacob. And family, I imagine."

"But he always looks so sad."

"You think he looks sad?" Tobias Stone had a stern, unsmiling face most of the time, and she could imagine he was the same in his dealings with most people, but her impression was that he'd shown nothing but kindness to Jacob.

Jacob nodded quietly. "He doesn't smile much. When you smile, your eyes go all shiny and crinkly. When Mr. Stone smiles, his eyes stay the same."

"I think he's still sad, honey."

"I would be sad forever if that happened to you." His eyes glistened and she hugged him close to her as she inhaled his sweet scent.

"It's not going to happen to me. I won't ever leave you."

"You promise?"

Her heart ached to see his lower lip tremble. "I promise." It was an impossible promise to make because what had happened to Tobias's wife had been out of her hands. But Savannah lived her life with the sole intention that nothing and nobody would ever separate her from her son.

"How about tomorrow we go ice skating?" She suggested wanting to make him happy again. Tomorrow would be the perfect day for it. Sure enough, it had the effect she wanted and as quickly as that, Jacob had forgotten the thing that frightened him the most.

CHAPTER THREE

***H**appy New Year*

It was a text from Naomi, thankfully that was all it said. No whiny, needy questions. Since their last interaction, she hadn't been in touch again until this morning.

It was about time she got the hint.

As desperate as he was for sexual release, Tobias no longer wanted her. He could have easily brought home any number of girls from the bar, except the one who continued to elude him. The one who most intrigued him, the one who seemed to have an intense dislike for him—she was the one he couldn't stop thinking about.

He stared out of his window at the silver sky and the frost-lined hard surfaces outside. He'd felt the sharp fall in temperature and braced himself. New York winters could be brutal. Yet the sun was struggling to break from behind the hard cover of the sky. Hopefully, it would, and then it would be the perfect day to be outside, if he dressed warmly. For once, Tobias didn't want to mope around the house by himself and he didn't have anyone to visit, not family or friends...or anyone special.

Work was out of the question. He could go in to the office, but where was the fun in that, especially when Savannah Page wouldn't be around?

What he needed to do was what all the well-meaning people in his life had been telling him for the longest time. He needed to get out into the world and mix with people. A walk along the Avenue of the Americas, maybe even a stroll along Madison Avenue where, hopefully, the crowds would be sparse.

It would do him good to get some fresh air. At the very least, it might even help him to get a few things clear in his head.

"I can do it, Mommy! Let go! Let go of me!"

Savannah wasn't sure how much Jacob remembered, though skating was like riding a bike and, once mastered, it was hard to forget. Still, she seemed hesitant to let go. It had been a while since they had last been, years in fact. But he seemed so sure and so, pushing her fears to the side, she begrudgingly let go of Jacob's hand.

"Stay close to the edge!" She watched as he glided away from her in his new military green coat and red woolen scarf, hat and gloves. Lights glittered around the outdoor skating rink in the Winter Village. Bryant Park was a place that Rosalee had mentioned many times. She'd come here in the summer, and had seen how expensive things were, and had deliberately avoided visiting, although most places in New York cost money to visit. But, walking around here today, she was thankful she had come.

Skating would have been free if they'd had their own skates, but even so, it was affordable now, for a one-time treat. She skated as close behind Jacob as she could. He tried to turn around, "See?" he yelled, before losing his balance and crashing to the ground. In an instant, she was around him, helping him to get up and protecting him from others who might have skated into him.

Thankfully, it wasn't as busy as she'd feared. She didn't like crowded places but this, today, was just perfect. In fact, all of the Winter Village with its music, cafes and benches had the right vibe. Smiling and relaxed visitors, recovering from the Christmas and New Year's madness, ambled around happily.

"We can take a break," she suggested, pulling Jacob's hat down over his head. This weather could trigger his asthma, and it was something she was always fearful of.

"No, Mommy. I want to go around again. We've got time, don't we?"

"Come on, then," she agreed, giving in. They had another twenty minutes at least. She had taken him a few times back home but they had never been ice skating in New York before. Maybe she'd try to come out here once a month at least, while the rink was open. She skated behind him, gliding gracefully over the ice, fearless and confident and feeling the blood rushing through her.

The sun glistened in the crisp blue sky. It was icy cold, but small slices of the sun's rays took the edge off the iciness in the air. She had warmed up now and Jacob, with his flushed cheeks and squeals, looked to be having the time of his life.

Last night they had gone to bed soon after midnight after seeing the fireworks in Times Square on TV. There didn't seem much reason to stay up and Jacob had almost fallen asleep on the sofa beside her earlier.

He'd woken up early this morning, excited about skating, and his Marvel figures hadn't gotten so much as a glance from him as he'd rushed to have breakfast and get ready.

She stopped and peered at the café in the distance; its warm and inviting lights looked welcoming and she was tempted to go there and have a snack. But Jacob had already told her what he wanted. On their way to the rink, they had passed some tiny boutiques and kiosks, like brightly lit shoeboxes lining the alleys around the park, all with a European feel to them.

Some sold hot chocolate and cylinder-shaped donuts filled with chocolate, some sold mac & cheese, lots of others had some kind of specialty. But Jacob wanted a nice hot dog, and come to think of it, she wanted one too. Fully loaded with greasy onions and drenched in mustard and ketchup. Her stomach gurgled as she skated past a market stall that was selling them and the tangy, salty smell of hot dogs floated over and seduced her senses. Maybe they would have some hot chocolate later as well, along with those donuts.

The fact that she could now consider doing these things, that she could even contemplate a day out here with her son, was a small but important milestone for her. It was a simple day out yet to her it represented a kind of liberation that only those who had lived with scarcity, who had scrimped and saved and hoarded their dollars—like she had done just so that they could have enough for a week's groceries—only those people would understand. She appreciated this one glorious day out with her son for that very reason.

Smiling at her good fortune, she caught Jacob waving at someone and looked over to see who it was. But she didn't see a familiar face as she stared at the crowds of people lined around the perimeter of the rink. Jacob soon came to a stop and waited until she had slowed down and was by his side.

"Who are you waving at, honey?"

"Mr. Stone's here!" Jacob pointed and waved again with a burst of excitement. Savannah turned and stared as her stomach knotted up like a cat's paw. There he was, in dark jeans, a dark sweater and a leather jacket straight out of *Top Gun.* She swallowed. He waved. She smiled feebly, unwilling to lift her hand and wave back, but Jacob was waving excitedly enough for both of them.

"Shall we go around a few more times? We don't have long left."

"Can't we go and say 'hello'?" Jacob insisted.

She hesitated, not wanting to, and examined the people around Tobias, hoping he would be with someone. But she was also partly relieved that he was not. He seemed to be alone. "They haven't told us to come off yet, Jacob. We have a little more time. Shall we skate until the very end? We can go say 'hello' then?" With any luck, Tobias would have wandered off, she hoped. She stared down in dismay at her jeans and big, loose cardigan and the same coat she wore to work. She really didn't want to see this man, especially not looking the way she did.

"Awww, Mommy. Let's go and see him *now.*"

It was pointless. Jacob wasn't to be deterred and from the looks of it, Tobias Stone appeared to be waiting for them.

"All right," she said, begrudgingly. "You lead the way."

They clunked their way over to the stands in their heavy skates, and Jacob tripped over and almost went face first onto the ground. Luckily, Tobias stepped forward and grabbed him before he hit the ground.

"Gotcha," he said, smiling at her son. "Happy New Year." He turned towards her and nodded.

"Happy New Year," she murmured, trying not to stare at him too much, or the way he looked in that big, chunky jacket.

"I didn't know you were such an awesome skater, Jacob." The boy smiled as though he'd won a medal.

"I learn from the best. Mommy's awesome. Did you see her?" Tobias looked at her again.

"I saw. She's pretty good." She nodded in return, even attempting a smile, as she once again lost the ability to speak.

"Can you skate, Mr. Stone?" Jacob asked, and then quickly, "Do you want to skate with us?" His voice rose to an excited pitch at this amazing new idea. Savannah's insides lurched.

"Our session's about to finish now, Jacob."

Tobias answered, "I'm not as good as you. I'd have a hard time keeping up."

"I can show you. Or Mommy will." Savannah's muscles tightened when Jacob volunteered her.

"I don't think that would be wise," Tobias replied on her behalf.

"I'm sure Mr. Stone has better things to do." Savannah's voice sounded oddly tight, even to herself, and she wondered if he had noticed. As always, his mere presence had an effect on her. One minute, she'd been skating happily around with the wind surging through her hair, filling her lungs, and turning her cheeks red, sending her heart soaring. The next moment, right after she'd found out about Tobias, she was suddenly self-conscious about herself and worried that her hair was bedraggled and her cheeks bright red and splotchy.

"Your mommy always thinks I have better things to do, huh, Jacob?" Her son giggled wickedly at Tobias's comment but she knew the remark was directed at her. He stood with his hands in his jean pockets, his bulky leather jacket making his frame look even bigger than she remembered. She wished she'd made more of an effort.

"Our time's up," she said, when the announcement came over the loudspeaker. She hoped the small talk would soon come to an end and that Tobias would move on. But he looked as if he had no intention of going anywhere.

"I call that perfect timing," Tobias announced, grinning at

them both. "You're finishing, and I only just got here." Jacob looked ecstatic.

"Thank you for Iron Man and the Marvel Quinjet, Mr. Stone. They're awesome!"

"You're welcome, Jacob."

"Your present was so cool! Mommy couldn't believe it was for us."

"Yeah?" Tobias threw a glance in her direction, making her already warm face feel hotter.

"Do you like hot dogs, Mr. Stone?" Jacob asked excitedly. "We're having hot dogs. Do you want one?"

"Hot dogs?" Tobias repeated, as if they were the most delicious food in the world. "They are one of my favorite things to eat, especially in a place like this."

"I don't think Mr. Stone likes hot dogs," Savannah said.

"I love hot dogs," Tobias replied. "It's been a long time since I last had one."

"So get one with us?" Jacob cried.

Tobias paused and looked at her as if he was canvassing for her reaction. Savannah felt pushed into a corner with Jacob chomping at the bit to spend more time with Tobias. She felt it would not do to turn him away. Her son was hungry for male company and since he wasn't exposed to it, she felt reluctant to ruin this opportunity. He was so excited to see Tobias again and clearly wanted to spend time with him. For his sake, she had to let go of the fact that this man was her boss, and someone she didn't, or shouldn't, frequent with. It wasn't only that, but she still hadn't forgotten how he'd reacted when she'd dared to think that Naomi was his wife. She never felt completely at ease around Tobias Stone.

Trust her to pick this day of all the days in the entire year to come to Bryant Park. And trust him to be here, too.

Didn't he have better things to do, like spend time with that overly groomed girlfriend of his? The thought of Naomi stabbed her like a pitchfork.

"Would that be all right?" Tobias asked, hesitating. She shrugged and held out her hands as if to express her helplessness in the situation.

"We're having hot dogs then," he said to Jacob and her son gave him the most endearing smile. "Tell you what. I'll get the hot dogs while you both—"

"You don't have to do that," Savannah interjected. "I'll go and —"

"It's fine. I'd like to," he countered, with a finality that had her back down. "What's yours? Plain or with onions?" he asked Jacob.

"Nothing but the dog and lots of ketchup, please, Mr. Stone."

Tobias turned to her, his gaze questioning. She would have said no, but the smell of the onions had already wafted over and tantalized her taste buds. "Hot dog, with onions, relish, mustard and ketchup, if you don't mind."

"I don't mind."

She slipped her hand into her coat pocket and took out her small wallet, ready to give him a ten-dollar bill.

He waved his hand. "No need," he said, dismissing her easily. She already felt indebted, and this added to it. Pressing her lips together, she slipped the wallet back; there was no point in making a scene about it. She didn't think Tobias would let her win in this case. "Thanks."

"Back in a moment," he told them.

"We'll be over by the benches near the pavilion," Savannah told him and guided Jacob over to the area where they could take off their skates.

"Isn't this fun, Mommy?" Jacob could barely sit still as she pulled his skates off.

"Isn't it?" she replied, hoping they wouldn't have to spend all day with Tobias.

"I really like Mr. Stone, Mommy. He's always so kind to us, isn't he?" She handed him his sneakers.

"I guess," she said, and began to take her own skates off.

"Can we spend the day with Mr. Stone?"

Her mouth tightened as she tied up the laces to her sneakers. "I think he's got things planned, honey. You can't ask people to do something just because it's what you want."

"Why not?"

She let out a breath. "Because, it's just the way it is. I want to spend my day off with you. Just the two of us. That's my plan for the day, and I think we should let Mr. Stone do what he set out to do." She smiled at him sweetly, and when he opened his mouth to say something, she quickly got up. "Stay here," she ordered, no longer able to keep Jacob's questions at bay. "I'm going to return the skates."

Alone with her thoughts, she wondered if Tobias had noticed that this was the same coat she had worn to work.

As if he would notice *her*.

As if he would pay any attention to what she was wearing.

She returned the skates back and smoothed down her hair as she walked back to Jacob. "Let's go sit on one of those benches near the Christmas tree," she suggested. "Mr. Stone will see us if we wave."

They sat down again, this time closer to the hot dog stand. "Here," she said, taking out her anti-bacterial hand wash and dropping a splodge on Jacob's chubby little hand.

Shit.

Why had she asked for a hot dog with all the works? It was going to be near impossible to eat without the onions and relish dribbling all over the place. As famished as she was, she should have stuck to a bottle of water.

CHAPTER FOUR

Tobias walked back to the bench where Savannah and Jacob were now waiting and handed them their hot dogs. Strange, to onlookers it would look like a normal family day out and yet the truth was so different.

"Thank you, Mr. Stone." The little boy's face said it all and reminded Tobias of how at that age even the simplest of things brought so much happiness.

"Thank you," his mother said, taking her hot dog and looking away quickly as if she was afraid to catch his eye.

"This was unexpected, meeting you both here," he commented, hoping to get the conversation going.

"Isn't it great?" Jacob replied.

Savannah stared back at Tobias and her lips lifted into a smile. Just about. He sensed her awkwardness, as if she found his presence hard to bear, and yet he hoped he could find a moment to speak to her, especially since yesterday had proved so elusive.

This—meeting her unexpectedly—had taken him by surprise, but he was glad that he had meandered off course from his walk and come here. He didn't venture out on foot much these days. He preferred to put his head down and deal with business, hiding under his work for most of the day, and if he needed to go anywhere, he relied on Morris to drive him. Occasionally, he also drove if he needed to.

On his walk this morning, the twinkling lights had attracted him, and the trees dressed in shimmering bulbs, with the brightly lit stalls that sprang up along the sides near the ice rink. He'd stumbled into the Winter Village, according to the signs he'd seen and so he had meandered in, mingling with people, families mostly or couples hand in hand. Wherever he looked, people were out in groups, and he was alone.

He'd seen them as he stood gazing at the ice rink. At first he'd been surprised, then he'd dismissed what he'd seen, thinking he was mistaken. But Savannah was hard to miss with her hair flying out behind her, her face flushed and dewy, and her lips red, like cherry. It was the familiarity of her, and then knowing that it really was her, that had brought the smile to his face. He'd seen Jacob in front of her. The boy was good. In fact, the mother was a great skater too. He'd watched them quietly, unknown by them, until Jacob had spotted him. Then Savannah had seen him, and when their eyes locked, she had looked uneasy, uncomfortable, almost as if she was avoiding eye contact.

And here they were, eating hot dogs together. It was indeed a strange turn of events. "I was hoping we could talk," he began, lowering his voice, as he leaned towards her.

"About?"

"About what I wanted to see you for yesterday, before my brother and Matthias interrupted."

"This wouldn't be an appropriate time or place for that," she said, lowering her voice as her gaze darted quickly towards her son.

He nodded; she had a point. They continued to eat quietly.

He was hungrier than he thought he would be, and damn it, this dog tasted like heaven. He grinned at Jacob whose fingers and mouth were covered in ketchup. Even the napkin he had was smeared in red.

"Here, buddy." Tobias handed him another one. The boy finished in record time though Savannah seemed to be taking her time daintily nibbling away on hers and had barely made her way through a quarter of it.

"Would you like another one, Jacob?" he asked. The kid seemed to have thoroughly enjoyed it.

"Have mine, honey. I'm not very hungry," his mother spoke up.

"Don't you want it, Mommy?"

Savannah shook her head.

"I'll get him another one," Tobias offered, stuffing the last of his into his mouth.

"That won't be necessary, Mr. Stone," she replied, and handed her hot dog to Jacob.

"Thanks, Mommy."

"I'm really not all that hungry," she replied, dabbing the corners of her mouth with a napkin.

That won't be necessary? Mr. Stone? She had a stiffness about her that he assumed she only reserved for the office, or maybe it was just for him?

He couldn't blame her. He could be intimidating when it suited him and he was acutely aware that he hadn't helped things much by the way he had behaved during their earlier encounters.

"You were hungry, hey, buddy?"

Jacob took the last bite of the hot dog and nodded. Tobias saw this as his chance to discuss a safer topic. "How was last night? With Matthias?"

She was about to tell him when Jacob interrupted. "Mommy, I'm really thirsty."

"Let me get some drinks," Tobias offered.

"I've got some bottled water." Savannah pulled a Marvel drinking bottle out of her backpack and handed it to Jacob.

"How was your evening?" she asked.

"My brother roped me into going with him to some rooftop bar."

She blinked at him, and he sensed that she had unasked questions lurking at the tip of her tongue, but she refrained from making a comment. He wondered if she thought he'd spent the night with Naomi. And then he wondered if this was his mind playing tricks on him because, unlike him, Savannah Page didn't seem to care two hoots what he did and whom he did it with.

"Matthias—" he started, hoping to prompt her again because he was anxious to know.

"Mommy, I'm thirsty, and this is finished."

"Excuse me," she said to him. "I'll get some more. Anything I can get you?"

"Water's good, thanks," he replied and watched as she wandered off towards the kiosks. He hoped to continue the conversation when she returned. He dragged his gaze away from Savannah to find Jacob watching him.

"Having a good day?"

"The best, now that you're here, Mr. Stone."

This touched Tobias, even though he knew that little children had a predilection for exaggeration. The words still meant something. "Thanks, Jacob," he replied. "It means a lot to me that you let me join you."

"I didn't want you to be lonely," the boy replied. Then, while Tobias was still trying to make sense of it, he asked, "Do you miss your wife?" The boy's words, spoken with an innocence that took the edge off their sharpness, surprised him and at the same time, diluted his anger.

A chill iced over him, making his chest tight and forcing him to work harder to breathe. "I do miss her, Jacob. I miss her a lot." He bent over until his face was level with the little boy's. "How did you know?"

"I saw it on Mommy's computer." The boy stared down at the floor, his face turning solemn.

"On Mommy's computer?" Tobias straightened up and ran a playful hand through the boy's hair. The thought of Savannah looking him up online lifted his spirits.

Jacob nodded. "I'm sorry."

The boy's apology brought him back to earth again. "Hey, buddy. Hey," Tobias slipped his finger under the boy's chin and tilted his face upwards gently. "There's nothing for you to be sorry about."

"But you look sad."

Tobias swallowed. Any mention of Ivy always made him sad. Anyone else asking would have been an unwelcome intrusion, but with Jacob asking, it didn't feel like that at all. "Sometimes things happen in your life that are out of your control." He stared into the boy's green eyes, needing him to hear his words. "This was one of those things."

"I'm sorry that you're alone."

"I'm not alone, Jacob. We ate together, didn't we?" asked Tobias, trying to keep his voice firm.

"I guess," Jacob nodded, still not looking convinced. "Do you like hot chocolate? Mommy was going to—" he stopped as his mother headed back with bottles of water for them all.

"Mommy was going to do what, honey?" Savannah asked, handing him a bottle.

"Is it okay if we get hot chocolate?" Jacob asked.

"Sure, we can," she replied. "Would you like to join us?"

She turned to Tobias but he shook his head. He would have taken them up on their offer but for some reason, he now wanted his own space. Perhaps it was better for him to continue with his walk, as he had set out to do this morning.

"Perhaps another time, Jacob. Thanks for the offer."

The boy nodded and Tobias turned to go. "Will you come again, Mr. Stone?" Tobias turned around. "Maybe next time you can come skating with us," Jacob offered.

Tobias hesitated before answering, and glanced at Savannah. "That would be good." He smiled, because it was impossible not to, especially when the kid looked at him as though he was his best friend.

He was tempted to ask Savannah what she had been doing looking him up online, but he decided that was a question best left for another day.

CHAPTER FIVE

The sound of a screaming siren drilled sharply into her brain, snatching her from Tobias's arms where she'd lain, their bodies naked and entwined.

Savannah's eyelids flew open, and she exhaled loudly, her hand automatically hitting the snooze button. She closed her eyes in the hope of retrieving and reliving those moments again but the last wisps of the dream had escaped and now passed beyond her reach.

Disappointed, she brushed her hand over her face and stretched out, reveling in the feel of the warm bed and dreading the thought of getting up and getting ready for her work and Jacob's school.

In her dream, she'd been in Tobias's bed and his leather jacket had been strewn carelessly on the floor. She felt a pull between her legs as heat swirled below her stomach. It was a feeling she hadn't experienced for a long time and it resurfaced now, giving her a want, a need and a desire for Tobias Stone and the curiosity of going with him to the thirtieth floor.

Not a chance in hell. But the fantasy, as far-fetched as it was, provided an excitement and thrill that her life currently lacked.

She could *not* have these thoughts about Tobias Stone. He would see right through her, especially with that penetrating stare of his and the metallic blue eyes that looked as if he could read her thoughts. She was torn between lying in bed and fantasizing about wicked things and jumping out of bed to get ready for the daily grind. The sharp reminder that it was the first day back to school told her she had to get up. The scramble to get her and Jacob ready and to school in time for the early morning breakfast club was already upon her. Christmas Eve seemed like a long time ago.

Wearily, she sat up, trying to mentally prepare herself for the trudge back to work while scorching hot thoughts, dripping with lust, coursed through her mind and pushed the grayness of January away.

Wondering what it would be like to wake up in bed with Tobias Stone had that effect.

"Don't worry," Briony reassured her. "There will be work and plenty of it but I need to produce a proper proposal and state my case."

Savannah wondered how long that was going to take, especially in a company of this size with its different departments and no doubt lots of pieces of paper that needed to be signed and dotted. It wasn't good enough.

The new recruitment agency had already replied and told her that they had submitted her résumé and were now waiting to hear back from the company that was recruiting for the position of a temporary office manager.

"You don't have anything else lined up, do you?" Briony asked her.

She wanted to keep her options open. "No," she replied,

telling the truth. But she needed to let Briony know that she couldn't sit around waiting for Stone Enterprises to take their sweet time in deciding whether they had a position to offer her or not. "But it would be good to know, you know, sooner rather than later," she said casually, "in case something comes up. I've sent my résumé to a couple of agencies, in the meantime."

"I understand," Briony assured her. "I'll see what I can do."

"Do you think there will be a chance of anything long-term?"

"I'm working on it. I have a proposal for Matthias."

"Do you know when it might come through, and for how long?"

"I know you need answers, hon." Briony combed her hands through her spiky hair, making it stand up as if a few hundred volts had passed through her. "But I have a heap of stuff I need to finish before I can spend any time on ironing out the job spec. Just bear with me, okay?"

Savannah nodded obediently. After all, what else could she do?

"Right now, the only things I can give you are little itty-bitty things," Briony continued.

"Thanks, I appreciate that you're doing your best." She was genuinely grateful for all that Briony had done for her but she was also relieved that she'd kept her options open and had been looking around.

Her livelihood and that of Jacob's depended on her working and earning as well as she could, given her experience. But it had been a lot harder than she had bargained. While this contract with Stone Enterprises had come at the perfect time and it had temporarily made things look up, and given her hope, Briony's responses had already dulled her expectations.

Now that she'd had a taste of working in an office, she could never return to her waitressing or supermarket jobs. Not only was the money better, but it was nowhere near as exhausting. For one thing she didn't have to be on her feet all day, nor did she have to suffer rude customers. Coming from an office manager's job back home, she was more than capable of handling admin work.

She stared down at her only pair of long boots. Thankfully they didn't look too battered. She'd worn a skirt and a black turtleneck top today. It was a little tight, but it was stretchy and when her whole outfit had been put together, with more care than she normally put into it, she didn't look bad at all.

"You've got enough to keep you busy for the next few weeks and if for some insane reason you finish it, knowing you," Briony raised her eyebrows at her, "come and tell me and I'll soon find you something else to do." Briony drew a line through her notes as if she was crossing something off. But it did nothing to dispel Savannah's gloom. She'd been basking in a false sense of security, believing that this contract would continue, because Briony had said it would. She needed something concrete and it didn't look as if Briony was in a position to offer that to her yet.

"Let me get that," replied Savannah, when the phone on her desk started to ring.

"Savannah?" It was Tobias. The sound of his voice, smooth like silk, made her insides somersault. It wasn't only his voice, but the way he said her name. So much had happened between them recently; small things, seemingly insignificant when taken on their own, but when put together, they made something bigger. She wasn't sure what to make of it but knew that the sight of Tobias Stone no longer made her just uneasy. It made her heart do little backflips, too.

"Hello," she replied cautiously, glancing at Briony who was still busy making notes.

"Could you come see me?"

Her insides turned hot, like molten liquid, and in the silence that followed, she heard a whooshing sound in her ears. "I'm in a meeting with Briony." She heard herself saying.

"For how long?"

"I don't know." The meeting with Briony wasn't so formal, but more of a casual chat. "Maybe an hour?" She knew it wouldn't last that long, especially since she and Briony had covered most things but Savannah wanted time to prepare herself before seeing Tobias. She had a feeling that he was anxious to talk, she'd sensed as much yesterday when, once again, the timing hadn't been right. Her heartbeat had already sped up—an effect, she was sure—of the crosscurrents of electricity that she felt between them.

This morning's sultry dream hadn't helped. Still, at least she had made a little effort to spruce up her appearance today.

Briony looked up. "We're done, pretty much."

"It appears you're done," Tobias reiterated, making her wonder if he had bionic ears. "You're free to come see me now."

Savannah bit her lip, unsure of why she was being summoned. "I'll be over in five minutes." Her stomach churned as she put the phone down.

"Who was that?" Briony asked, scratching her nose.

"Tobias."

Briony drew her brows together and stared at her. "What did he want?"

"He, uh ... he had some problems with his Word templates last week and I helped him out."

"Hmmmm." Briony got back to her notes and scribbled some more. "Was there anything else you wanted to talk about?"

Savannah had a lot of things she wanted to talk to her about but it didn't seem as if Briony was in a position to give her a solid answer. The decision was not hers to make. "No. I'm fine for now."

Briony got up and hugged her file to her chest, crossing her arms over it. "I think it would be a good idea to do this every Monday, don't you? A quick weekly meeting where you and I can catch up."

"Sure," replied Savannah and waited for the door to close once Briony had left. She needed a few moments alone, to get herself together.

CHAPTER SIX

Was that a new skirt? He raked his gaze over Savannah as she walked in.

"Good morning."

"Good morning." Her voice was shaky, almost like a floating whisper, and she looked more casual and sexy, he decided, his eyes taking in her appearance from top to bottom. Her face was flushed and his gaze quickly dropped to her snug top which fit like a second skin. He looked away and tried not to wonder how those breasts might feel between his fingers...

Get over yourself, Stone.

He stared down at his planner, at the random scribbles he had made, then swallowed and glanced back at her again.

"Was it a problem with your Word template?" She'd jumped right into it, making it about work right from the get-go and stood tentatively in front of him, choosing not to sit down as she normally would have.

"Take a seat, please."

"I—" she seemed unsure, as if she couldn't wait to get away, and those shimmering hazel eyes of hers glanced at him briefly before she nodded at his screen and sat down. "There was something you wanted me to fix the other day," she began, sitting down slowly.

"That's right." As well as things he needed to say and questions he wanted to ask her.

"Can I fix it now?"

"Go ahead," he replied, getting up and moving out of the way so that she could access his computer. She seemed to be so concerned about the goddamn Word templates that if it helped to put her at ease, then so be it.

Sitting in the chair she had vacated, he enjoyed the vantage position and the view it afforded him—one from which he was better able to observe her discreetly. So far neither of them had mentioned yesterday, the fact that they had spent time at the park, unintentionally and accidentally, but still—they'd eaten hot dogs together.

"How's Jacob?"

"Good. He had a great time yesterday."

"I did too." He let the moment stretch out and when she said nothing in return, he added. "He's a good skater."

"Kids seem to pick it up so much quicker. I think it's something to do with their center of gravity being lower."

"Is that what it is? I thought it was because they weren't afraid of getting hurt."

"That too."

She typed away on the keyboard, allowing him the luxury of letting his gaze roam along her side profile. He felt he had come to know her, that she wasn't merely 'that temp' anymore. And yet he didn't know her.

But he wanted to get to know her better, had been trying to get a moment alone with her for days so that he might glean some idea of what *this* was. His interest in her had deepened from wanting to help her to something more, and even though he couldn't understand or explain why—for their interactions had involved no glitzy nightclub, nor a dimly lit bar, no drinks, no sexy dress or flirtatious talk—he found himself drawn to her.

Things were getting to the point now where he couldn't stop thinking about her.

"It was strange, wasn't it?" he asked, drawing in a long breath. "Running into you both at the park."

She nodded, still staring at the computer screen as she typed away. She seemed to be weighing her words carefully before answering. "It *was* strange. Jacob liked seeing you and eating hot dogs."

He laughed.

"What were you doing around there?" she asked, slowly turning to face him.

"I went for a walk."

"Do you live around there?"

"No, I live on the Upper East Side." *You should come over some time.*

"That was a long walk."

"I needed to clear my head."

He waited for her question but instead she said, "All done," and got up quickly. "I can show Candace what I did to fix it." She passed by the desk then hovered near him.

"I prefer to call *you* each time I have a problem."

Surprise flickered across her face, and her brow furrowed. "But I thought—" She stopped, as if deliberately holding back what she wanted to say.

"You thought what?" He got up slowly. "Say it." He stared longingly at her lips, full, and pink, and more than a little appealing right at this very moment. His breathing quickened, making him feel like a teenager in high school again and he found himself caught in a spell which slowed down time. When the phone rang, he didn't move.

"Aren't you going to answer that?"

"No." *More goddamn interruptions.* "What were you going to say?"

"I—" the ringing continued and she frowned when he still refused to answer it. "It's Candace," she said, reading the caller display screen.

"What were you going to say?" he demanded, but two knocks were followed by the door opening and the charge of Candace's footsteps.

"Tobias, you didn't—"

He turned around quick as a shot. "Not now."

"But," Candace stuttered. "It's—"

"I said *not now*." His words dripped cold venom and he gave her a look that could easily leave a bruise. Candace backed away quickly, then glanced at Savannah before she closed the door.

"You seem nervous this morning, Savannah." He lowered his voice and took another small step towards her.

"Nervous? Me?" She braved a smile. "I thought that Candace was—"

"You worry too much about Candace," he told her, sliding his hands into his slacks before he accidentally tucked the stray curl that now grabbed his attention behind her ear. The more he looked at her, the more he wanted to touch her face and run his thumb along her lip.

"There's something I wanted to say to you last week, before you left." He noticed that her gaze trailed to his lips before darting back up to his eyes again; the quick motion wasn't lost on him, and it gave him hope, as weak as it might have been. *Jesus.* He had never been in this position before and it was something he wasn't used to.

"It sounds as if people need to see you urgently," she said, her voice still a whisper.

"This is more important." But two more knocks followed on

the door. "I said 'NOT NOW!'" he bellowed. Savannah looked scared, and shrank back just as Matthias walked in.

"I'm sorry," Matthias began, holding out his hands as if to calm Tobias's temper.

Fucking unbelievable. Tobias bit his tongue to stop himself from shouting out. "I'm *busy,*" he barked at his colleague and didn't miss the incredulous look on Matthias's face.

There was something else too, the element of surprise; something Tobias couldn't yet fathom, as the other man looked at them both slowly.

"I didn't mean to *interrupt* you," said Matthias slowly, before acknowledging Savannah. "Hello, Savannah. Sorry, Tobias, but this is urgent. Xian Yanling wants to talk to you now. This could be a game-changer."

Xian Yanling? Tobias squeezed his eyes shut. "Put him through."

"He's *here,*" Matthias said tightly, as if his teeth had been wired together. "As in he's staying at the Four Seasons."

Tobias stared back in surprise. "He's in New York?"

Matthias nodded. "He's requested a meeting with you."

"See when Candace can fit me in." Tobias kept his hands firmly entrenched in his pockets. The man was in New York and he expected them to come running to him?

"Tobias, this could be a deal maker."

"I'm busy. Set it up for tomorrow."

"But—" Matthias looked at him in surprise.

"I've finished," Savannah said in a quiet voice and nodded at both men as she walked towards the door.

So much for clearing that up, thought Tobias, in irritation.

"Set it up," Tobias told him.

"I thought you wanted this deal? This could be huge."

"Then set it up." Tobias repeated slowly, grinding his teeth together.

"You don't seem eager to meet with him," Matthias remarked. "I thought you had big plans for this year?"

"My plans haven't changed."

"He said he can meet in the next half hour."

"I'm ready," Tobias replied.

"Then we need to discuss a few things now before we meet with him."

Tobias sat back down in his chair and smoothed his fingers over his slate gray silk tie.

CHAPTER SEVEN

She sneaked away with relief, glad to be out of his office. Being witness to Tobias's anger up close was an eye-opener, even though she hadn't been in the direct line of fire this time.

Yet just before that she'd felt something else—a simmering heat, not anger, more like a magnetism that pulled her towards him. He'd held her captive the way his intense deep blue eyes had bored into her, reeling her towards him and reminding her of the dream she'd had earlier. And just like the dream, he'd left her with a slow-burning fire in her belly just now.

Even while she'd been fixing his templates, she sensed that he was watching her. She could almost feel the heat of his stare while she had tried to look busy, but the tingling in her skin had heightened her alertness. It was as if he had taken a feather and traced it along her naked body.

This was what being in a room alone with Tobias felt like.

"Hi," Candace snapped, breaking her reverie as Savannah walked past the elevator bank. She carried a bundle of files in her arms and a handbag on her shoulder.

"Hey." Savannah smiled quickly and attempted to walk past but Candace had stopped in front of her and for a moment Savannah was transfixed by the silver-gray thick Russian fur hat she wore. It was as if a fox had curled up and fallen asleep on her head.

"What were you doing in there?" Candace asked, the tightness in her lips noticeable.

"Where?" asked Savannah, feigning innocence.

"In Tobias's office—or was it Matthias you'd gone to see?"

"Are you keeping tabs on me?" she asked, wondering what it was that had ruffled Candace's feathers.

"Whatever for?" Candace tossed back, her voice sweeter than honey.

"You seem to be overly concerned about me. Or are you always that nosy?" Savannah was fully aware that Candace had never liked her from the start.

Tobias's PA narrowed her eyes and pressed her lips together, but said nothing.

"If you really must know, Tobias wanted me to look at something," said Savannah, revealing enough to keep her guessing.

"What?" Candace's tapered fingers slid over the files she was holding.

"You're really worried, aren't you?" Savannah tried to figure out if it was Tobias Stone that Candace was after or if she was worried about her job. Then, relenting, "If you must know, it was some documents. There was a problem with a few Word templates. Why do you need to know every little thing? Does it bother you that he asked me?"

"Careful, Savannah. You're only a temp. Don't go getting any high and mighty ideas about your role here."

"I have no illusions about my role, or my position. I know

I'm a *lowly temp.*" She wondered what Candace would make of it if she knew that Tobias had joined them, purely by accident, yesterday at Bryant Park. She had to stop herself from grinning.

"What's the matter?" Candace asked curiously. "Why are you smiling at me like that?"

"No reason. If it makes you feel better, I told Tobias that I would show you how to fix the template."

"You don't have to show me a thing. I know everything I need to know about Word. I'm a PA, not a temp."

"That's what I thought. There's not much point in being a PA if you can't handle your Word processing." She returned Candace's false smile with her own and then heard the sound of the door opening behind her.

"You're still here, Savannah?" Matthias asked teasingly as he walked out of Tobias's office. "It seems to me that you have your eyes on an office on this side of the floor." Before she had a chance to refute his allegation, as playful as it seemed, Tobias walked out, wearing a long black coat and giving her a look that burned right through her.

"I'm very happy in 218, Matthias," she replied as she dragged her attention away from the man who had the ability to make her heart stop and speed up at will. "I don't have any desire to be on this side of the floor."

"Seems to me that everyone's feeling grumpy today," Matthias commented. "I'll get my coat and meet you downstairs," he said to Tobias then rushed off as did Candace.

"I haven't finished speaking to you," Tobias whispered, taking a step towards her and making her mouth turn dry.

"Was there something else?"

"You know there was."

Before she could reply, Matthias returned, slipping on his coat and carrying a briefcase in his hand.

She unintentionally gave him a once-over, in an attempt to focus on something else and move away from the intensity of Tobias's closeness, but when she turned to face him again, she found herself staring into Tobias's hardened face.

"Good luck," she said and slipped away as fast as she could.

CHAPTER EIGHT

"Did you see Mr. Stone today?"

It was a question Jacob had asked her every day so far. She turned around, slowly removing her rubber gloves, to find her son wearing his Age of Ultron Iron Man Mask. "I did," she replied, carefully. "But like I told you, honey, he's been awful busy this whole week. I only saw him getting into his car. He's not been in the office much lately."

Jacob's shoulders drooped.

"Why do you keep asking?" She placed the folded up gloves neatly on the side of the sink.

"I wanted to know when he can come skating with us next."

"*That's* why you've been asking me?" She twisted her hair around and brought it over her shoulder.

Jacob shrugged silently.

"He's a busy man, Jacob. I don't expect he'll have much time to come skating with us."

"But he said he would!"

"I know, but sometimes grown-ups say things they don't mean." She couldn't read his expression behind the Iron Man mask.

"That's not nice."

"I'm sure he would love to come, one day," she added, eager not to crush his hopes. "But when grown-ups say 'one day', they're trying to be nice so that they don't hurt your feelings."

"He lied to me." Jacob's voice was flat and monotone as he removed his mask. She bent over so that her face was barely inches from his.

"He wasn't lying, honey. I don't think he said anything he didn't mean. I have a feeling that Mr. Stone likes you."

"I like him too. He's nothing like Daddy and I wish we could have more days in the park with him." There was a touch of anger in his voice, and a temper she had never seen on him colored his childish-features.

"What is it, Jacob? Why are you upset?" Clearly something was going on and she needed to get to the bottom of it. He'd been quiet lately and she put it down to him getting tired after being back a full week at school but looking at him now, her son looked anxious. "Jacob?"

He coughed a few times then told her. "Both of Henry Carson's parents came to see him at the Christmas concert. Henry said my dad didn't 'cause he hates me." She thought back to that night, to the Nativity play in which Jacob had been a sheep. A cute and delightful sheep who said nothing but smiled like an angel the whole time. She didn't remember Jacob being upset that evening and he hadn't said anything to indicate that. In fact this was the first she'd heard of it. He seemed to be settling in fine at this new school and she'd been hoping things had gotten off to a good start.

"Your daddy doesn't hate you," she replied quickly. She liked to think that Colt cared for his son, on some level—buried way down deep—but just not *enough*. But her son didn't need to know that.

"Then why isn't he here?"

"Do you *want* him to be here?" Her heart tripped a beat and anxiety flowed through her knowing that his father wasn't in the slightest bit concerned about him. She was always mindful that the boy *had* a father but Colt had never expressed much interest in his son. He hadn't even called on Jacob's birthday a few months ago.

It was all so different from how things had been when they had first met. He'd always been arrogant and cocksure of himself, but in the early days there had been a gentleness about him which had disappeared when the factory he'd been a foreman at had closed down. It had affected him badly, and she had never realized that his self-esteem had been wrapped up in his position. He'd refused to take on other jobs as a forklift operator or a handyman, even to get by. His pride had gotten in the way.

"Do you, Jacob?" she asked again. "Do you want your Daddy to be here?"

Jacob shook his head. "He scares me, Mommy. But I don't understand, if he doesn't hate me, why does he hate *you*?"

Savannah clenched her teeth together, thinking about her response. "He doesn't *hate* me, Jacob. Daddy wasn't very well back then." She ran her hands through her hair, causing her neatly twisted hair to shake loose again. She scooped Jacob up in her arms and held him close.

In a couple of years or so, he would be too big for her to carry, and another part of his childhood would fall to the wayside. She buried her face in his hair and carried him to the sofa. Sitting down with him on her lap, she held his warm, chubby hands. "Daddy just likes being by himself. Just like you and me like being by ourselves."

She felt his arms tighten around her.

"Do you miss being with Grandma and Grandpa?" Maybe he was lonely for family?

"Sometimes. But I wish I had a mommy *and* a daddy. A *nice* daddy. Everyone else does." She didn't know what to say to this; she'd known that one day he would have questions but she hadn't thought he'd have them so soon.

"Is that what's bothering you?"

"I don't want a daddy who makes you and me cry. I want someone nice like Mr. Stone."

"Honey," she slipped her arms tightly around Jacob's small frame but he soon wriggled out of her hold.

"Why can't Mr. Stone be my daddy?"

Ok, enough madness. "Because he can't, Jacob." She lamented the lack of positive male models in his life. Aside from her father, there were none. She had no brothers, and neither did Kay. They didn't keep in contact much with her father's side of the family and she had no male friends she could occasionally 'borrow' who would take Jacob to a game, or to watch a movie. And now to make matters worse, to remind him even more of what he didn't have, Tobias Stone had stolen into her life, and into her son's heart and had shown him, in vivid technicolor glory, the very thing that was missing from his life.

"Why not?" Jacob persisted. "He was all by himself that day at the park, and we were all by ourselves and we had a good time together, didn't we?"

Damn Tobias Stone. She nodded, because she knew Jacob had had a good time, but she had to knock this nonsense out of his head. "It's not as simple as that." That meeting last week at the park had been freakily weird. "I know he seems like a kind man, honey." At this Jacob's face clouded over. "I mean, he *is* a nice man and he's wonderful and all that."

"*Do* you like him, Mommy?"

"What? No, that's not what I mean." She shook her head, worried that her son might get the wrong idea. "I'm saying he's wonderful to work with," she struggled to keep her chain of thought, "but he's a very important man at work, and everyone listens to him, and I'm just one of the little minions. He's in charge of hundreds of people." She wasn't sure where she was going with this, in her quest to put Jacob off.

"Hundreds?" Jacob asked, full of admiration. Tobias Stone just went up another notch in Jacob's book. "I want to be just like him when I grow up."

Eager to change the subject, she told him, "People like Henry Carson don't know that your mommy loves you two hundred million times as much. I'm sorry you feel alone, honey. But you're not alone and it's wrong of other kids to say things like that, but people sometimes say nasty things to other people because it makes them feel better about themselves."

"Why?"

"Who knows, honey. Some people are just made that way."

"I told him he was being unkind because he had a big nose."

"Jacob!"

"He has! It's a real hooter."

"Jacob Samuel Page. That is being unkind, picking on someone because of the way they look. You don't say things like that to other children."

"Why is that unfair? He was nasty to me because I don't have a dad."

"You *do* have a dad."

"Not one who cares about me."

"He does..." She bit back on her tongue as Jacob buried his head in her shoulder.

"Henry said my daddy didn't love me, and that's why it was just you and me." His muffled words stabbed her heart.

"Your daddy loves you but it was better for him to be alone, and for us to be alone. Don't you agree?"

He nodded and she ran her fingers through his floppy

brown hair. It was darker than hers, more like Colt's, but unlike his father's, Jacob's was fine and soft. "I like it here."

"I like it too," she said, gently stroking the back of his head. It killed her, his worries and his sadness, especially over *this*.

The divorce hadn't been painful, not as painful as staying too long in the marriage, hoping things might get better. But what had hurt was the finality of it, that a partnership that was supposed to last forever had been severed and a boy had been effectively left fatherless. She was doing her best for her son and trying to make theirs a life that wasn't one full of struggle, but being a single mother had shown her the reality of just how hard it really was.

Not that Colt had ever been there much, especially in the later years, but if he'd been the same man she had married, even half that man, they might have somehow survived. If the emotional abuse, and the times he had lashed out at her, had never happened, they might have had a chance.

She was even more worried now that she had uncovered the worries Jacob had been carrying around on his tiny shoulders. In her struggle to make ends meet, she'd lost sight of the things her son desperately wanted; a home, a family, a father.

"So when can we see Mr. Stone again?"

Goddamn it.

He coughed again and this time she heard the low rumble in his chest. "Jacob Samuel Page, did you wear your scarf and hat and gloves today?" It was the tone and her saying his full name that expressed her gravity. Losing her married name and giving Jacob her maiden name hadn't been as hard as she thought it might have been. She'd been determined that her son didn't bear the name of a man who didn't really want him.

"Jacob?" His looking at the floor, and refusing to answer her question, set off alarm bells. She leaned her head against his chest. "Does your chest feel tight?"

He shook his head.

"Can you breathe easy?"

He nodded.

"I don't care how excited you are to go outside and play, Jacob. You still have to make sure you put your hat and scarf on first, do you understand?"

He nodded.

"I can't hear you," she said, lifting his face up.

"Yes, Mommy."

"And always make sure you—"

"Have the inhaler on me. I know, Mommy." He parroted the words she said all the time, fearful that one day he'd need it and not have it. He yawned and rubbed his eyes. "Can you read to me, Mommy?"

"Sure I can. Come on. Brush your teeth and change into your PJs. I'll be over to tuck you in."

"And read to me," he reminded her.

"And read to you."

He scampered away to get ready and she walked over to the coffee table where the laptop was and hit the keyboard, jerking it back to life. She reread the email from the new agency telling her the company was interested in interviewing her, and that they would get in touch with her soon.

CHAPTER NINE

"I still don't trust him." Tobias stared out of the car window, his brow creasing into tiny grooves.

"You don't trust Xian Yanling?" Disbelief echoed in Matthias's voice.

Tobias turned to face him. "No."

"Why the hell not?" his colleague asked, stunned. "You've been interested in him for a long time. You said yourself that Yanling is a big player in the Far East."

Tobias gave him a steely look. "I want to generate the best return for my investors, but I'm not so sure we can do that by continuing to invest in China and Hong Kong."

"You're bullshitting me now, aren't you?" Matthias laughed nervously.

"I'm dead serious."

"But we've spent the last week and a half in meetings with him and his associates. Couldn't you have said something sooner? He thinks we're in."

"It's too convenient," Tobias replied in a smooth voice. Ever since he'd been summoned into a hasty meeting with Yanling, his gut had told him that something wasn't right, but he'd persevered in spite of his reservations and because Matthias had been adamant that this was a good deal for them both. Tobias had used the meetings to observe Yanling and his people and had come away with the notion that they were desperate. Watching the Far Eastern markets, as he had been doing in the last quarter, the falling share prices of the top companies spelled doom despite what Yanling and Matthias said.

"What's too convenient?" Matthias's voice balanced on the edge of laughter.

"Our deal falls through just before Christmas and a few weeks later, Yanling's here in the US demanding that I see him on the spot, and things are fine again."

"It's not just you. He's seeing other companies too. He's looking for more investment. Why wouldn't he?"

"It's the sign of a desperate man." Tobias replied, grabbing his suitcase as Morris parked the car. Both men got out and walked into the Stone Building.

"Know what your problem is?" Matthias shot at him. Tobias didn't care to know. Something didn't smell right and he was going with his instinct. "Paranoia," his friend continued. "You don't trust anyone."

"It's served me well up to now," Tobias answered and then did a double take at the slim figure that hurried out of the elevator. Savannah Page rushed towards them.

Matthias stared in the same direction and let out a low whistle. "Wonder where she's rushing off to."

Savannah stopped in her tracks as if she had sensed that they were talking about her. Tobias could have sworn she blushed a little. She looked pretty damn good, he thought, raking his gaze up and down the length of her body. She'd done something to her hair. It looked neater, straighter and shiny, and the tousled look he was beginning to admire had disappeared. It was lighter too. And she was dressed in beige colors. Was that a new coat? Rich brown wool, it was open at the front and she was belting it up as she walked.

She looked like a new woman. Not that there had been anything wrong with the other Savannah.

"Hey." She glanced at them both, giving him a fleeting look. He hadn't seen her since that first day back, and now the sight of her stole his breath away in little pieces. They still had unfinished business to deal with. Or rather, *he* did. But he'd been caught up with Xian Yanling and finding time to talk to Savannah was still as difficult as ever.

"Is this a new look?" Matthias waved his hand up and down the length of her body in unashamed admiration. *Way to go,* thought Tobias. *Now there's a great way to embarrass her.*

"What? No!" She blushed furiously, just as Tobias had predicted, and then she avoided his stare, the second thing he had predicted. "January sales, and start of the year resolutions," she said quickly, her eyes darting to the exit. "I'm in a rush, actually, and I need to go."

"Then go," said Matthias, leaning towards her and giving her one of his hungry looks which Tobias had come to know. "We must catch up at some point. Maybe drinks one Friday?" Matthias called out, as she sped off. "She looked like a different person," he remarked as they stepped into the elevator.

"She looked the same to me," Tobias commented drily.

With the second week at work almost over and no further news from Briony about future projects, Savannah was getting anxious. The only light in her tunnel of doom was the interview she had been called for.

"I'll make up the extra hour at the end," she had promised Briony.

"You're working late on a Friday night?" Briony had looked surprised. "You don't have to." True, she didn't but it would be an hour's wage that she would lose and, given her recent shopping splurge, not to mention letting Rosalee talk her into getting her hair cut and highlighted from her hairdresser friend, Savannah definitely couldn't afford to lose an hour's wage.

But she had been more than happy with the outcome. For the first time in years, her hair had shape, and long bangs which she swept to the side, though she wasn't sure about the highlights yet. They seemed too drastic a change for her, and she had almost decided against the coloring, but the hairdresser had persisted, and because the woman's own hair had looked celebrity-worthy, Savannah had given in. The end result had been quietly spectacular, just the way she liked it. It lifted her hair from dull brown to brown with gold bits. It even made her eyes look brighter and more noticeable.

She'd had the new makeover done when she'd heard from the agency last week. "You sound perfect on paper," the recruitment consultant had told her, "but ideally we'd like to see you in person to see if you're the right fit."

The only problem was that she had to squeeze in the interview during her lunch hour and she'd arranged for Rosalee to keep Jacob for an hour longer than normal so that she could make up the time.

She slipped on a plum-colored lipstick and pinched her cheeks. Any more makeup and she'd feel overdone. With that, she rushed out of the elevator.

But the first person she saw as she walked across the lobby was Tobias. That man would be hard to miss in a crowded stadium. He had that kind of presence about him. Tall and with a magnetism that seemed to get stronger each time she saw him, she knew she couldn't pretend she hadn't seen him, even if she rushed across the marble lobby super-fast. Eyes the color of gunmetal burned through her. It had been over a week since she'd seen Tobias, and only now that she'd laid eyes on him did she acknowledge that she'd been looking out for him every single day since.

Snippets of conversation and information she'd extricated from Briony and the others told her that he'd been busy working on a deal with a foreign company.

She knew Matthias had seen her, the way he flashed a large toothy grin at her and she stopped to talk. Matthias commented on her appearance, and in the fog that now enveloped her brain —thanks to the way Tobias was silently looking at her—she mumbled something in return. She forced herself not to look at Tobias and feigned interest in everything his partner had to say.

This was crazy. Whatever *this* was. Tobias Stone had an effect on her that, as time went by, turned her into a throbbing and pulsating combination of bones and blood.

After a little while, she made her excuses and escaped; thankful to have gotten away unscathed.

She flew through the revolving doors and stopped to take a deep breath outside. It wasn't the thought of the interview that had sent goosebumps creeping out all over her body. It was seeing Tobias.

CHAPTER TEN

"We're one of the top ten hedge funds in the United States. I want us to be in the top three by the end of the year." It was an ambitious plan. After all, Tobias was young compared to the other hedge fund managers who had been in this business for decades.

They had all looked at him as a one-hit wonder when, the year after Ivy's death, his company started to creep into the top one hundred. Working like a madman in order to cope with his grief had made him take more risks than he would have liked. But it had paid off. Now Stone Enterprises looked like a strong contender. And he had bigger goals.

"We have the chance to attract new investors, and to offer more products, so we all need to be ready. That means you need to let me know if you need resources to help you. I don't want excuses, I want results. Any questions?" He looked around the table at his management team as they sat in the glass conference room. Matthias, to his right, smoothed down his tie and nodded back at him. On his left, Candace took the minutes of the meeting. Briony and the other managers shook their heads at him. He took this to mean a 'No'.

He liked holding these weekly meetings last thing on a Friday. It meant the managers would be thinking and planning ahead so that their start back at work on Monday would be more action-oriented and not the usual slowly-getting-back-to-work-on-Monday mindset.

Most managers would have held meetings on a Monday, but Tobias knew this would be the time when most employees' thoughts would linger on what had happened over the recent weekend. Friday meetings, just before the end of the day, when most were anxious to leave, meant he had everyone's full attention and there would be no needless discussion of points back and forth.

It worked like a charm.

"Then we'll call it a day." Everyone rushed to get up and leave, including Matthias. The room began to clear quickly and as he got his file and pen together, he heard Briony talking to Matthias.

"I need to speak to you about segmenting the client data for your marketing purposes. I want Savannah to work on part of that project and we need to talk about budgets and timeframes. The sooner the better." Tobias's ears pricked up at the mention of Savannah's name and he listened intently while pretending not to.

"That's a good idea," Matthias replied, giving her an understanding smile. "We could do with an extra pair of hands."

"Savannah would be working for *me.* I need someone helping me out," Briony told him. "But an extra pair of hands, to collect the information and to enter it online, would make for a more efficient process. She could help with the marketing effort as well."

"Let's talk on Monday. I have places to go and people to see," Matthias replied, his tone suave and smooth. "Check my calendar and book me for the first available time on Monday. Let's get together then."

"Thanks and have a good weekend," Briony replied.

"You too." He turned to Tobias, "Don't work all weekend," he said, then waved his hand and left.

Tobias nodded and left the conference room with Briony.

"You're looking to fill a full-time position?" he asked.

"I am. I'm going to speak to HR. I know we can't fabricate positions out of thin air and you need a case for hiring a new person and—"

Tobias cut in. "As I said in the meeting, I don't want money or lack of resources to be a reason for our business not hitting its expected goals this year. I have high expectations and I'm aiming for a sharp increase in revenue. Nothing can jeopardize that."

"I understand, Tobias. Savannah's the person I have in mind —she's working late tonight, as a matter of fact—but before I can put my case forward, I need to have ironed out exactly what I need. That's why I figured if I can get Matthias to commit to the workload he's assigned for me, which always seems to grow over the timeline of the project, then I can justify her position."

Tobias listened. "Don't leave it too late," he told her, as he entered his office. Closing the door behind him, he pressed the pressure points below his eyebrows and held it there, closing his eyes. Two weeks back at work and already it seemed like a month. He would work for a few more hours and then maybe order some food in once he got home. The thought of going back to an empty place held no appeal. Neither did going to a bar.

Savannah was working late, was she? Maybe now would be a good time to get it out of the way; the talk he'd been trying to have ever since New Year's Eve. He wasn't sure he wanted her working alongside Matthias, either, even though Briony had implied that she'd be working for her.

He didn't like the idea of Savannah working for anyone else, period.

The offices emptied early on a Friday evening, at least they did on the twenty-first floor. Tobias offered big enough bonuses and incentives to his employees and he knew that on other floors, the offices would still be busy, Friday or no Friday. Yet senior management, who were already offered more than generous health and financial perks, cleared off faster than anyone else. As long as they delivered, he saw no reason to fire them.

He picked up his phone and called Savannah. "Could you come see me?"

"Now?" She sounded surprised.

"If you can." *I need you to.*

"Uh—sure."

He put the phone down and wondered whether he should have gone to see her instead. He ran his hands through his hair and paced around the room, his nerves jangling in anticipation. A few moments later when she knocked, he opened the door to see her looking anxious.

Close up, her eyes were brighter and his gaze scanned over her fitted cream dress. "Hello," she said, her voice almost a murmur.

"Hi, come in." She threw him a quick glance and he could see something tighten around her eyes when she looked away. He closed the door, a lightning flash of heat pierced through his body. His heart rate quickened as he admired the view from behind of Savannah walking towards his desk.

She was having that effect on him again.

This wasn't going to be easy.

He didn't walk around to his chair but instead balanced on the edge of the desk, facing her, and even now he could see that she looked hesitant as she wavered by the chair. "Sit down, Savannah, I don't bite."

CHAPTER ELEVEN

She mustered a half-smile and did as asked, then backed the chair away slightly.

"Did you want me to fix your document? From last time?"

He shook his head, trying hard not to stare too obviously at her face and hair. She'd done something, lightened it a little, maybe had it cut and styled. She looked good, and she was working late.

Was she staying late to meet someone?

"The document can wait," he told her, and noted the way her eyebrows pulled together, and the way she quickly dropped her gaze to the table. "Why are you working late tonight?"

"I lost an hour during lunch," she replied, lifting her head.

He nodded, remembering their brief encounter in the lobby. "You were in a rush earlier."

"I was," she replied, and didn't elaborate, but he could tell from her voice and the way she avoided looking at him that she wasn't comfortable talking about it. "What did you want to see me about?"

His body stiffened. How could he say it without making it too big of a deal? Was it a big deal? Or was he using it as an excuse to try to figure something out—between her and him, something which he wasn't sure was real enough. And here she was in a cream dress which had ridden up slightly as she sat with her legs crossed, wearing shiny sheer pantyhose, and making his breath hitch when she stared at him with her bright eyes. For a second, he imagined trailing his fingers down the length of her legs and sliding them back up again. Slowly. He folded his arms and coughed lightly.

"I've been trying to speak to you since New Year's Eve. It's nothing serious," he said quickly, seeing her eyes widen. "I wanted to apologize for my behavior the day before, when you asked about my wife."

She sat forward, uncrossing her legs and looked at him in surprise. "You don't have to, Tobias. Really, it's not necessary."

"But it *is* necessary. It was wrong of me. It was downright rude and insensitive. I shouldn't have reacted the way I did."

"I'm a tough cookie, Tobias, it takes more than words to hurt me."

He inclined his head, wanting to know more, but she remained silent. "I hurt you physically and I'm sorry." His gaze dropped to her wrists and once again his mind drifted as he pictured his lips brushing feather-light kisses along the insides of her wrists ...

He quickly dragged his gaze away.

"Apology accepted," she said, her hands on her armrests as though she was eager to leave.

"Are you going somewhere?" he asked, surprised that she hadn't asked him any further questions. "You look as if you're in a rush." He'd been expecting her to say something else, to ask more about Naomi, or Ivy, or that day.

Was it Matthias she was meeting? She was all dressed up and obviously eager to leave. Matthias had rushed off too. "I have some things I need to finish before I leave," she answered.

"Surely you can relax?" he replied, laughing a little and leaning forward as he balanced on the edge of the desk. "It's Friday." He was going to have to coax the information out of her. The idea of her and Matthias was not easy to swallow, especially since he'd noticed that she always had time to talk to Matthias. It grated on him. He couldn't stop thinking about this woman, yet she didn't seem to give a shit about him.

She pushed off the chair and stood up, her gaze almost level with his. She stood closer to him now and he felt it; the way his heart sprang into life beneath his ribcage. He was close enough now that he saw for the first time the specks of amber in her hazel eyes; eyes he wanted to look at when he woke up in the morning. His gaze lowered to her lips and he tried to block the image of what she might look like under her dress. He blinked, tried hard not to think about her lips, or the thought of his tongue over them, not to think about her breasts, or his fingers stroking them...

What was the matter with him?

"Some of us have things to do, Tobias," she attempted a smile as she folded her arms and mirrored his pose.

"As your boss, I'm ordering you to take it easy and slow down. Briony says you're finishing everything quickly she's giving you. Surely, you can't have much work to catch up on? I imagine Jacob's waiting for you at home." He smiled at her, attempting to inject a dose of humor into his words but he still wondered. *Where was the boy's father?*

"As my boss?" she asked, lifting an eyebrow.

"As your boss's boss," he clarified, then stood up slowly. "Briony reports to me." She gazed back at him silently, her face flushed, and her eyes bright.

"So, we're okay about that day? No more questions?" he asked, giving her one last chance.

She shook her head slowly. "You made it quite clear that

your past and personal questions were off limits. But now that we're on the subject, I want you to know that I only asked because..." she seemed to brace herself. "Because the gift box was there, on your desk, and I had seen Naomi in the elevator. You and I kept running into one another that week, and so when I asked you, I was only making conversation. I would never think to ask such personal questions otherwise. You'd made our Christmas special with your generous gifts and I was curious to ask you about yours. That's all it was, Tobias." She lifted her shoulders as if to say: *I wouldn't have really bothered, otherwise.*

"How is Jacob?"

"He's well and back into his routine now that school's started."

"That must keep the little fella busy."

"It does. He liked seeing you that day at the park."

"I liked seeing him." *And you.* "Maybe we should do it again sometime?" The breath stilled in his chest and his lungs suddenly stopped functioning. It was an innocent, harmless question but he knew what was at stake here. The prickly sensation trickling along his spine was as uncomfortable as seeing the look of complete surprise on her face. He was leaving himself open—to her laughter, to rejection, to a '*No*' or '*whatever for?*'

To getting shot down.

The almighty Tobias Stone was being brought to his knees. But it had come to this, and he was tossing it out there because keeping it inside him was getting so goddamn hard.

Her head jerked sharply towards him. "Jacob said he would like to..." Her words surprised him, because he hadn't expected that. "I guess it's because..." She stared back at him, biting her lip.

"Because?"

"Because he had a good time."

"Then maybe we should?" His insides quivered as he waited for her answer.

"I don't know," she said, holding back once again and prompting his next comment.

"I guess Jacob's father might not like that idea," he ventured as he tried to get his breathing under control. It felt as if his life hung in the balance.

"He doesn't have much to do with us," she said, avoiding his gaze. "It's only me and Jacob." She glanced out of the window while he breathed again, and hope gurgled through his veins. He had suspected as much, but had needed to hear it from her. Three, maybe four, silent seconds passed by as they stood almost facing one another, and in that hopeful moment, he was overcome by the desire to grab her and kiss her. Yet he knew he could not, even though the blood in his veins drained south, leaving his mind in disarray.

He wanted to know. "Are you going out tonight?" Then, without giving her a chance to reply, "You look as if you are, the way you're dressed." His voice was soft as he stared at the amber flecks in her eyes, reminding him of the yellow in the marbles he'd played with as a young boy. His heart pounded when she looked at him; the thump as loud as a cartoon caveman's wooden club.

"This?" she replied softly, glancing down at her dress.

"Yes, this," he said, and fought the urge to skim his fingers along her arms. He moved his hand back into his pocket and shifted slightly, conscious of her nearness, and her resolve not to reveal any more about herself. But he couldn't go another sleepless night. He needed *something*, and it had been a long time, decades, since Tobias Stone had had to chase after anyone.

All thought of ethics, his position at work, and hers, crashed out of the window. This was new territory for him, unfamiliar, and as exciting as it was scary. He hadn't thought it through, didn't know what he had expected, had no idea what he wanted, except for the desire to hold her. He wanted her body and lips, soft, wet and yielding, against his. His insides ignited in a riot of wanting. When she didn't answer, he had to ask, "Is it Matthias?"

"Matthias?"

"Drinks on a Friday night?"

She cried out in sharp surprise. "No! Why would you think so?"

"Because you always seem to have time for him."

She waved her hand, her mouth twisting as she tried to express her alarm at his suggestion. From her response, she was either very good at creating an elaborate denial or there really was nothing between her and Matthias. "What makes you think I would go on a date with him? What makes you think he would ask me in the first place?"

"New Year's Eve," replied Tobias. "He asked you then and you went running. It's an observation," he said, taking refuge in his words.

"I didn't go. I went straight home in the end."

"You did?"

"Yes. But why do you care what I do and whom I date?" Now she had him.

Not wanting to answer that question, because he wasn't so sure of the answer himself, he lied, "I don't care. Like I said, it was an observation. You and Matthias seem awful easy around one another."

"He's good with people. Some people have that flair." She looked daggers at him.

"I know what Matthias is good at."

She angled her head. "You're very quick to throw accusations around, Tobias. You seem to think you can ride roughshod over people's emotions and that you can say and do as you please."

Her words made him suddenly defensive. "I *can* say and do as I please. I can do anything I want, Savannah."

Her eyes blazed at him and all he wanted to do was to kiss her; the tantalizing way in which her lips moved, soft and supple, the way she was, unknowingly gutsy and sexy, and decent, made him want her more than ever. She seemed to know what mattered, seemed to know what was important, and she wasn't blinded by who he was, unlike the plastic mannequins who tried to dig their talons into him.

Savannah Page didn't seem to care, and that made him desire her all the more. He craved to touch her, to feel her, to own her.

"You think you can," her voice turned sharp. "But there are limits and, failing that, there is the law."

"Anything can be bought, Savannah, and everything has a price."

"Only in your universe, Tobias." She turned to go, but he grabbed her wrist again, lightly this time.

"Ask me anything you want," he insisted.

"I don't have any questions."

"You did the other day."

"And you made it very—"

"It doesn't matter what I said then. Things have changed. Ask me."

She gave him a pointed stare. "What's changed?"

He clenched his jaw, wondering how it was that she always had him in a corner, he who was so good at brokering deals and getting his opponents at a disadvantage first. "What's changed?" she asked again, and when he said nothing, she pressed further, "Between New Year's Eve and now?"

You. In my head. The whole time. But he remained silent.

Exasperated, she looked around and threw her hands up in the air. "I don't even know what I'm doing here. I have to go, Tobias. This feels surreal."

"Being here?"

"Having this conversation with you."

He didn't want her to go. "I want to see you."

"You're looking at me," she blurted out, lifting her brows.

"I want to see *you*. Have drinks with me, tonight." It was the closest thing he knew to making an offer, though he wasn't sure what he was offering, or what she made of it. She stepped back, clasping her hand to her chest.

"See you?" she whispered. "As in—go *out*? For a drink?"

She felt something, he could see it as clearly as if she'd told him. He'd had enough women throwing themselves at him to be able to easily recognize true desire, and Savannah Page displayed all the signals, even if she was in denial about it herself. "You're with Naomi."

"Says who?" He straightened his body and stood tall so that she was forced to tilt her head upwards, revealing more of her neck, a direct invitation to his senses. For a moment, his gaze lingered along the curve of it, and he imagined sliding his fingers under her dress and feeling her soft skin. He moved forward, closing the already small gap between them. Her eyes widened like a gazelle's. "*Aren't* you with Naomi?"

He shook his head. "Do you think she means anything to me?"

"I don't know. I'm liable to get my head bitten off if I ask too many questions. Remember?"

"I already told you, ask me anything you want and I promise not to bite your head off."

"I can ask you anything?" She licked her lips.

"Anything. No holds barred." He licked his lips, and watched her lips part; he had to bite his tongue to rein back what he wanted to do with her mouth, and what he wanted to do with the rest of her body.

She glanced at the door. "What if someone comes in?" Her voice was seductive as was the spell he found himself caught up in, the one that drew him to her with a desire that was beginning to spiral out of control.

"It's only a question..." he said slowly. "Unless..." He had great control of his body, and most situations, but this was new, and soon enough she would see how excited he was. "I can take you to the thirtieth floor, if you're worried about privacy..." She shook her head quickly, the color creeping into her cheeks, painting her face rose-colored, making him wonder if she would look like that when he made her come.

"That's not what I meant," she said, looking away. Then, "Naomi."

"Is that your question?"

"You said you're not with her."

"She's a high-class call girl and I pay her for sex." He heard her gasp. This secret that he hadn't divulged to anyone up until this moment now tumbled out of his mouth easily. Savannah's mouth fell open, drawing his full attention to her lips which he so badly wanted to savor.

"You pay for sex?"

"Anything can be bought, Ms. Page, even you."

She slapped him hard across his cheek, catching him completely by surprise, his heart giving a huge THWACK! against his ribcage. Excitement coursed through his bloodstream and he pulled her to him. She flinched back, the expression on her face one of horror and excitement—in that microsecond of emotion, he couldn't tell which it was. But he refused to let go.

"You disgust me," she whispered, but she stopped pulling back and her dark, hooded eyes stared back at him, and not in anger either. If this was disgust, she had a strange way of showing it.

"You're so turned on. I can tell by the way your eyes are so dark. You want me, Ms. Page."

She panted in response and the stiffness in her wrist vanished. Emboldened, he slipped his arm around her waist, and inched her closer until her breasts rested against his chest. Silent, she stared at his lips, her mouth parted, and this time he couldn't hold back.

"Do you know how much I want you, Savannah?" She licked her lips, her mouth an invitation he could not refuse. "I want to flip you over right now and take you hard against this desk."

The image burned into his brain. He didn't think with Savannah Page, he *felt*. And the moment he said it, the moment he revealed his baser emotions to her, he saw a flicker of anticipation behind her eyes, more than anticipation, it was one of want.

She let out a soft moan, then trapped it, her eyes glistening. God help him, but when she licked her lips for the second time, it wasn't with fear, it was with excitement. He'd bet his bottom dollar that if he slipped his fingers inside her panties, she would be soaking wet. His cock twitched with hungry anticipation. She wanted it too. Unable to hold back or think cautiously, his hand moved slowly towards her face and he traced a line around her mouth with his thumb, heard her breath, slow and long, like one of pent-up frustration being released, and took it as a sign.

"Tell me to get lost, if you don't want this," he said. Not because of who he was, not because he was the CEO and she was a temp, but because he needed to know, needed to hear it from her lips.

She parted her lips, and their breath mingled, hot desire heating their bodies. She huffed out a sigh, more like a soft mewl, the sound of post-sex contentment. He leaned forward, and pressed his lips gently over hers. This time, she moaned deep and low as their soft lips melted together. Her fingers sank into his biceps.

She fell into his kiss but he had to keep his wits about him even though he'd dropped his CEO mantle the moment she had walked in. He wasn't so careless that she might slap a lawsuit on him so fast for harassment. But her soft body fell against his, and the kiss that started slow and sensual, as their lips and tongues slid softly, feeling and caressing, soon turned into electric-white heat. She pressed her body hard against his, and her kisses turned urgent, like passion unleashed, her tongue lashing hard against his as if she hadn't tasted such kisses for a long time. Soft moans, hungry moans fell from a place deep inside her; he didn't so much as hear them as he felt the vibrations of them.

He wanted to claim her here and now, but he knew he had to bide his time. She had already set him on fire and he wanted more, but all in good time. At least he now had his answer, and he knew that she felt the same way. Her lips, her body, her soft moans of delight all told him that she did.

But the dizzying moment suddenly stopped. She pulled back, her eyes glistening with excitement, her lips swollen and wet.

"Not everything can be bought, Mr. Stone."

She pulled away, leaving him steel hard and surprised.

What the fuck was this?

She walked away, and out of his office, leaving him with a rock-hard dick, and in such a state of shock that he could barely move or speak.

CHAPTER TWELVE

She had made out with the CEO.

Tobias Stone had touched something inside her that she had long buried and forgotten about. The dampness between her legs was evidence enough of how badly she had wanted that kiss.

She staggered into her office, and leaned against the closed door, catching her breath and letting the delicious feeling of excitement calm down. Her breasts had peaked, and she closed her eyes, living out the fantasy of Tobias's mouth sucking them hard. She had felt these strange undercurrents between them and now she knew he felt them too.

She had been excited, more than eager and a little intrigued when he'd called her to his office. A flame had spread out from her lower belly, warming each inch of her body the whole time they had talked. Something had happened between them, but she couldn't pinpoint it down to a direct moment, or a day, or a conversation. Not only had Tobias Stone infiltrated her mind and dreams, he now crept into her thoughts during the day.

He wasn't one to show his emotions, or lose control, and the fact that he had done so made her think that the desire she had started to feel for him wasn't one-sided.

Oh, dear God, she wanted more of it, this fleeting moment of madness she'd shared with him had been unlike anything she'd experienced before. Dropping her head to her chest, she breathed in deeply and replayed their stolen moment. Her cheeks heated at the thought of his words and, with her eyes closed tightly, she imagined him thrusting into her as she bent over his desk—the way he said he'd take her. Losing her mind along with her senses, she half-wished he had carried out his desire, but knew that he wouldn't come after her.

An urge deep within her compelled her to go back to him. She wanted him to do the thing he had threatened to do.

But she couldn't go to him, could she?

He was the CEO.

She was nothing.

And yet ... his lips had claimed hers with an intensity she'd only read about in romance books. His hardness had been the proof that he desired her.

Reveling in the afterglow of her excitement, she heard her phone vibrate on the desk and rushed to answer it.

"Come quick!" Rosalee screamed. "Jacob is sick. I'm in the ambulance with him now."

"What?" It was as if her heart had slipped through her stomach and fallen to the floor.

"I've been calling you." Rosalee sounded scared. "Come to the hospital. Hurry!"

Savannah grabbed her coat and her bag and fled.

She rushed out of the taxi and barreled through the main entrance doors of the hospital, rushing to the ward where Rosalee had told her they were. Jacob lay on the bed with a mask over his face. Savannah's insides hardened like concrete at the sight of her sick child lying with his eyes closed and the oxygen cylinder beside him.

"Oh, baby," she moaned, holding his hand tightly. His eyes lifted as he looked at her, unable to talk. "What happened?" she asked Rosalee.

"He was fine when I picked him up from school. We went back to my apartment but I noticed he was coughing and then he started to wheeze, as if it was getting difficult to breathe. I told him to take his inhaler but it didn't seem to help. One minute he was watching TV and the next moment he was fighting to breathe. I was scared and called 911, and then I called you but you didn't pick up. I tried so many times." Savannah closed her eyes and tried to picture the scene of her boy fighting to breathe. And she'd been in Tobias's office, doing other things.

A doctor entered the room and gave her a solemn look. "He's going to be fine, Ms. Page. He's in good hands now. Young Jacob's asthma quickly worsened to the point that the inhaler wasn't having an effect."

"He's been coughing and I didn't pay too much attention." Savannah murmured. It was her fault, she should have kept a closer eye on him.

The doctor walked over to Jacob and smiled. "It's fairly common. His lungs are congested and we want to get them clear so that he won't have any problems breathing. He should be good to go home in a few days' time."

She looked horrified. "A few days' time?"

"The mucus has been building up for some time. The

inhaler wasn't working as effectively. When was the last time a doctor saw his asthma care plan?"

"Not for a year. He's been fine."

"Asthma can creep up quickly, you need to keep an eye on what triggers it. It may be a combination of the lingering cold and the weather has likely made things worse."

"Does he need stronger medication?"

The doctor nodded. "We've increased his dose for now and we'll continue to monitor it while he's here. The inhaler he has is fine and I'm not keen to increase the dose ongoing but he hasn't been using it when he should have. This has exacerbated the problem."

She opened her eyes. "He doesn't like taking it, but he knows he has to if it becomes hard to breathe. How can you tell he hasn't been taking it?" She looked at Jacob who had closed his eyes. Guilt smacked her hard across her face. She should have checked, instead of taking Jacob's word for it. He'd been coughing and his chest had sounded blocked but that had been over week ago. He had seemed fine lately.

"Because he told me. Don't worry, Ms. Page, your son is going to be fine." The doctor walked away from the bed and towards the door, motioning Savannah to follow. "Will your husband be coming?"

Savannah shook her head quickly.

"Could I have a word with you outside, please, Doctor?" He nodded and she followed him out of the room and into the plastic blue and cream-colored corridor.

"Jacob's father and I are divorced and it's highly unlikely that he'll come to see Jacob."

"I see."

She was sure that in his capacity as a doctor, he had seen all sorts of stories and witnessed many similar scenes. Then she asked the question she had been dreading. "How much will this set me back?" The thought of it had been eating away at her stomach like acid. She was too scared to find out, but not knowing was worse. At least if she had a figure to work towards, then she could decide how to go about settling the final bill. "I want him to get well, and of course he'll stay here for as long as it takes, and you give him all the medication he needs."

The doctor smiled. "We always plan to."

"I need a rough figure, Doctor."

"Do you have government assistance?"

"No." She could have kicked herself and wished that she had applied for it earlier. But no, she'd been so determined, so pigheadedly stubborn and stuck-up about wanting to make a living for them both, that she had turned her nose up at any assistance, or form of welfare.

"How much, Doctor?"

"Let me hand you over to the nurse, Ms. Page, and she can answer any questions you might have," was the doctor's diplomatic answer.

Returning to the room, Savannah walked over to Jacob and gave him her widest smile.

"We're going to stay here tonight, honey, and maybe tomorrow night, too." She watched as he shook his head. "It will be fun," she said, dismissing his sad face. "And before you know it, we'll be back home. No school for a few days, and no work for me either."

Jacob's face brightened. She gave his hand a squeeze and wanted to ask him why he hadn't been using his inhaler, but that could wait until later. The main thing now was that he recovered fully so that they could go home.

She went over to Rosalee and sat down in the chair next to

her. No words were necessary as she threw her arms around the woman and hugged her, holding on to her because she needed the comfort.

"I don't know what I would do without you," she said, moving away and trying to put on a brave face. "I can't ever thank you enough, Rosalee, for being there. For being there when he needed me. I'm sorry to put you to so much trouble."

"Please don't say that." The elderly woman wagged her finger at her. "It's no trouble at all. Jacob is like my grandson to me. I am glad he is fine and that he is getting better. That is all we want."

Savannah's eyes moistened. "I'm so thankful that you're here," she whispered, looking at Jacob, who had closed his eyes. She fell back against her plastic chair, hard beneath her body, and as her head and shoulder drooped, she felt a warm, comforting arm around her shoulder. She leaned into it and Rosalee tightened her hold.

"He's going to be fine, and so are you. You must believe that, Savannah."

She nodded and attempted to put on a brave face. "You go on home now, Rosalee." She reached into her handbag and pulled out some bills. "This is for the cab ride home." She thrust them into Rosalee's hand but the woman shook her head.

"I am taking the subway home."

"You're not." Savannah was adamant. "I'll call you a cab myself if I have to." But still Rosalee refused to take the money.

Savannah wasn't having any of this. It was bad enough that Rosalee had come to the hospital, and that her evening had been ruined. "Rosalee, this isn't fair. If you help me, you must be prepared for me to help you." She slipped the bills into Rosalee's tightly fisted hand, forcing the woman to take the money. Rosalee kissed her on the cheek then blew a kiss in

Jacob's direction and disappeared, leaving Savannah in the dark and dingy room.

She was alone now with her thoughts, and the worry of mounting bills. The nurse hadn't been able to give her an exact figure since they didn't know how long Jacob would be in for, or what other course of medication he would need between now and his release. But the figure was 'in the thousands' already.

She didn't have that kind of money lying around. She'd pretty much used up what she earned, give or take a few hundred dollars that she'd been trying to save. But she didn't have hospital-stay kind of money, not when she was still paying off her credit card bill with the years of debt stacked up on it and suffocating her. She'd had two cards and had only recently gotten rid of one, leaving another one, with almost ten thousand dollars of debt on it, for her to work through.

She watched Jacob sleeping and sought comfort in knowing that he was fine now, and would soon be well enough to go home. She knew how fatal asthma attacks could be. Closing her eyes, she expressed silent thanks and gratitude that her son was alive and sleeping peacefully.

Everything else, she would think about later.

Including Tobias Stone.

CHAPTER THIRTEEN

She had rushed out of his office, leaving him with a boner the size of the Statue of Liberty.

Tobias still wasn't sure if Savannah was being a tease, or if she was confused, or why she had broken off so suddenly and left. But he was determined to find out. That evening and all through the weekend, he had thought of nothing but Savannah. That kiss and the taste of her lips were branded upon his mind forever. It wasn't enough, he wanted more. He wanted to have and taste all of her.

If he'd been unsure of her interest before, he now had his answer. She felt the same way, or at least she felt *something*. He wasn't sure of what or how much, but it no longer seemed like a one-sided daydream.

Sometime during the weekend, Naomi had texted him, asking if he wanted the key to the penthouse back. Talk about perfect timing. He'd sent Morris to get it and with that chapter over, he no longer expected to hear from the high-class escort again. That was how these arrangements worked. He didn't have to deal with questions about why it had ended or how they could fix it.

Despite the way Savannah had left him—the worse for wear with a need that had gone unrelieved—he hadn't been tempted, not even by Naomi.

His craving now was only for Savannah—a woman who at first sight would have been light years from the type of woman he thought he'd find attractive. Now, his curiosity was as insatiable as his urge to possess her and he needed to know if what he imagined matched the real thing. He liked to think he knew Savannah, but he also knew she could surprise him, and that element of surprise, with her eager body, and her fiery personality, were the things that both tortured and paralyzed Tobias the entire weekend.

He'd been left wondering why she'd suddenly walked out on him and though he had her number—because he had access to her work records—he'd held off the temptation to call her.

Maybe he'd scared her, maybe she felt ashamed. Or was the real surprise going to be the lawsuit she might finally serve him with? It was difficult to tell with women, even those who were passionate enough to want the sex. Sometimes money pulled harder.

He didn't think Savannah was that type of woman—he knew how badly she wanted that kiss. He wanted to believe in the way she had quickly succumbed and fallen against him, soft and gentle, and hot and needy all at once. Her lips and tongue had sought his with an urgency that had surprised him. Women didn't moan like that if they didn't want something that badly. But he knew better than to assume she wanted the same thing he did. He wanted to think it was because she felt something for him in return.

But he'd learned a lot in life and business, and the most powerful lessons were not to trust people so easily and not to take anything for granted.

He was anxious to know how things stood between them,

and when he returned to work after the weekend, he was desperate to seek her out again. But his day had been full from the start. Meetings with managers and clients kept him busy. He emailed Savannah, but she hadn't replied and by late afternoon, he was bristling with irritation.

He wanted her.

He had a good idea that she wanted him.

And the penthouse beckoned.

He shook his head, trying to throw the sordid thought away. *Slow down, Stone. She's not that kind of woman.*

She wasn't Naomi. Nor did he want her to be. With Savannah, the possibility of something beckoned. Small wisps of light that called out to him and gave him hope.

He checked his inbox throughout the day but still there was no reply from her. By late afternoon, he was so pent-up with frustration that he couldn't think straight. Returning from yet another meeting, he knocked on her office door and when she didn't answer, he walked in anyway, expecting to see her surprised face looking up at him.

Except that the office was empty and looked as if it hadn't been in use today. Back in his office, he called Briony. "Did you put together your case for a full-time worker?" It was a flimsy attempt to elicit the information he needed without asking the obvious. Briony's momentary silence indicated her surprise at this sudden question. These trivial matters were things he would have never chased up before. Except that Savannah Page was not a trivial matter.

Briony laughed instead. "Not yet, Tobias. I'm busy scoping out the exact job spec for the role." Dissatisfied with her reply, he was about to ask where Savannah was, when Briony offered up the information. "Savannah's not in today, anyway."

"She's not?" Tobias repeated, hoping to hear more.

"I was going to have a word with her when she gets back."

It would sound suspicious if he enquired further, and he was mindful that whatever it was that had happened between them, it could not be spoken of, nor was it to become public knowledge. He scratched his jaw, and knew there was only one thing to do now, as difficult as it was. And that was to wait.

CHAPTER FOURTEEN

It couldn't be, $3,583.95?

She stared at it as if it was a death sentence. It might as well have been.

A two-night stay in a hospital was $3,583.95.

The bill floated out of her hands as she slumped to the floor in her bedroom. She didn't have that kind of money.

Holding her head in her hands, she tried to figure out her options. She couldn't put it on her existing credit card because the one she had was already maxed out and she had closed the account on her other one now that she had paid off the debt on it. She'd cut the newly paid card into tiny pieces. Congratulatory confetti. Except that it would have come in handy now if she'd had it.

She had been on her laptop for most of yesterday, while Jacob had been resting, trying to apply for another card online but had been denied. Today was her chance to resolve this problem. It was better to do this from home because it wasn't the sort of thing she wanted to deal with at work. She didn't want Briony or Tobias walking in while she scrambled to find money to pay a hospital bill she had no hope in hell of settling, unless a miracle fell into her lap.

With her breathing shallow, Savannah folded her arms and hugged them to her chest. She felt the urge to rip the sheet of paper into shreds but she couldn't do that. Wouldn't, because she knew her problems wouldn't disappear as easily. Money problems crushed her hopes and spirit, making her feel a thousand times smaller. She hated sinking into that limitless black hole that drained her completely and reduced her future to bleakness again.

The ray of light had been that the agency had called her this morning to tell her that she had been short-listed with two other candidates and they were still making their decision. All this interviewing for an office manager's position. She'd already decided to take it, if it came her way. Stone Enterprises, and Briony, bless her, with her good intentions, could not beat slightly better money, a six-month contract and the chance to go full-time.

Still, she needed thirty-five hundred dollars in the next few weeks, not in the next few months. If only she'd signed up for government assistance, instead of stubbornly trying to prove that she could do this herself. Her heart was heavy, as if tar had been poured over it and the worry of debt and unpaid bills pinched her insides like cockroaches eating their way out.

But when Colt's image flashed inside her angry mind, she got up, spurred into action and called him from her cell phone.

"Savannah," he drawled, picking up eventually as she was about to hang up.

"Jacob's been sick."

"Yeah?"

"He had a bad asthma attack and was in the hospital for two days."

"How's the little runt now?"

She gritted her teeth, trying not to let Colt push her buttons. "He's recovering. I'm keeping him at home for a couple of days so that he can get his energy back."

"He always was a weak little thing. Takes after your side, I reckon."

"He's not weak," she snapped. "He never was. He's sensitive." *Unlike you*, she wanted to say, but stopped herself, not wanting to get into another argument again. "The hospital bill came through. It's over $3,500."

He said nothing for a few moments, then, "Why're you telling me? Ain't like I can help you out. I'm still trying to find work."

"Maybe you should try a little harder." It had already been years. She had a feeling that getting a job was low down on his list of priorities because it would mean he'd have to pay something towards child support. "You already do nothing for him, it's not like I'm beating down your door for alimony." She had trouble keeping her voice calm. "But a little help—"

"Can't do it. You're working now, ain't you?"

How did he know? Savannah flared her nostrils. She'd have to tell her parents to keep their mouths tightly closed, although she had a feeling it had probably been her mom. Her dad hated Colt with a passion and barely acknowledged him. "Sounds to me like you're doing okay, living in New York and all that." He drawled on, making her wince.

She didn't want him to know more than he needed to but hearing him talk, any worry she'd had that he might have had some interest in coming to see Jacob was instantly dismissed. This man never had and never would give a shit about their son.

She pressed the heel of her hand into her chest and thought of her little boy, and all at once she wanted to slam the phone down and be done with this man. But she was stuck. She was so broke, and holed up in a corner with nowhere to run, that she'd had to call the man who'd hurt her and sworn at her and made her life a complete misery. And all because she wanted to get some money from him. She should have known better.

How had her life hit rock bottom so quickly? One moment she was getting by, the next she was feeling grateful, but the first sign of an emergency and she had fallen into the gutter. She had no rainy day money, she'd only ever had *getting-by* money.

"It's not cheap here. I can barely get by."

"You shoulda thought of that before you moved your ass out of North Carolina."

I wanted to get as far away from you as possible.

"You can't help me out at all? Not even with your beer money?"

"You're scraping the barrel, sugar, if you're coming to me asking for money."

"He's your son."

"Is he? Sometimes I'm not so sure myself."

"You bastard. You know I've never been with anyone but you."

He snorted at her and she knew why she'd been putting off calling him. It hadn't even occurred to her to call him to let him know that Jacob had been hospitalized. Colt Brookes didn't care for anyone except himself. He'd put her off men for life.

Almost.

Tobias's kiss floated back to her, and she closed her eyes for a few seconds. "Thank goodness I never waited around," she said, fighting to keep the vitriol out of her words.

"Waited for what?"

"For you to turn into a man." She hung up on him and this one simple act gave her a feeling of small triumph. She stared at the phone, wondering what it was she'd ever seen in him.

Desperate, she called her parents next. They had called every day, from the moment they'd found out about Jacob going into the hospital and they, along with Rosalee, had been her only source of comfort. She wasn't sure if Briony would have understood, not having a child herself, but she'd left her a voicemail message yesterday telling her that Jacob wasn't well. She would explain fully when she returned to work. The only people who could really help her would be her parents, and even though she hated to do it, she had no option. The urge to pay off the soul-sucking hospital bill stuck in her throat like a sewing needle. She couldn't rest until it had been dealt with.

She called her parents' home and dropped her head into her hand when her father picked up. It would have been so much easier to ask her mom for the money. She didn't want to worry her dad because she knew he already worried plenty about her; both her parents did, but her dad worried all the time. If she told him about her money worries, he would do whatever it took to help her and get the money to her, and she didn't want to put that kind of burden on him.

But she had no choice.

"Hey, Dad."

"Hey, Ruby Red." He sometimes called her by the nickname he'd given her when she was a child. It had come from her favorite ragdoll of the same name and she'd been inseparable from it. "How's the little man doing?"

"He's resting up, Dad. I'm keeping him home from school today as well but he'll be fine to go back tomorrow."

"Only two days? Why don't you give him the whole week off and let him recover properly?"

She brushed her hand over her forehead. "I don't want to take more than two days off work, Dad. I don't get paid if I don't show up."

"It's so hard for you, Red. It breaks my heart to know that you're struggling alone."

"We're better off alone, Dad." She forced herself to sound

stronger, even though her soul had been bruised. "It's not so bad, really it isn't. The job I have is great. This is a minor setback but he's okay now and things are looking good." It couldn't be further from the truth, but it was better not to spread her woes around.

"Are they?" She heard the anxiety in her father's voice and knew that he was already worried. Her idea of asking for financial help choked in her throat.

"Did you call his father and tell him?" Her dad found it hard to refer to Colt by his name, ever since she'd shown up at her parents' doorstep with a black eye and Jacob in a stroller. It had taken her mom and the neighbors to stop her father from going over and 'kicking the shit of out him.' She'd convinced them not to call the police either, fearful that Colt might twist facts to suit himself. Lying came easily to him and she knew he wouldn't hesitate to make out that her father had hit him. Colt could have made things worse for her or her parents. In the end, with the decision made to leave him, she thought it best to leave the home town in North Carolina where she had lived for most of her life and go far away. Kay and Aunty Sylvie were a godsend.

"I did."

"I don't expect he's coming up to see the boy?"

Her head fell to her chest and she squeezed her eyes shut. "No, Dad."

"Did you ask if he might pay for the hospital bill?" The real reason her dad had wanted to know if she'd called Colt. Already he was worrying about her bill.

"No need, Dad." She exhaled sharply. "The place I work at can help out."

"They can? I didn't think you had any insurance, being a temporary worker and all."

"They can help." She hated lying to him.

"That's something, Red. Do you need any extra?"

"Uh." She couldn't make herself say the words. *Do you think you could loan me some money please, Dad?* "I think I'll be okay."

"You let me know if you need a helping hand. Did you get the Christmas money?"

"Yes, I did. Thanks, Dad. I already told you." That was two hundred dollars she could put towards it. She chewed her lip. One hundred, now that she'd spent some on her wardrobe and getting her hair done last weekend.

Her father lowered his tone. "I've booked a cruise from Miami to the Bahamas in the summer. Your mom always talked about going on one and we've never been. One of her friends has just come back from one and she won't stop going on about it. So I bit the bullet and booked one for your mom and me to go on." He sounded so proud of himself.

"Aaaw, dad. That's a fantastic idea."

" 'Course, it's going to set me back some, but she's worth it. It's a surprise for her sixtieth, so don't you go saying anything to her."

"I won't, Dad." Her eyes filled with tears. Thirty-two years of marriage and he still wanted to surprise his wife. "That's such a thoughtful idea, Dad. Mom will be over the moon." There was no way at all that she could ever ask for the money now.

"Your mom and I want to visit you and Jacob, but I'm waiting to get my energy back. This infection knocked me out over Christmas, otherwise we would have come and spent time with you guys."

"I know, Dad. It's good you didn't come. The weather here's been getting colder. I think it set off Jacob's asthma. There's no point coming until you're fully well."

"We were thinking maybe during the mid-term break. You let us know when."

"You can come any time you want." She pursed her lips together into a tight line, felt the lump stick in her throat, and fought back a sob. "I miss you guys. We can't wait to see you."

"Same here, Ruby Red, same here."

She hung up and crossed her arms over her pushed-up knees and buried her head.

She had nowhere else to turn to, unless...

Unless she could get the company to somehow help her out. Maybe she could ask Tobias Stone.

She rocked her head from side to side, considering the idea. She had been feeling jittery about her first day back at work, confused about how to face Tobias, but how could she now approach him and ask about money on top of everything that had happened between them?

Was it wise?

But did she have any other choice?

At the hospital while she'd sat by Jacob's bedside, it had given her plenty of time to analyze *that* kiss. She had wondered, with that dream she'd had about him, whether her slow-building interest in Tobias had been a one-sided fantasy, or whether it was something that he also wanted. Each time she now relived that moment, she sensed that it was something he had initiated; something he had wanted, too. Wasn't he the one who had insisted she could ask him anything? And the way he'd stood so close to her, with his piercing eyes burning into her soul—the way he'd grabbed her again and pulled her towards him, wasn't that him coming onto her?

He wanted her.

There was no use lying to herself about it anymore—she wanted him as much. The man had a magnetism about him which had slowly reeled her in. She didn't know how it had happened, or when it had started. Had it been that night at the toy store? Or when he'd accused her of stealing the Dalton file?

Or when he'd sent her the gift basket...or all of that week when it had been only the two of them at work?

Heat coiled between her legs at the thought of him and she shivered as goosebumps prickled over her arms and chest. His penchant for paying for sex both intrigued and repulsed her.

But not only was he the CEO of the company she worked for, he was also a troubled man. The death of his wife had scarred him and she had no idea what she was dealing with. As much as she wanted to believe there was a decent man buried beneath that cold exterior, he was also someone who blew hot and cold.

In her mind, she'd shared his bed, explored his body and let him use hers. She had dreamed up fantasies so hot that she had trouble sleeping. Thoughts, dirty and delicious, had left her so turned on she was ashamed to be sitting in the room next door to her son, fantasizing.

Did Tobias want her—for her? Or was he after her because she wasn't so easily obtainable? Not being sure of where she stood made her uneasy and her earlier idea to ask for his help vanished as easily as it had appeared.

She had no idea how she was going to react when she saw him again. She had no idea what he wanted, or what would happen, but the more she thought about him, the more her body hungered for his touch.

CHAPTER FIFTEEN

Wednesday rolled around quickly and it was back to the frenzy of juggling school and work again.

"Why can't I take the whole week off, Mommy?" Jacob had asked her as she ordered him to get ready for school.

"Because you're perfectly fine now, Jacob." She'd checked obsessively that he had on his scarf, hat and gloves, and that his coat was zipped up to the top and they had gone to school together, him looking like a little Eskimo.

Rosalee was like a second mother to Jacob, and Savannah couldn't put a value on the help the woman provided for her. Each day Rosalee picked Jacob up from school and some days he would go to Rosalee's place, other days Rosalee would bring him back to the apartment. Savannah paid her a small amount for her trouble.

This morning Rosalee offered to help again, but Savannah had wanted to take Jacob in herself just as school started, instead of leaving him at the Early Bird Breakfast club and rushing off to work like she normally did.

Now, as she walked into work, she felt better for having

spoken to his teacher about his asthma attack and making sure that the school was aware of his asthma care plan.

As a result she'd shown up at work a little later than usual but this time she was determined not to stay after work in order to make up the time. She popped her head into Briony's office as soon as she got in, to the chorus of 'hey, how are you?' and 'feeling better now?' from the other women.

"Yes, thanks." Savannah replied. "Is Briony around?"

"She's in meetings all morning. You won't see her until after lunch."

Crestfallen, she murmured her thanks and left. Returning to her office, she closed the door behind her. Days had passed since she'd last been here, standing in this very position after that encounter with Tobias. Unable to think straight, her first reaction had been to run away and she'd rushed out of his office after their kiss, feeling dazed, confused, and giddy. Even if Jacob's asthma attack hadn't happened, it would have been awkward enough, facing Tobias again.

And now?

How was she going to do this?

What kept her going was the thought that he had helped them before, with the Christmas gifts, and the advance payment into her account a month early. Maybe it wasn't completely crazy, this idea of hers. Maybe he would understand since he already seemed to have an understanding of her circumstances.

But, as she switched on her PC and settled down to work, she was surprised, and a little reassured, to see a couple of emails from him sent a few days ago.

We need to talk, and I promise that's all it will be.
Tobias

He'd sent that on Monday and a day later:

I see you are away for a few days. Not avoidance issues, I hope. I need to speak with you on your return.
Tobias

What did he want?
Was he ashamed of what had happened between them?
Was that it?

She shook her head. It couldn't be. Things were electric between them, or at least in her head they were. It couldn't have been one-sided. He'd initiated it and she'd given in, but he had initiated it first. Then she remembered the time when the boxes had fallen on her and he'd come rushing to her side. She recalled his fear that she would slap him with a lawsuit.

Was that what he was afraid of?

Not knowing was as insanely crazy as the thought of knocking on his door and asking to speak to him. His emails had left her none the wiser. She had to bury her thoughts of what he *might* want, and put on her best professional face and ask what she had to. Yet the memory of that searing kiss, and along with it her fantasies of him naked in her bed still lingered at the forefront of her mind. She was suddenly scared that he'd read her easily.

An advance for a few months' wages wasn't asking for too much, was it? Even though, technically, her contract was due to run out in a few weeks' time. She was desperate, and in her desperation she was choosing to hold onto Briony's words that 'she was working on something' to keep Savannah at Stone Enterprises. She would worry about her contract expiring later, for now she needed the money.

If she sat and thought about it, it would haunt her all day long. She would be in a state of frenzy within the hour. Her inbox was already full of emails, and she no doubt had a stack of queries to deal with as well.

Her hands trembled, and her legs felt like jelly as she forced herself to stand up and walk towards Tobias's office. Bile soured in her throat and she was tempted to run away but of the many lessons her life had taught her, facing her fears and jumping in, despite her anxiety levels, was the one that had made the most difference. She would not allow herself to be talked out of doing what she needed to, not with the weight of thirty-five hundred dollars sinking her soul.

She knocked on his door, once, twice, three times. But there was no answer.

"He's in meetings all morning." Candace told her with a smug smile. The door to Candace's office was wide open. "You can leave a message with me."

Savannah's insides churned. Leaving any message with Candace was out of the question. Seeing the PA's sour face was exactly the impetus Savannah needed to bolster her resolve. "I need to speak to him."

"About what?" Candace asked.

"About something that's none of your business." Candace was the least of her problems. Savannah walked away, closing her eyes and letting out a silent sigh of relief but as she turned the corner and headed towards the elevator bank, she found Tobias walking towards her.

He stopped as their eyes met. She looked back at his face and it was as if small sticks of dynamite exploded in her chest.

Boom, boom, boom.

She'd been crazy to do this. Desperate *and* crazy. He nodded, acknowledging her, his lips twisting, but no words came out.

"You wanted to see me?" Her voice shook, despite her best

efforts to keep it level, and the trembling in her stomach spread out towards her legs.

"I did." He had one hand in his pocket and brushed his other one through his hair. "Come," he told her. Once inside the elevator, she was too fraught to question why they were heading up to the thirtieth floor.

In the silent minutes it took to reach the door to the penthouse, she tried to control her breathing which had rocketed out of control.

Tobias stepped inside the penthouse and she nervously followed him in. The open space, the spiral staircase, the huge windowed wall showing off the silver-gray sky, all caught her attention while the rush of blood pounding through her ears slowed time down. She heard him close the door first, before she heard the thumping beneath her ribcage, and the crazy flips in her belly.

They stared at one another for a few heated, questioning seconds.

"What was it about?" she asked, wanting to hear what he had to say before she asked him about the advance. She couldn't ask him immediately because the memory of being alone with him knocked the sense right out of her head and sent blood pooling between her legs. He was about to say something, but she looked away as searing images of him and what she longed for him to do to her colored her thoughts.

He stepped closer to her. "About Friday night...what happened then..." His voice was lower than she'd ever heard it. "Look at me, Savannah." She held her head up high, even though adrenaline burned beneath her ribcage. He paused, shoving both his hands in his pockets, and she could see the words didn't come as easily to him. It gave her time to catch her breath but her nipples hardened, as if in anticipation, and she let out a silent, slow breath.

"Friday night?" She couldn't go there, not at this moment, otherwise she would never get around to saying what she had to. It was already difficult enough to make her request.

"I couldn't stop thinking about you all weekend, Savannah." His voice was a murmur that was both husky and sexy, and should have been outlawed.

She hadn't been prepared for *that.* The intensity of his words, like his gaze, pierced deep inside her and she couldn't breathe, couldn't focus, couldn't speak. Sparks of electricity seared her skin and bones, and she licked her lips, trying to pull herself together, trying to think about the task at hand before he seduced her further. Had it been a different time, she felt sure that she would have done anything for him in this moment—such was his power over her. All he had to do was ask.

God help her, it had been difficult enough asking for money from her parents, but from Tobias Stone, even if it was an advance for a job she wasn't sure would even stretch out that long, it was now almost impossible.

"I—" She wanted to tell him that she'd thought of him too, in her moments. That she wasn't sure why she'd rushed away that evening; that she too had been thinking about him.

But her dilemma ripped her in two. Damn this mess she was in. Not Jacob being sick, but her being too dirt poor that she couldn't provide for them; that she couldn't weather any storm, that she couldn't pay her hospital bill. She stared up at him. "I don't know what came over me that day," she managed to say.

Something tightened around his mouth. "You don't know what came over you that day?" His voice was hard. "You mean you didn't feel anything?"

She stared at his lips again, wanting him to claim her with his mouth. He lifted his head. "Is this about Naomi?"

Puzzled, she stared back, trying not to get caught up in the intense blue of his eyes.

"Naomi? No, I—" She swallowed. "I wanted to ask—" She stopped, and even though she was standing, she had the overwhelming sensation of falling to pieces in all scattered directions.

"What did you want to ask me?"

She blinked a few times, unsure how to say it. "I wanted to ask you for a favor."

"A favor?"

She could see the tension as his shoulders seemed to stiffen, and she stared glumly at her hands, unable to face him. She already regretted asking to speak to him but it was too late to back out now. "I was hoping that maybe," she cleared her throat. "I wondered if it would be possible to ask you for an ... an ... advance?" The last few words were almost a choked whisper.

"An *advance*?" He looked puzzled, as if he had no idea what she was going on about, and how would he? She'd been worried sick about her boy the entire weekend and he'd been caught up in how they had left things on Friday night. She squeezed her eyes shut, as if the explanation pierced her deeply.

"I wanted to ask you if you could advance me a couple of months' wages."

"An advance in wages?" There was a hardness in his eyes that hadn't been there before. "What exactly are we talking about here?"

Maybe she should have considered returning to waitressing and working at the supermarket on the weekends instead of *this*. Tobias Stone glared at her.

"You're not making this any easier for me, Tobias."

"You want money from me? Is that it?"

God, no, not when he put it like that. "I've had a setback, and I need to come up with some money. Fast. I don't know who else to turn—"

"How much?" he sneered, making her feel like a dirty little tramp.

"Thirty-five hundred dollars," she whispered, unable to lift her gaze. "I thought if you could maybe—"

"Is this because I told you I paid Naomi for sex? Is that it?"

She lifted her head sharply, taken aback by his sudden outburst of anger which seemed disproportionate to the request she had made.

"No! This has nothing to do with Naomi," she replied hotly, not even sure what he was getting at.

"I bet," he murmured and scrubbed his hand across his face. Her humiliation burned through her skin.

"It's for—"

"You want to slap me with a lawsuit for sexual harassment? Is that what you're going to make of that night? Is this your idea of blackmailing me?" His words landed in her ears like a fist to her head. "You kissed me back, it wasn't a one-way thing."

She was shaking and shivering all over as his words cut into her like razor blades. Heat swept over her face, coloring her shame and she tried to swallow but her throat muscles seemed to have packed up.

He stepped closer, his eyes blazing with hatred, the muscles along his jaw flexed. "Do you expect me to pay you for sex, Ms. Page?"

His words landed in her stomach, heavy, like cannonballs, and sunk deeper into her gut, settling there and filling her with coldness and fear. She lowered her eyes in misery, unable to face him.

"I never expected *this* from *you*." He jabbed his finger at her and walked away towards the center of the room. She wanted to run as fast and as far as she could. But something snapped inside her. Anger and humiliation mixed with her sense of being wrongly accused.

Goddamn it.

He wasn't going to get away with this.

"I'm not a whore, Tobias. I'm disgusted that you would think that of me." Enraged, she stood her ground, her eyes burning back into his. Not only was he wrong, but he was also sick and twisted.

She wasn't *that* desperate.

"I told you that anything can be bought, Ms. Page," he murmured, walking back towards her with his eyes hard and unsmiling, digging into hers. "And everything has a price. It seems to me you just found yours."

"You sick man," she hissed. She stepped back but he stepped towards her again, his voice low.

"Think how convenient it would be to slip up here every so often. I would fuck you for hours, and pay you well for your services, and nobody would know."

She flexed her fists to keep her hand from slapping him again. "You're disgusting. I can't believe you're talking to me like this." Her words came out low, like an angry whisper, as if she were sharing a dirty secret, her hopes falling to the floor like broken glass. "I'm sorry I ever laid eyes on you." She tried to muster up as much menace as she could, but his words had wounded her deeply. Rushing out of the door and towards the elevator, she stabbed her finger at the elevator button, but it wouldn't light up.

She heard the sound of the door closing behind her and his soft footsteps along the carpeted floor. Forcing herself to stare ahead, she cursed the sudden moisture that had filled her eyes.

"You need a key to access this floor," he muttered, invading her personal space as he reached over and lifted the button she had been pressing. Underneath was a slot into which he inserted a key and seconds later the elevator arrived.

She got in and stayed close by the door, refusing to look at him, her insides on fire as humiliation filled every cell in her body. Silence filled the elevator as she stood with her back to him, her breath coming out faster than she could let air in. She closed her eyes until the elevator stopped at her floor and as soon as the doors opened, she fled, seeking the sanctuary of her office.

CHAPTER SIXTEEN

"Is everything all right?" Candace asked, as she closed her folder and clipped her pen to it.

"Why?" Tobias barked.

She took a few steps towards the door. "You've been wound up all day."

"I hate meetings that drag on for hours."

Candace nodded sympathetically. "Savannah Page was looking for you this morning."

"I know."

"Was it anything I could have helped her with?"

"No."

She seemed to hesitate, as if she had more to say, but he wasn't in the mood to hear her whining. "I don't need anything else, Candace."

"Fine." She picked up her briefcase and made to leave. "I'll see you tomorrow."

He grunted a "Yes."

So much for looking forward to returning to work. It had turned into a fuck-awful day. Never mind the meetings with investors who wanted the impossible for their greedy and already fat little pockets. Now Savannah Page had shown her true colors as well.

He swiveled his chair around and stared out at the Manhattan skyline. He would never have figured her for a gold-digger. She had seemed so different, so decent, so honest and so honorable; filled with the salt-of-the-earth goodness. And yet also fiery, and sexy, and not really aware of it.

Now she'd gone and punctured his hopes.

Tobias had always been on the alert for people who wanted things from him but it was something he had never expected from *her*.

The moment he'd discovered that she'd come looking for him, his insides had heated, like bubbling lava. His hopes had come to life because *she* wanted him, or so he'd thought. He'd wondered if maybe they might have a chance to see how things would turn out.

But the moment she'd spoken about money, the moment she'd asked for an advance, his insides had hardened like cast iron. His excitement quickly pulverized into nothingness, and instead something icy had slivered and snaked its way up from the pit of his stomach, leaving a trail of frost in its wake.

All weekend he'd thought of nothing but her and had wondered how things would be. He'd imagined what it would be like to hold her and to have her and he'd taken plenty of cold showers when the images in his head could no longer be reined back.

And now this.

Of all the things she could have wanted from him, she'd come begging for money.

Fuck it.

A million times over.

He had finally met a woman who had not only captured his interest, but who was special, and meant something to him, but in the end, she was no different from the rest of them.

He would never again find someone as honest and as decent as Ivy. A woman like that was a rarity. They'd known one another since they were sixteen, way before he'd made his money. She'd known him when he'd been dirt poor and lived on ramen noodles. For her it had never been about the money.

Too bad the rest of them wanted to leech off him. This was why he had never wanted to get involved. Paying for sex had suited him just fine.

Until Savannah Page had come along and caught his eye.

Thinking about it now, he'd crippled her. He had seen it from the way her body had crumpled, like a battered ragdoll flailing weakly, but it hadn't stopped him from holding back.

It was a goddamn shame that she had turned to be nothing more than a gold-digger in the end. Disgusted with himself for thinking there might be a chance of something, a stab at something, he now wanted to wipe all traces of her from his memory.

And he'd gone and dumped Naomi too. Tonight would have been a fine time to have her over. God knows he needed it.

"Come in," he shouted at the sound of a knock on his door.

"What's going on?" Matthias asked. He was dressed in his coat, ready to leave for the day.

"Whaddya mean?"

"You snapped at most of the managers in that meeting."

"They need to produce results quicker."

"They are, Tobias. You know they all work hard. You'd have fired them by now otherwise." Matthias frowned at him. "Seriously, Tobias, what's going on? Is it Naomi?"

Tobias looked up sharply. "Hell, no. But thanks for your concern."

"We can still be on target to achieve the goals for this year. It might take a bit more aggressive marketing and investing in places we discussed. Don't write Xian Yanling off so easily."

"I'm in no mood to discuss Yanling." Tobias stretched his neck from side to side. He needed to fuck. Naomi did that very well, and she gave one hell of a sensual massage as well. His mind ignited at the thought of it but in his head Naomi's image was replaced by one of Savannah, naked and oiled.

"I signed off the proposal for an extra person in Briony's team." Matthias told him, tactfully changing the subject.

"Why did *you* sign it off?"

"Because you weren't around. Why, is it a problem?"

"No."

"Briony's been on at me this whole week. With an extra person to help her, she can help me without her department falling to pieces. She's got Savannah Page in mind."

Tension crawled along Tobias's spine, making his shoulders bunch together. He hated the sound of that name. Matthias walked towards the door. "Shame about her son."

"Whose son?"

"Savannah Page's boy," replied Matthias, holding onto the door handle. "He was in the hospital for a few days. Had a bad asthma attack apparently."

The color drained from Tobias's face.

"He's okay now. But, yeah. Having her on the team would be good. I like the look of her, and she's not bad at her work either. See you tomorrow, buddy."

Tobias sat frozen, staring at the door. He shrank into his chair and then into his body, and let the guilt wash all over him. He wasn't sure how long he sat there but he recalled the exact moment he had turned into a total prick.

A jerk and a douchebag, a man who would never be able to make it up to Savannah if he tried.

A man he felt sure she would never want to see again. He

couldn't have read the situation more wrong.

He got up and scrubbed his face with his hands, his insides twisting when he remembered what he had accused her of. What had he done?

Savannah Page would never let him back in again. Ever.

Unless he made her an offer she couldn't refuse.

Thank you for reading THE GIFT, BOOKS 1-3! I hope you love Tobias and Savannah as much as I do. Their rollercoaster love story continues in **THE OFFER, Books 1-3**

He begins to thaw. She begins to trust. It's almost too good to be true...
A misunderstanding between Savannah and Tobias causes things to turn sour.
But Tobias isn't used to failing, and he always gets what he wants.
And what he wants is Savannah Page.
Winning her back is one thing, keeping her is another.
Get THE OFFER, BOOKS 1-3 now!

Sign up for my newsletter to find out about new books:
http://www.lilyzante.com/newsletter

I appreciate your help in spreading the word, including telling a friend, and I would be grateful if you could leave a review on your favorite book site.

You can read an excerpt from **THE OFFER, BOOKS 1-3** at the end of this book.
Thank you and happy reading!
Lily

AN EXCERPT FROM THE OFFER

I'm sorry I rushed off but something urgent came up. I'll be back tomorrow.

She'd sent that text to Briony as soon as she had arrived back home, not long after lunchtime.

Tobias's words cut into her, sharp like shrapnel, leaving her so devastated that the only thing she could think of was to get the hell away. She couldn't run the risk of seeing him again. She'd tried to soldier on at work, had managed to stumble along for a few hours but his unpleasant words and that venomous look on his face refused to leave her and made it unbearable for her to remain at work.

The hours had crawled miserably towards lunchtime. She'd gone out to grab a sandwich but had ended up coming home and cleaning her oven instead.

It was spotless now. Because when all else failed, when she couldn't stop replaying that scene over and over in her mind, or stem the endless recording of Tobias's poisonous words, her urge to clean, the desire to put order into things she could control, helped focus her mind. So she had cleaned her oven until she could see her face reflected in the shiny window of the oven door.

I'll fuck you for hours and pay you well.

His words stabbed into her psyche, throwing her into further misery. Each time her mind drifted to *that* scene again, she scrubbed harder, forcing herself to concentrate on the task at hand.

It was bad enough that money worries kept her from sleeping ever since she'd found out how much the hospital bill had come to. This morning, she had worked herself into a frenzy as she'd left for work and was already hesitant about asking Tobias for an advance. Yet he had so graciously helped her through a tough Christmas period and it was this that had convinced her to go forward with her request.

But she hadn't been prepared for his response which had knocked the life and breath right out of her, as if he'd landed a solid punch to her midriff. She had rushed away, unsure which was worse: Colt's punches, or Tobias's words.

She never wanted to see him again. Never. Sucker that she was for attracting only jerks and douchebags.

Her cell phone rang, snapping her back to present and when she saw Briony's number, she was half-tempted to ignore it but she knew she couldn't do that to one of the few people she liked and trusted.

"Hey, Briony."

"Is everything okay? I just got back from a meeting and I saw your text."

"I'm fine," said Savannah, eager to put her boss's mind at ease. "I'm sorry I left but something came up."

"Are you okay?"

"Yes." *No.*

"I wanted to make sure. Tobias was looking for you earlier; I didn't know where you were."

"Does he know I went home early?"

"He's been in meetings all day. He wouldn't even know if your room caught fire."

Savannah feigned a laugh. "I'm sorry. I can explain tomorrow when I come in."

"Don't worry about it. I know you've had enough to deal with recently. Is Jacob all right? I thought for a moment—"

"Jacob's fine. Thanks for asking. What did Tobias want?" Her anxiety began to climb. What more could he have to say after the disgusting accusations he had leveled at her?

"I'm not sure and I didn't care to ask. He didn't look too happy."

"Maybe he had a problem with his Word templates," Savannah suggested, knowing that it wasn't the reason he'd come looking for her.

"I don't know why Candace can't deal with those problems," Briony muttered. "But that's not important. I wanted to make sure that you and Jacob were okay."

"We're fine." Savannah reassured her, quickly glancing at her cell phone screen when she heard the beep of another call waiting. Her eyes flickered with excitement. Bella from Southwood Select, the new recruitment agency she'd been dealing with, was on the line. "I've got another call coming through," she said. "Do you mind—?"

"No, go. I'll speak to you tomorrow."

Savannah quickly switched to the other call.

"Savannah?" Bella's crisply efficient voice greeted her, raising her hopes. "I've got good news."

"Yes?" Her mood suddenly brightened.

"You've got the job!" Words that lifted her from her misery.

"I did?"

"You sure did. They loved you. It wasn't only your experience to date and the fact that you've held this position before, but they liked your personality. They think you'll fit right in." Savannah placed her hand on her chest as if she was unable to contain her happiness. This news was more than a small ray of sunshine in an otherwise shit-filled day.

"That's the best news I've heard all week! I'm so excited. I really am." She felt a lightness in her chest and couldn't help but smile. "How soon can I start?" *Tomorrow?* She hoped. She was desperate to leave Stone Enterprises at the first opportunity.

Bella laughed. "You *are* eager to start. I like that! Unfortunately not tomorrow, but maybe in around two weeks' time. I've been told that they're looking at the beginning of February."

"Are you sure?" asked Savannah, suddenly anxious again. "Because when I spoke to the manager during my interview, he told me that they needed someone as soon as possible."

Bella paused. "I'll look into that for you. I can ask, certainly. But first, let me get the paperwork over to you—"

"I can come by during my lunch hour and sign all the necessary paperwork." Forget waiting until lunchtime, she might even rush out an hour after she arrived at the office to get that paperwork signed.

"That works for me. I'll see you tomorrow. Congratulations, once again."

"Thanks." Savannah put the phone down and hung her head in sheer relief. It was strange how today life had shown her two extremes on the emotional spectrum. *Not only two,* thought Savannah despondently, hugging her arms around her body. She'd suffered a whole heap of emotions in between. So much so that she was now ravenous, as well as drained, after the tumultuous ride that the day had turned into. She still hadn't eaten lunch.

Feeling happier, she opened the refrigerator and pulled out some cheese and a jar of relish with which to make a sandwich.

As she opened the lid to the jar, she was again reminded of Tobias Stone; this had been in the Christmas gift basket he'd sent her.

Back when he had cared.

Get THE OFFER, BOOKS 1-3

BOOKLIST

The Seven Sins:(New Series) A series of seven standalone romances based on the seven sins. Steamy, emotional, and angsty romances which are loosely connected.

Underdog (FREE prequel)
The Wrath of Eli
The Problem with Lust
The Lies of Pride
The Price of Inertia

The Billionaire's Love Story: This is a Cinderella story with a touch of Jerry Maguire. What happens when the billionaire with too much money meets the single mom with too much heart?

The Promise (FREE)
The Gift, Book 1
The Gift, Book 2
The Gift, Book 3
The Gift, Boxed Set (Books 1, 2 & 3)

The Offer, Book 1
The Offer, Book 2
The Offer, Book 3
The Offer, Boxed Set (Books 1, 2 & 3)
The Vow, Book 1
The Vow, Book 2
The Vow, Book 3
The Vow, Boxed Set (Books 1, 2 & 3)

Indecent Intentions: This is a spin-off from The Billionaire's Love story. This two-book set consists of two standalone stories about the billionaire's playboy brother. The second story is about a wealthy nightclub owner who shuns relationships.

The Bet
The Hookup
Indecent Intentions 2-Book Set

Honeymoon Series: Take a roller-coaster journey of emotional highs and lows in this story of love and loss, family and relationships. When Ava is dumped six weeks before her Valentine's Day wedding, she has no idea of the life that awaits her in Italy.

Honeymoon for One
Honeymoon for Three
Honeymoon Blues
Honeymoon Bliss
Baby Steps
Honeymoon Series Boxed Set (Books 1-4)

Italian Summer Series: This is a spin-off from the Honeymoon Series. These books tell the stories of the secondary characters who first appeared in the Honeymoon Series. Nico and Ava also appear in these books.

It Takes Two
All That Glitters
Fool's Gold
Roman Encounter
November Sun
New Beginnings
Italian Summer Series Boxed Set (Books 1- 4)

A Perfect Match Series: This is a seven book series in which the first four books feature the same couple. High-flying corporate executive Nadine has no time for romance but her life takes a turn for the better when she meets Ethan, a sexy and struggling metal sculptor five years younger. He works as an escort in order to make the rent. Books 4-6 are standalone romances based on characters from the earlier books. The main couple, Ethan and Nadine, appear in all books:

Lost in Solo (prequel)
The Proposal
Heart Sync
A Leap of Faith
A Perfect Match Series Books 1-3
Misplaced Love
Reclaiming Love
Embracing Love
A Perfect Match Series (Books 4-6)

Standalone Books:

Love Inc
An Unexpected Gift
An Ordinary Hero

ACKNOWLEDGMENTS

I would like to thank the following wonderful ladies who look through my manuscript checking for errors, typos and other strange things that might have found their way into my story:

Marcia Chamberlain
April Lowe
Dena Pugh
Charlotte Rebelein
Carole Tunstall

I would also like to thank Tatiana Vila for creating my awesome covers: **www.viladesign.net**

ABOUT THE AUTHOR

Lily Zante lives with her husband and three children somewhere near London, UK.

Connect with Me

I love hearing from you – so please don't be shy! You can email me, message me on Facebook or connect with me on Twitter:

Website http://www.lilyzante.com

Email lily@lilyzante.com

facebook.com/LilyZanteRomanceAuthor
twitter.com/lilyzantebooks
instagram.com/authorlilyzante
goodreads.com/authorlilyzante
bookbub.com/authors/lily-zante
amazon.com/author/lilyzante

Printed in Great Britain
by Amazon